MOLLY AND THE MACHINE

ERIK JON SLANGERUP

ALADDIN

New York   London   Toronto   Sydney   New Delhi

ALADDIN
An imprint of Simon & Schuster Children's Publishing Division
1230 Avenue of the Americas, New York, New York 10020
First Aladdin hardcover edition June 2022
Text copyright © 2022 by Erik Jon Slangerup
Jacket illustration copyright © 2022 by Oriol Vidal
All rights reserved, including the right of reproduction in whole or in part in any form.
ALADDIN and related logo are registered trademarks of Simon & Schuster, Inc.
For information about special discounts for bulk purchases, please contact Simon & Schuster Special Sales at 1-866-506-1949 or business@simonandschuster.com.
The Simon & Schuster Speakers Bureau can bring authors to your live event. For more information or to book an event contact the Simon & Schuster Speakers Bureau at 1-866-248-3049 or visit our website at www.simonspeakers.com.
Jacket designed by Laura Lyn DiSiena
Interior designed by Ginny Kemmerer
The text of this book was set in KazimirText.
Manufactured in the United States of America 0422 FFG
2 4 6 8 10 9 7 5 3 1
Library of Congress Cataloging-in-Publication Data
Names: Slangerup, Erik Jon, author. Title: Molly and the machine / by Erik Jon Slangerup. Description: First Aladdin hardcover edition. | New York : Aladdin, 2022. | Series: Far Flung Falls | Summary: In the summer of 1983, kids of Far Flung Falls are disappearing one by one, including Molly's brother, so aided by a crew of unusually determined pets, Molly sets off to find her brother and discover who the mastermind is behind the abductions. Identifiers: LCCN 2021032188 (print) | LCCN 2021032189 (ebook) | ISBN 9781534497993 (hardcover) | ISBN 9781534498013 (ebook) Subjects: CYAC: Brothers and sisters—Fiction. | Missing persons—Fiction. | Robots—Fiction. Classification: LCC PZ7.S628847 Ml 2022 (print) | LCC PZ7.S628847 (ebook) | DDC [Fic]—dc23
LC record available at https://lccn.loc.gov/2021032188
LC ebook record available at https://lccn.loc.gov/2021032189

✿ CONTENTS ✿

For Krissy,
the brightest, bravest girl I know,
and I know a few

PART I

OUTSIDE

CHAPTER 1
WARNING SHOT

The intruder paused midstep, fixing his attention on a party of finches who'd been eyeing him from their perches up ahead. Well, they weren't eyeing *him*, he reminded himself, so much as *the thing he was in*. A curiosity, to be sure. And weighing in at two hundred tons, it would be hard to miss. Even out here, in the middle of nowhere.

He clicked the image magnification dial to the right, telescoping in on the flock until he could count each bird's feathers if he wanted. They had stopped chirping, every one of their dark little eyes intent on this stranger's next move. He stared back, admiring them through two circular screens that dominated the curved wall in front of him, each one nearly ten feet in diameter.

Hello there. Even though not a soul—bird or otherwise—could actually see *him*, he considered for a moment how strange he must look, suspended by a leather harness in the center of a gyroscope that swiveled in tandem with his every movement. Not to mention the tangle of cords, the panels of blinking lights that encircled him. He shifted his weight to one side, careful not to let his feet push the omnidirectional pedals below. They were calibrated to respond to the slightest pressure—a feature he was still getting the hang of.

In spite of his precautions, the finches sensed something. A vibration, maybe? In a blink, they were gone.

The intruder hadn't come all this way to bird-watch. But still. Their sudden departure left him feeling even more alone in his command center than he had at the outset of his trek. Now all he had to keep him company were the flickering readouts of the console.

Stay on mission, he told himself. The digital displays all glowed under his nose, giving him a steady flow of information.

He checked his latitude, longitude, altitude, wattage, engine temperature, hydraulic pressure. There were measures for everything. Then he looked at the readout above them all, the one labeled **TIME/DATE**. It read:

06:14:37 AM / WED 06-22-1983

A short grunt of surprise. The sun would be up any minute. Where had the night gone? For the next twenty-three seconds, he watched the last two digits in the **TIME** column continue their endless tick upward until the minutes turned over to :15 and the seconds reset to :00 to start all over again.

Below that, one more readout caught his eye, labeled **OCCUPANTS**. Unlike all the other numbers, it remained unchanged:

01

He nodded. Time to get going.

With great care, he resumed the practiced movements from his harness. Each step he applied to the pedals activated one of the colossal mechanical legs far below, hundreds of times heavier than his own. When he did it right, the hushed sounds of the machinery were almost imperceptible among the constant creaks and cracks of the old forest—which was impressive when you considered the size of the thing.

Whirrrrrrr . . . tick . . . grong . . .

Whirrrrrrr . . . tick . . . grong . . .

Whirrrrrrr . . . tick . . . grong . . .

Everything running smoothly.

In this patch of Ohio, far south of the cornfields, the woods grew especially dense, and with each mile, the terrain had become more unpredictable. Steep drop-offs and gorges crisscrossed through the hills and hollows, many of them hidden under a canopy of leaves. For every two trees that held upright, there would be one leaning over at an angle, too old or too tired to stand without help. Other trees were laid out flat entirely, slowly becoming part of the forest floor.

For a metal giant, it made for precarious steps. An ever-changing obstacle course. But also not a bad place to hide. And from where he dangled, the view was nice. At a hundred feet up, he could see just ahead where the trees finally thinned and the earth smoothed, giving way to a string of small houses along a narrow two-lane road.

He approached from the back of the neighborhood. The homes were simple and squat, with low pitched roofs and tiny windows. Easy to miss—and step on—if you weren't paying close attention. But he was.

The backyard directly ahead distinguished itself with a tire swing in one corner and a trampoline in the other. Both appeared to be well-worn. All good signs.

The intruder checked his map to confirm the location, marked it, then continued forward, zeroing in. The houses were well spaced apart, separated by stretches of grass. But they were close enough that the sound of someone causing a commotion could still travel between them.

He slowed his steps.

One colossal foot came down on a newly fallen tree, snapping it in two. He immediately tried to correct his footing, but too much in the opposite direction. Wider than a dump truck, the steel sole slipped, sending the log, along with several others, rolling down a moss-covered slope, into a ravine that cut diagonally through the wood. A quick chain reaction of thumps and crashes. The intruder froze.

Somewhere, a dog started barking.

Up ahead, a light blinked on through one of the tiny windows. Then another.

The intruder tilted both handles downward to assume a crouch position as he maneuvered partway into the gorge, still allowing him to peek through the tops of the trees. He waited.

With a sharp creak, the back door burst open, and a broad-shouldered woman pushed her way through. Her body was draped in a spectacular teal and gold muumuu, with the hair on both sides of her head wound tight in rollers, which somehow made her look even more formidable. She ambled down the porch steps and tromped across the length of the backyard, dog by her side, stopping at a chain-link fence that met her at the waist.

The woman held something in her hands.

He zoomed in. *Click, click, click.* It was a double-barreled shotgun.

Uh-oh.

The edges of the sky grew pink, and he suddenly became

aware of how, in just a few moments, the sunlight might glint off the top of his metallic shell. He crouched down even deeper into the gorge, metal legs scraping against the outcropping of stone. No longer able to see over the trees, he aimed both audio sensors straight ahead.

The woman was shouting into the shadows.

"An' ya better stay off our land, if'n ya know what's good for ya...."

He slipped his hands off the main grips that controlled locomotion, pressing his palms together. They were a little sweaty. Didn't want to cause any sudden movements that gave his position away. *Statue still.*

The woman carried on with her threats in his general direction, along with the dog. Then, through his speakers, he heard the amplified metal *clink* of a gate being unlatched.

"Go get 'em, Boz," she said.

Boz took off like a rocket, crashing through the under-brush. By the sound of it, the dog was quickly closing the distance between them.

The intruder's hands danced over the control panel,

toggling the switches that caused the articulated limbs to contract in on themselves, section by section. But there were limits to how small he could make a giant. The tractor-size claws that served as hands dug into the earth, crunching felled trees and underbrush. He powered down.

Now his view barely cleared the ravine's edge. He was just above ground level.

Two minutes later, a snout poked through the bushes to the left, followed by the head, body, and tail of a very large hound. Boz. After a few tentative sniffs at the lifeless giant, the dog started baying with renewed vigor. His howls were long and loud. Whatever the metal intruder smelled like, Boz clearly did not approve.

"Ar-ar-aroooooooooooooooo . . . ," the hound persisted.

Not good. The operator considered his options. He flipped a switch, powering the primary systems back up. A sharp hum of energy filled the small clearing around the gorge. He pressed a few more buttons. With a low groan, the massive head swiveled on its bulky, neckless body. Now they were face to face.

"Aroo—"

Without warning, the two gigantic, perfectly circular eyes went incandescent. The dog's terror-stricken face was frozen under a bright green glow. He managed one whimper before turning tail to run.

Beyond the trees, a shotgun fired, echoing through the predawn air. The blast was quickly followed by the unmistakable *shunk-shunk* of a reload.

"Next'un won't be no warning." Muumuu was still on duty.

The intruder took three deep breaths before extending the giant's limbs back to their full length. Rising up, he stole one last glance at the tire swing and trampoline before looking back down at the control panel. The displays all danced before him, save one that remained fixed. **OCCUPANTS: 01**. Heart sinking, he leaned to one side in the harness, pushing his weight to the right pedal while squeezing the left-hand control to pivot.

In perfect sync, the massive metal foot turned on its heel. Stepping out of the ravine, the giant robot kept low as it made its retreat, the first traces of daylight chasing behind.

TWO AND A HALF DAYS LATER

CHAPTER 2

FLYING SOLO

Thirty-Six Miles Northeast

Molly skidded to a stop in front of the empty cement driveway.

The bright green confetti of cut grass was everywhere. It clung to her sneakers and tires, made her wonder if maybe she'd missed a parade. She saw the clippings repeated in regular semicircles up the drive, showing the recent about-face tracks of a mower. The fresh scent of yardwork hung heavy in the air. Molly sniffed. Was that a trace of gasoline? The combination made her hopeful. Seemed likely somebody could still be home.

Molly and the Machine

It was later in the day, but the summer heat held firm. Under Molly's braid, a trickle of sweat worked its way from the base of her neck down her back. She squinted. The windows of a beige split-level stared back at her, revealing nothing. This was Margo's house.

"Go find your own fun," Molly muttered under her breath, repeating the command her dad had made from the couch just a few minutes ago. She couldn't really blame him for saying it. She and her brother Wally had been trading insults for a solid hour, with no end in sight to the bickering. Wally could get on her nerves so bad sometimes. Most of the time, actually. So "go find your own fun" felt less like a punishment and more like a relief. Or maybe a dare. And Molly was always up for a dare.

Margo's house felt like her best bet, or at least the closest.

With a two-car garage, porch swing, and well-tended lawn, it definitely ranked nicer than where Molly lived, just a mile or so down the road. Molly looked back and considered briefly that maybe the distance between their houses was greater. Sometimes it felt like it might be.

Molly shifted her weight. In one fluid motion, she flipped her kickstand and slipped off the banana seat. Walking up to the door, she slowed down to admire the bushes that had been trimmed into impossibly neat little box shapes. Molly wondered how big a pair of scissors you needed to do that. Or maybe they just grew that way? Definitely not how anything grew back at her house, which was somewhere between overgrown and out of control.

She turned back to make sure she'd positioned her bike at a good viewing angle for when Margo came to the door. Bright pink from end to end, it had been a birthday present from her Great-Uncle Clovis—or "Gruncle," as he preferred to be called—a few months before, and she still loved showing it off. Clovis had built it from scratch, so there wasn't another one like it anywhere. Other kids had asked her what all the extra buttons, levers, and compartments were for, but she kept those secrets to herself. Her great-uncle had told her that vehicles this special deserved names, and he had dubbed it Pink Lightning when he gave it to her.

From the porch, Molly couldn't hear anyone inside. The shades were drawn. She knocked and waited.

Not a sound from within. So she tried the doorbell.

"They're not home," a voice shot out from behind her. "Didn't Margo tell you? They went up to Michigan, I think."

Molly turned to see Arvin leaning over his handlebars, parked on the other side of the street. Arvin was a year older than Molly, so he'd be going to middle school next year. Dark, unruly hair stuck out from under the *Empire Strikes Back* cap he always wore, or at least what was left of it. The edge of the bill had frayed into fuzz, and the faint outline of a giant mechanical Land Walker was almost completely faded from view. Molly remembered those things giving her nightmares when the movie first came out, but that was three years ago, and she had only been eight at the time. Now they just seemed kind of silly.

Molly realized she hadn't responded. "Went to Michigan?" she finally repeated. "Like ... forever?"

"Naw, butt brain, they didn't *move*. Gah, you're such a

bozo." But he smiled when he said it, so it sounded slightly less mean, at least for Arvin. She hadn't forgotten that he was one of the kids who had capitalized on the fact that you could rhyme *Molly McQuirter* with *diarrhea squirter*. He had teased her mercilessly a couple of years ago, but as far as Molly could recall, few kids hadn't. It had been a bad time for a lot of reasons, but it seemed like a long time ago. For Molly, it almost seemed like another life.

Arvin was kind of a ringleader with teasing, but he dished it out equally to just about everyone. And she hadn't been the target in a while.

He was still talking. "They left for *vaaay-caaa-shun*." He drew out the last word, like it was something she wouldn't know. Which wasn't true. She knew the word, even if she had never actually experienced it. She imagined what Michigan was like, pictured Margo and her family having the time of their lives, riding roller coasters or eating cotton candy, or whatever they did up there. Vacations were something other families went on.

Her family, if it still was one, never went anywhere. At

least not anywhere fun. In fact, Molly's dad rarely even left the house anymore, not since . . . well, not for a long while. Molly had overheard other kids' parents openly speculate if he could even fit through the front door—which Molly knew he could.

She couldn't believe that Margo hadn't even told her she was leaving. She felt embarrassed for not knowing, and a little hurt in a way she couldn't explain. They weren't *best* friends, but they talked on the bus on the way home from school, which had been out for more than a week now. How was it that Arvin knew, and she didn't? She looked back at him across the street.

"Oh. Yeah, that's right," she said, acting like she'd forgotten. Molly made a show of palming her forehead to emphasize her point, then started walking back toward Pink Lightning like it was no big deal. She eyed Arvin, who didn't move. What was he waiting on? Arvin might be her last choice for a friend, but she wasn't ready to give up on her dad's dare. *Go find your own fun*, she thought. Maybe it was time for plan B.

"Whatcha doing today?" she asked.

"Ehhh, nunya." Arvin shrugged. He was built thick, like a fire hydrant.

Molly folded her arms in response. She knew that one, and she wasn't about to give Arvin the satisfaction of asking him "what?" so he could say "nunya business." Instead, she stared at him.

Arvin stared back, finally giving in.

"I'm waiting for Leonard. We're gonna head up to 7-Eleven, maybe get a Slurpee. Plus, I heard they finally fixed their *Donkey Kong* . . . sooo, I need to show 'em what a real high score looks like. Again." Arvin patted the front pocket in his shorts, making the stash of quarters jingle inside.

Molly walked back toward her bike, thinking Arvin might ask her to come along. Instead, he pantomimed like he was playing, one hand shifting an invisible joystick back and forth, the other repeatedly slapping the jump button. He made some quick "doo-la-da-*doo*-doo, doo-la-da-*doo*-doo" sound effects and shifted his shoulders for dramatic effect. It wasn't necessary. Every kid on Far Flung Falls Drive knew that Arvin could beat them at any arcade game in 7-Eleven. *Donkey Kong,*

Pac-Man, Galaga, you name it. For some reason, he was always more motivated than others to win.

"Okay, Arvin...Shadrach...Simmons," she said.

Arvin grinned. That was his full name. Everyone knew that too. He had once explained that the middle name belonged to his great-great-grandfather or something. But what was of bigger interest were his initials, a detail his regular church-going parents must have overlooked when they picked out the combination. Arvin took it as a source of pride that his very own monogram doubled as a bona fide cussword, like it gave him a special license to get away with something others couldn't.

So when the screens on the arcade games flashed their top scores, you could expect to see Arvin Shadrach Simmons's three initials at the top, typically several thousand points ahead of the next runner-up. For him and his friends, it never failed to get a laugh.

Arvin didn't invite Molly, and Molly didn't ask. Nonchalantly, she reached into the front pockets of her cut-offs, knowing she wouldn't find any quarters in there. And watching other kids play got boring fast, especially if the player was Arvin. He could make one quarter last forever.

Molly and her brother had an Atari at home, but it had been broken and collecting dust for months. Molly was sure it had been Wally. He broke everything.

"Well, see ya 'round," Molly said, flipping up her kickstand.

"Okay," said Arvin. "Nice bike."

Molly looked down and nodded. It *was* a nice bike, probably the nicest in the neighborhood. Definitely the only thing she owned that carried that distinction. Molly turned it around to head back home, defeated in her attempt to find a friend—or her own fun.

It was going to be a long summer.

CHAPTER 3
EVIL WIZARD

How was it that people in your life could just pick up and leave without even telling you? Molly wondered if this was how it was for everyone, or just her. She passed a car idling in a neighbor's driveway. The engine was sputtering, a little too loud, like the muffler had long since given up. The sound triggered a memory, pulling her back in time to a moment from two years before. She had only been nine then, but she could still perfectly recall when she'd heard another vehicle make that same heavy sputter.

She had been sitting in her bedroom, alone. After listening to her mom and dad get into yet another argument over supper, she had quietly slipped past them unnoticed to the refuge of her room and closed the door. She was pretty sure her brother Wally had done the same. It had become their evening routine.

Back then, her parents could find anything and everything to fight about. Molly remembered that this one had started over how much salt her dad was putting on his Salisbury steak, which her mom took as a personal insult. Dad salted everything, so this was a recurring theme. But this particular argument had then evolved to Dad's high blood pressure, which the salt wasn't helping anyway.

Even from behind the closed door, she could hear their voices getting louder and louder, rising toward a crescendo like they were performing a scene, one they'd rehearsed many times. They never hit each other—at least not that Molly could tell—but amid the shouts, they'd make their points by stomping a foot, pounding a fist, or slamming a cupboard door. It had made Molly feel scared.

That night, she struggled to make out the details, but over the racket, in a voice that sounded more tired than angry, her mom had said, "For heaven's sake, Stanley, why can't we . . . *just be happy?*" Molly remembered thinking that sounded like a pretty reasonable thing to want. Prior to that moment, she had never really considered if her parents were happy or not. Wanting to hear her dad's response, she pressed her ear to the door.

But the question hung in the air unanswered. In fact, after that, the whole argument had abruptly come to an end. Somehow, the silence made her feel even worse.

A little while later, Molly heard a car engine idling somewhere outside, one she didn't recognize. It sounded like it needed a new muffler. Molly had spied out her bedroom window, which offered a partial view of the street. The rumble was coming from a purple van at the end of the driveway.

It was parked at an angle, the corner of the front fender barely crossing their property line, as if it was unsure if it should venture any farther. What first caught her eye was the mural on its side. An evil-looking wizard with a long white beard had been airbrushed with great detail. His glowing eyes peered out from under a dark hood, and in his hand he gripped a gnarled staff that shot lightning out in all directions. The entire scene was surrounded by a cloud of mist.

Who in the heck is this? Molly thought. *And why is he waiting at the edge of our driveway? Must be lost.*

Movement from the driver's-side window caught her eye. There was a man behind the wheel, someone Molly had never seen before. He had been so still at first, she hadn't even noticed the van had a driver. He sat in the shadow, but the flick of a lighter briefly illuminated the man's face as he fired up a cigarette. Long, narrow nose, stubbly chin, a thick mane of hair that flowed past his shoulders in a fantastic mullet. Something silver dangled from his left ear.

The man took a long drag, exhaled, then smiled. He wiggled his fingers in what could have been a wave. Had he seen her? Molly slunk a little lower. Whoever this guy was, she was quickly coming to the conclusion she didn't like him. She *definitely* didn't like the tattoo on his shoulder. A cracked skull with a snake curling out of one of the eye sockets. *Ew.*

He hadn't been waving at Molly.

To her surprise, she saw her mom walking out toward the van. *Maybe she's going to give him directions,* Molly thought. Something looked different about her mom. She wasn't stomping anymore. In fact, she seemed to be practically skipping. And she had changed clothes. Was that a new skirt? Her mom skip-walked over to the driver's-side open window, and Molly could see them talking. Mullet Man said something, and her mom threw her head back in laughter. It looked like he was laughing too. Then her mom turned around and walked back a few steps out of view.

To Molly's confusion, her mom came back carrying a small suitcase. She watched her mom go around to the other side of the van and pull back the sliding door. Then she just stood there. Mullet Man said something, and her mom laughed again. Finally, she threw in the suitcase and shut the door.

Molly wondered what her mom could be giving this stranger with a skull tattoo. Her mom was looking back at the house now. And then she climbed in the van herself! This couldn't be right. What was she doing? As soon as her mom closed the door, Molly watched the van make a wide turn, bouncing over the curb. The last thing she saw was the license plate:

WIZWHLZ

Wizard Wheels, driven by Mullet Man. It had been the last time she'd seen her mom. And as sad and mad and confused as it had made her feel, she knew it was even worse for her dad. He hadn't been quite the same since.

Why can't we just be happy?

"Hey, Molly! Watch out!" Somebody was shouting at her, yanking her out of the memory. Wizard Wheels disappeared.

Before she even saw the speaker's face, she recognized him from his Def Leppard tee. It was Leonard, riding his own bike in the opposite direction. She hadn't been paying attention and was barreling straight for him. Pink Lightning wobbled as she skidded to a stop. Leonard veered off to the right, braking beside her.

"Oh, sorry, I—" Molly started.

"No problem," Leonard said, peeking out from under his blond bangs. "You okay?" His band tee was at least two sizes too big. Probably a hand-me-down. The wind kicked up and it caught the air like a sail. Across the front, block letters spelled **PYROMANIA** under a picture of some building going up in flames.

If not for Leonard's pale, ropelike arms poking out of the sleeveless armholes, he might pass for tough. Still, he tried. Leonard told everyone who would listen that he'd seen the band live in concert up in Cleveland, but Molly had her doubts. Who took a fourth grader to see Def Leppard? Besides, wouldn't that melt your ears?

"I'm good. I was just..." She didn't finish.

Leonard cocked his head and brushed his bangs to the side. "Rad bike," he said. It's what he always said now when he saw her, ever since she got it.

"Thanks," Molly said, smiling. "Rad shirt." This is what she always said back. It was a little ritual they had started.

"Thanks," he said, waiting for the next part.

"Even though Van Halen's better," she said. She didn't actually believe that—she just liked getting a reaction. Every time, she'd challenge him with some other band she'd pull out of the air. Maybe Iron Maiden, or Judas Priest. It didn't matter; Leonard never failed to flip out. Or at least pretend to.

"Wha—? Than Def Leppard?" Leonard said, slapping both hands on his grips in mock surprise. "Pshaw! Nobody rocks harder than Leppard."

Molly left it with a shrug. "Have fun with Arvin," she said as they parted ways. Molly pedaled Pink Lightning even faster than before. The pink streamers on the ends of her handlebars fluttered backward like flames from an exhaust.

Who wants to play some dumb old arcade games in a crummy 7-Eleven anyway? Molly thought. *Who needs Leonard, or Arvin, or Margo, or Michigan, or Mom, or anything at all?*

Not her. She had better things to do.

She just wasn't sure what those things were—yet.

CHAPTER 4
DUCK 'N' COVER

Molly continued down the middle of Far Flung Falls Drive. The houses got noticeably shabbier the closer she got to hers. Finally, at the end of the road, she spotted their mailbox peeking out between a pair of overgrown shrubs. It drooped forward, like it was trying to catch a breath, or maybe struggling to hold the mail inside.

Molly brought Pink Lightning to a stop and pulled the chain that dangled below the box. One quick yank, and a thick stack of letters magically slid forward, pushing the hinged door open from the inside. Molly scooped them up with her other hand before letting go of the chain. Immediately, the invisible track slid back in place and the mailbox slammed shut.

The mailbox-opening chain was one of Molly's earliest enhancements to the McQuirter property, and it remained one of her favorites. It was born of necessity, after reaching in one day to grab the mail and getting surprised by a big fat frog that had mysteriously found its way there. Molly had screamed, of course, but not because Molly minded frogs. She just didn't like being surprised by them.

Nobody ever fessed up to the prank, but Molly was convinced it had been her little brother Wally. Who else? And she didn't buy the idea that the frog had somehow managed to get there on its own.

Anyway, however small, the invention had felt like a victory. Never again would she have to reach into the darkness of the mailbox to check the mail. Instead, the mail came to her. She thumbed through the stack, thinking maybe there'd be something from her mom, but it had been nearly six months since the last postcard, and Dad said it was better not to have too many expectations.

Molly and the Machine

The postcards had come more often at first, nearly every week right after she'd hopped into the Wizard Wheels van. They always came in pairs, one for Molly and one for Wally. She and her brother had tracked their mom's travels with Mullet Man from where they lived in Ohio down into West Virginia, through the Carolinas to Georgia, and then finally to Florida, where she'd been for the last year or so—at least according to the covers on the postcards.

But that initial bounty of mail was more than two years ago. And since then, their frequency had trickled from monthly, to every other month, to what seemed like forever.

As good as Molly's invention worked, it couldn't make mail appear.

A few of the envelopes caught her eye with their angry red type. They said things like **PAST DUE** or **FINAL NOTICE** in all caps. She had fished out letters like these from the mail many times before. Molly wasn't sure exactly what they meant, but she figured they couldn't be good.

She stuck them in the basket on the front of her bike and rode up the gravel driveway to her house. The paint had chipped off in so many places, it looked almost camouflaged with its surroundings. Weeds had entirely taken over the front yard, some of them taller than she was. Molly guessed the whole place was about a year away from achieving complete invisibility. She continued into a narrow passage between the stacks of boxes, random junk, and debris that filled the tiny carport. There in the back, right next to a broken-down lawn mower, she had made a secret parking space for Pink Lightning.

Carefully angling her bike alongside the back wall, Molly flipped down the kickstand and slipped off the banana seat. She gave Pink Lightning a quick once-over, checking for any new scuff marks. Her eyes narrowed. *There!* A tiny piece of gravel was lodged in the tread of the back tire. "Gotcha," she whispered, prying it out with a finger. Molly inspected the bike one more time, smiled, then turned to head inside. Before she even opened the door from the carport to the house, she could hear the TV blaring.

It was the news, Molly's least favorite thing on television. Why couldn't there be less news and more cartoons? The anchor was droning on in a deep, serious voice: "Tensions between the United States and Soviet Union have continued to heighten since earlier this year, when President Reagan, in a recorded speech, called the communist country an *evil empire.* ..."

Darryl, the family dog, came to greet her, tail wagging. He was part border collie, part who-knew-what, with a big brown spot that encircled one eye. A happy mutt. Six years ago, Molly had found him lurking in the woods behind their house, without a collar or tag. Back then, he was shy, skinny, and scratched up. But he'd taken well to Molly's attentions, and he reciprocated. Now he gave her shin a vigorous lick.

"Okay, boy, that's good."

Darryl wasn't easily deterred. More licks.

"Geez, Darryl, enough already." Gently, she pushed him away.

Molly walked past the small kitchen into the living room, where her dad had sunken into the middle of the couch, which drooped under his weight. He was eating a frozen TV dinner, eyes fixed on the screen. Molly looked up at the clock on the wall. It was half past two. Pretty early for dinner.

"Hey, Dad."

Still chewing, he mumbled something back.

"Late lunch, or early dinner?" she asked.

He finished chewing, swallowed. "Oh, this? Just a snack, I guess."

From behind the couch, Molly put a hand on her dad's shoulder, gave it a gentle squeeze. She looked down at the top of his head, noticed his crown poking through where the hair had started to thin a little. Sometimes, she wondered if her dad was still in there, or if now it was all just a dad-shaped shell filled with TV dinners.

Her brother Wally was sitting in the corner, playing Legos with one hand and digging into his nose with the other. She took a moment to try to figure out exactly what he was building. A spaceship? Or a castle? Maybe a space castle. It was hard to tell. He looked up at her briefly, his glasses catching the reflection of the TV, so his expression was tough to read. A moment later, he got back to work on the Legos... and his nose.

The nose digging was something her brother did all the

time, and that wasn't an exaggeration. There never seemed to be a moment's rest from his search for some lost treasure lodged up one of his nostrils, just waiting to be discovered. And the worst part was that Dad never seemed to notice. He didn't notice much of anything, really... other than when his favorite shows were on. But Molly noticed. Wally, born nearly four years after his sister, had always been completely and totally gross from day one.

No wonder Mom left, Molly thought. Why wouldn't anyone escape if they could? Ever since Wally had come into the picture, things had gotten worse. It had been years, but sometimes when she walked in the house, she could swear it still smelled like his dirty diapers. Could they have missed one somewhere, maybe? There had been so, so many. Molly gagged a little at the memory.

The screen flashed to a clip of President Reagan smiling and waving at a crowd of reporters, hair slicked back in a perfect pompadour, unmoved by the helicopter behind him. There were dozens of microphones in front of his face.

"Oh, mail," she said, dropping it on the pile of unopened

letters that already covered the cushion beside her dad.

"Hmmph," he mumbled, not taking his eyes from the TV. He was still wearing his navy coveralls from the repair shop where he pulled a couple of shifts a week. His hours had been cut, which lately meant more hours glued to the set. An embroidered patch over his left pocket read *STANLEY* in script letters. But Molly was pretty sure her dad was off today. Had he not changed clothes since yesterday?

Molly had always loved the fact that her dad was a repairman. Back when she was little, he would bring home smaller jobs in the evenings. She remembered sitting beside him at the kitchen table after dinner, feeling his excitement as she watched him turn an old clock or transistor radio into a pile of parts, find out what was broken, then put it back together again. It was usually her job to locate a particular circuit board or mainspring from the spread. Her dad would hum funny little tunes while they worked. Those were happy memories, and Molly missed them.

She used to think there was nothing her dad couldn't fix. But families were more complicated.

Darryl finally decided on a spot in the middle of the room, circled a couple of times, then lay down. Crank, the cat, eyed him suspiciously from her perch on the arm of the couch until he was still. She was a fourteen-year-old graying tabby, but she seemed like she'd been around much longer than that.

The anchor hadn't stopped talking: "According to experts, the combined nuclear arsenal between the two countries has now reached the capacity to destroy all life on the planet nearly twenty times over. . . ."

The image cut again, this time to a giant mushroom cloud rising up over the horizon. Molly had seen this footage several times before. They were always playing it on the news, which her dad watched continuously, with headlines like "World War III to Come?" or "Is This How It Ends?" Next, a grainy image of a small house, about the size of theirs, disintegrated sideways into smoke and dust.

Molly's dad took the last bite of his corn dog, plopping the empty stick down on the frozen TV dinner tray that rested on his belly.

"Are the Russians gonna nuke us?" Wally asked, not looking up from his Legos.

"Shhhh, TV's on," Dad said.

"But are they?" Wally asked again.

"Are they what?"

"Are they gonna nuke us into smidgereens? Cuz of what the President said?"

"It's *smithereens*," Molly corrected him.

"That's what I said. Smidge-er-eens," Wally said.

"Well, those commies might just be dumb enough to try. But we'll be fine here in the great state of Ohio," Dad said. Molly watched as he pulled a can of RC Cola out from a spot where he had it wedged between the cushions and took a long swig, followed by an equally long, only semi-muffled belch. "Just remember to duck 'n' cover like they taught you in school."

Molly groaned. She'd hated all the drills they made her do during the school year, crawling under her desk and curling into a ball on the floor. What was the point? Nuclear war sounded pretty terrible, sure, but if the Russians dropped a bomb on their school, did it really matter if she ducked and covered? Either way, they'd spend several minutes like that on the dirty tile floor, knees tucked in, facedown, hands covering the back of their heads. Her teachers always told them to make themselves as small as possible and called her out as a good example. Probably because she was small to begin with.

"Gerald Bumgarner says that the radiation from the bombs will turn all the survivors into psycho mutant zombies who eat each other's brains," Wally said.

No one paid any attention, so he lifted his arms up and gave his best zombie impression: "Maaaaaaaaaaahhhhhhhhhhhhh..."

"Well, at least you'll be safe, Wally," Molly said.

"Why's that?"

"Because you don't have any brains."

"Dad! Molly said—"

"Uh, why don't you kids go to your rooms or something if you can't get along," their dad said. Without taking his eyes from the TV, he lifted the empty stick back off his tray to take another bite of corn dog, realized he'd already eaten it all, then dropped it again.

Molly watched her dad, missing him even though he was only a few feet away. *Looks like the zombies already took over,* she thought. She got up without another word and made the short trek to her bedroom at the end of the hall. Crank stayed put, but Darryl got up and followed. When she and the dog both made it in, she closed the door behind them.

She climbed onto her bed and opened the drawer in her nightstand. Inside, there was a short stack of postcards, mostly from Florida, held together with a rubber band. The most recent one was at the top of the stack. It had a picture of flamingos on the cover and a list of "Fun Flamingo Facts" on the back, including an explanation of why they stand on one leg, tucking the other up in their body to preserve heat.

Molly read over the fun facts like she had countless times before, then the handwritten words below them:

Miss you, Angel. Love, Mom

Five words. That was it. Five lousy words. In total, the Fun Flamingo Facts comprised forty-two words. *Here is a fact,* thought Molly. *Somebody cared a lot more about flamingos than my own mom cares about me.* She dropped the postcards back into the drawer and curled into a ball on her bed, making herself as small as she could. Who had time to worry about nukes when so many other things were messed up?

Darryl sidled up close to Molly's shins, but he refrained from any more licks.

CHAPTER 5
KITCHEN STANDOFF

The next day wasn't faring much better. At least not yet.

Sitting at the tiny breakfast table across from Wally and her dad was a special kind of torture. *At least I don't have to look at them,* Molly thought. Watching Wally dig for gold in his nose while she ate would be too much. She'd carefully arranged all the cereal boxes around her to block any direct view. Unfortunately, her breakfast fortress wasn't soundproof.

Just a few feet away, Wally was smacking, slurping, and spilling a bowl of Cookie Crisp all over the place. *Ugh, why didn't I get up earlier?* It was more than anyone should bear.

But Dad said nothing. He probably couldn't hear over the crunch of his own Grape Nuts, which sounded like he was eating gravel.

Crank took her position in the empty chair that Mom used to sit in. Keeping her head low, the crotchety cat waited patiently, her eyes bouncing back and forth, looking for anything to fall or spill from the table. (The chances of that happening were usually pretty good.) Darryl lay on the floor for anything Crank missed.

Sometimes it was hard for Molly to decide who bugged her more, her brother or her dad. But instead of voicing a single complaint, she quietly finished her Lucky Charms (the best cereal of all time, even if it had yet to bring her any luck), put her bowl in the sink, and got on with her day. It was already late morning, and Molly had plans.

She slipped in and out of the back door a few times unnoticed, grabbing some last odds and ends she needed from around the house and putting them all in place out in the backyard. Darryl and Crank, who did notice, snuck out alongside her to see what was happening.

This invention was going to be the raddest of all time. And present company was definitely not invited. Having endured breakfast across from her brother, she was ready for some time without any other humans around. Or at least none named Wally.

Between trips, Molly heard her dad get up, make a little groan, and shuffle into the living room without a word. He wasn't very talkative in the morning, or any other time of day, really. He left his bowl on the table, right next to one from yesterday's breakfast. A moment later, she heard the unmistakable sound of the television being turned on.

All Molly needed now was a rolling pin. She slid open the drawer and grabbed it, along with a spool of twine, a spatula, and a handful of clothespins. Why they were all kept in the same drawer was a mystery, but not one she planned on solving today. *Stay on mission*, she thought, inching to the back door. *So close to freedom.* She clutched the rolling pin like it was a magic scepter.

Unexpectedly, her dad returned to the kitchen and started rummaging in the cupboards for something. For the first time, he noticed Molly by the door. Then he started to make his thinking face. *Oh crap*, thought Molly, *this is usually when he makes the absolute worst suggestions, like ...*

"Say, Molly, why don't you take Wally along with you to do ... whatever it is you're doing?" He gestured vaguely at the rolling pin, unable to pinpoint what exactly she *was* doing.

She nearly dropped everything. *What? Wally? To destroy my best invention ever? No way*, Molly thought. She felt the heat rising in her chest and neck at the mere suggestion. She was probably starting to get splotchy. That usually happened when she felt stuck. For what seemed like a full minute, no one said a darn thing.

The applause that trickled in from the TV in the next room broke the silence.

"Darle-e-e-e-ne Jaronski! . . . Come on down! . . . You're the next contestant on ... *The Price is Right!*" The announcer sounded overjoyed, which couldn't have been more opposite to the atmosphere at the McQuirter residence.

Molly knew she had to do something. But if she came off too angry too fast, it could backfire. So she played it cool and . . . slumped, head down. She needed to look really disappointed. She slumped some more, taking a moment to study the stained linoleum floor below her, following one of the cracks that ran under her feet and zigzagged its way to a trash can that was overflowing. After enough time had passed, she sighed a long, loud sigh, hoping this would get through to her dad that letting Wally tag along was a bad idea.

It didn't work. Her dad was still rummaging. He hadn't noticed a thing. How hard was it to pick a snack?

Molly straightened up, stood as tall as her fifty-four and a half inches would allow, and tried something else. She wasn't about to give up her chance at a little peace away from her brother. She put her hands on her hips and shot a hard look at Wally, then back at her dad, whose heavy, rounded frame made the kitchen feel even smaller.

For the first time, Molly noticed that the faded curlicue floral pattern on her dad's shirt was almost exactly the same as the faded curlicue floral pattern of the wallpaper behind him, like he was trying to blend into the house. *Is that on purpose?* Molly wondered. Then she shrugged. At least he had changed clothes. But she wasn't about to let herself be distracted from her plans to exit alone. Wally took account of her stare, briefly pausing from the demanding business of digging in his nose.

The fact that Wally had stopped picking meant that he was paying attention to what was going on—at least more than Dad was. He might fool their dad, pretending not to care, but Molly knew he was dying to join her experiment—and ruin it! That was Wally's specialty.

Molly made a quick mental inventory of her brother's biggest offenses. There was the water rocket she'd carefully built out of old soda bottles, only to have him launch it into the woods and lose it. There was the secret ghost trap she'd set out by their haunted-looking shed, only to have him get tangled up in it and break it, along with his big toe—which she got blamed for. Then there was the Atari that mysteriously stopped working after he'd been playing Space Invaders by himself.

Molly knew he never meant to, but Wally seemed to have a knack for messing up everything he touched—like their family. It might not be fair, but if she was being honest, she blamed him for breaking that, too. Molly only had a few memories of life before Wally came along, but they were happy ones, or at least happier. And how else could she account for the fact that after Wally came into the picture, Mom just up and left?

In the other room, the game show cut to a commercial, pulling Molly out of her reverie. "... Two boys go missing in the last twenty-four hours," the news anchor was saying, "and neighbors have some theories you won't believe. How can we be sure our streets here in Far Flung Falls are safe? Details at the top of the hour!"

Suddenly, Wally appeared to notice that Molly was studying him, and without so much as a warning, he began digging in his nose again, only harder than before. His eyebrows scrunched together as he gave this task his full concentration.

"Grody...," Molly muttered under her breath. She could swear he got past the second knuckle on his picking finger. Why was she even looking? She turned back to her dad, who finally seemed to have found what he was looking for. A jumbo-size bag of BBQ chips.

"Aw, Dad, do I hafta?" Molly pleaded, refocusing her efforts.

"Yeah, ya hafta, Mollz," answered Molly's dad, only half listening while he shook loose the contents of the bag into a plastic bowl.

"Why can't he go with you?" Molly asked.

"Because . . ." Her dad shoved a few chips into his mouth, then started talking again. "Because I'm not going anywhere."

"That's the problem, you're never going anywhere." It came out sounding much harsher than she had meant. And she immediately regretted saying it.

Her dad stopped. He caught Molly's eye for a moment, then looked down. Now it was his turn to slump. Molly wished she could shove the words back in her mouth, rearrange them, and try them again in a way that sounded less mean. But it was too late. She tried something else.

"Dad, I . . . I just don't want him to mess it all up."

"Mess all what up, sweetie?"

"Everything!" Molly's voice started rising again. He just didn't understand. She could feel her splotches getting bigger and redder by the second. "I'm putting together my raddest creation ever, with Darryl and Crank . . . and Wally will ruin everything! I just know it!"

"You should be lucky you even have a brother at all, young lady."

"Yeah, but he's so . . ."

She didn't finish. Even compared to Darryl and Crank, Wally was the dirtiest, most disgusting creature in the house, if you asked Molly. But he was still her brother, and life hadn't been easy on him lately either.

"Well, Miss Molly Jean McQuirter, I am watching my show. So. I. Need. You. To. Watch. Your. Brother. Please," Molly's dad called over his shoulder as he shuffled back into the other room. He had to pivot a little to the side to squeeze through the narrow doorway. As he slipped out of sight, Molly knew the conversation was over.

The two siblings eyed each other for several seconds.

"Dad said," Wally finally offered.

"I know what Dad said."

She understood that grown-ups made the rules, but

lately it seemed that all the grown-ups in her life were mostly breaking them. Her dad didn't even put his own cereal bowl in the sink! Deep down, she knew he was going through a hard time too, but it didn't seem fair that the rule makers were also the rule breakers. And it was getting harder to listen to them. Especially when that meant she kept getting stuck on Wally duty.

CHAPTER 6
CONTRAPTION

Defeated once again, but not surprised, Molly turned on her heel so fast, the single copper braid that hung to her waist whipped around behind her head, nearly hitting her brother right in his gross, nose-picking face. This would have been great, but unfortunately Wally dodged the blow.

"C'mon," Molly mumbled to her brother. *Another day of unpaid babysitting.*

She tromped out of the kitchen and into the backyard, letting the screen door slam shut. Wally opened it back up and followed closely behind. He was trying not to smile, even though he was clearly feeling victorious at the moment. Molly was always left in charge of the annoying little sneak while their dad sat in front of the TV watching "his shows." It didn't matter what was on. Dad just wanted to zone out like the couch potato he had become.

"Just don't touch anything," she warned as they made their way to the far corner of their backyard.

"Okay," said Wally.

"And no nose picking."

"Um, okay."

"Or anything else that's, well, gross."

"Like what, exactly?"

Molly frowned. Why did Wally want a specific list of no-no's? It wasn't like he could stay clear of being ... himself.

"Like ... well, you know ... all the usual gross stuff." She didn't want to inadvertently give her brother any other ideas that weren't already cooking up in that evil brain of his. "Got it?" she asked.

Wally nodded, squinting to see what she had assembled. Finally, they had arrived.

"That's close enough," she said.

But the warning wasn't necessary. Wally had already stopped in his tracks to take it all in, mouth dropping open in a state of awe. Molly's latest contraption was by far the biggest the McQuirter residence had ever seen. The mishmash of parts and pieces sprawled out across the back stretch of the yard. End to end, it was the length of two cars at least.

Molly pretended not to notice her brother's reaction, but it was hard not to feel proud. She busied herself with the finishing touches, slipping the recently borrowed rolling pin by the handles between two upside-down coat hanger hooks. The hangers dipped a little from the added weight but held their position, just inches above a precarious stack of volumes one through seven of the *Encyclopædia Britannica*.

Molly let out a breath. "Perfect," she said.

Wally marveled at the jumble of plywood scraps, all affixed with loops of metal wiring. As he followed along, the wires gave way to some sections of old garden hose that had been cut to various lengths and propped on a stack of hubcaps. Beyond that, a water balloon hanging from a string. A xylophone turned on its side. An old boat propeller with a fork taped to each blade.

His eyes hopped around, pulled from one marvel to the next, but they seemed to never end. There was a six-foot tower of PVC piping that pointed straight up like a smokestack. Next to that sat a massive A-frame of nailed-together two-by-fours. A folding metal chair. A truck tire. Two shovels capped with an upside-down pair of galoshes. A braided rope tied to a metal pail holding a fluorescent green bowling ball.

"What ... is ... all ... this?" he finally asked.

"It's a Rube Goldberg machine," Molly said. "Duh."

"A rude whatzit?"

"No, a *Rube* Goldberg machine. You know, where one thing leads to another ... and another ... and another. I designed it myself."

"Hmmmmm." Wally craned his neck. "What's the bowling ball do?"

"It gets launched by a trebuchet," she said.

"Oh. What's a ... trebuchet?"

"It's like a catapult."

"Then why didn't you just say *catapult*?"

"Because it's different."

"Okay."

"Everything about my machine is different," Molly said. "For instance, mine will also include participation from . . ." She lowered her voice. ". . . *live animals*."

"Animals? I don't see any ani—"

Wally stopped when he saw Molly looking over at Darryl and Crank, both watching from a few feet away. The two had found a nice shady spot on top of an old picnic table tucked up under an enormous oak. Darryl's tail wagged at the acknowledgment. He let out a little whimper of excitement. Crank ignored them.

"There's not another one like it in the whole world," Molly said, checking the tension on the rope.

"How do you know?"

"I just do."

Wally admired it for another moment, then asked, "What's it for?"

"For you to not mess with. You'll see. Just keep your distance. I don't want you getting hurt—at least not by anything that would be my fault."

"Uh-huh."

Molly set back to work, securing a few other loose ends with the stash of clothespins she had just snatched. Once that was done, she taped the spatula to the raised karate-chop arm of an action figure.

"Hey, that's my—"

"Shhh." Molly gave him a look.

Lastly, she added the twine.

Today was just a practice run, not intended for anyone else to see. But Molly had to admit that she enjoyed seeing Wally's reaction to her creation. Even if he needed a little convincing about having, uh, *donated* an item or two, he appeared awestruck. Wally took a step closer, noticing even more details.

There was a model train track. A kitchen knife duct-taped to a broomstick. A meticulously arranged domino chain. Wally's eyes widened.

"Hey, you took all the domino—"

"Shhhhh," Molly said. "I'll put 'em back when I'm done."

"But Moll—"

"Wally, it's for something really important."

"Like what?"

Molly smiled. "Science."

As she said it, Molly's eyes traced along the line she had painted on the ground a few days before. It started at the bowling ball and ended at the upper half of a mannequin propped up on top of a crate some thirty yards away. The mannequin's head was partly covered with an old blanket, like a hood. Along its jawline, she'd glued several strands of toilet paper to approximate a long white beard. The crate was labeled **EVIL WIZARD**.

A series of concentric circles had been painted around the mannequin's chest. It was clear that Evil Wizard was a target.

Wally's eyes followed Molly's.

"Oh, science," he said. "Okay."

Wally hadn't actually seen the Wizard Wheels in their drive two years ago, but he had been given some version of what happened from Molly. Somewhere along the way, in the telling and retelling of the story, the staff-wielding character on the side of the van and its mullet-wearing driver had merged into a single villain responsible for their state of motherlessness. And together, they had grown in their shared hatred of bad wizards—at least the kind that carried off moms.

"Yeah, science," Molly said.

Strictly speaking, the science part wasn't untrue, but if Molly was honest with herself, she knew she'd given that answer before whenever she just wanted to do what she wanted. Which in this case also wasn't untrue.

Wally nodded like he understood, then walked over and took a seat beside Darryl and Crank in the shade. It offered the three of them front-row seating, even if the bench had seen better days. The paint had long since chipped away, and it looked like the whole thing might collapse under the weight of the current occupants. But it held.

All three spectators looked unsure what would happen next, too afraid to get in Molly's way. The show was about to begin.

CHAPTER 7

DOMINO EFFECT

Molly eyed her little brother. For a moment, he looked so small sitting there. Had she been too hard on him? Was he really that bad? But maybe everything just looked small under the shade of that massive oak tree. It was by far the oldest and biggest thing standing on the plot of earth the McQuirters claimed as their backyard. Molly figured it was a couple of acres.

The actual property lines, if there were any, had always been a little fuzzy to Molly, hinted at here and there by a random pile of engine parts or a lone tractor tire. She had watched these remnants from long-departed vehicles get slowly overtaken by weeds, rust, and the incessant creep of nature. But there was no mistaking that the ancient oak marked the back corner of the lot. Beyond that, the forest quickly grew denser and darker, the slope of the earth falling away without warning to steeper angles—a much less friendly terrain for science experiments.

She looked again at the spectators. In addition to Wally, Darryl, and Crank, there was one more. He was keeping a low profile in a private glass cage in the grass. His name was Don Carlos, the newest member of the family. Don Carlos was a chameleon that Molly had won at school the previous year in an essay contest. Her winning essay was about why lizards make excellent pets. Since winning, Molly had secretly questioned her essay's premise, as Don Carlos didn't do much except hang out on a stick and eat bugs.

Wally noticed the chameleon and jumped—then quickly pretended he hadn't.

Maybe I can go a little easier on him, she thought. Now that he was there, she realized she didn't mind having an actual human around. Dogs, cats, and lizards didn't always appreciate her creations. Honestly, a few more humans might be nice sometime. The problem was that the McQuirter house was just so out of the way where it sat alone at the very end of Far Flung Falls Drive, on the edge of town.

Their nearest neighbors, the Kowalskis, were more than half a mile away. And they were all boys anyway, most of them older—except for Leonard. The Simmonses lived even farther down than that. And Arvin's sisters rarely came out. Come to think of it, they didn't really live very close to anyone or anything at all. Even Far Flung Falls—the actual place the road was named after—was a few miles away. So Molly had to make do with who she had.

She surveyed her machine one last time. There was something very satisfying about having everything set up and in its rightful place. It gave her a sense of order in a world that didn't make sense lately. She thought briefly about sharing this sentiment with her brother. But when she looked his way, he was picking his nose again. She decided to keep it to herself.

Besides the nose picking, he was bumping the machine with his feet, making the dominoes wobble.

"Watch it, Wally! You're gonna mess it up."

"Fine," Wally said. He stopped.

"Fine," Molly repeated.

She walked over and carefully picked up Crank, setting the tabby on a little patch of carpet in the center of all the equipment. "There you go, Miss Crankers. Stay right there." Crank didn't look too happy about the forced relocation, but she gave the new spot a few tentative scratches and appeared willing to stay in place. Next, Molly brought Darryl over to the front of the machine and had him sit on a platform marked with a big black X. Lastly, she pulled Don Carlos from his cage and balanced him on a broomstick next to a small curtain.

"Here we go," Molly said. She turned her attention to Darryl. "Who wants a treat?"

Immediately, Darryl's tail started wagging, hitting the propeller positioned behind him and causing it to spin. One of the forks taped to the propeller's blades tipped over a thimble, sending a marble down a chute. The marble traveled down a set of winding wire tracks, then through a garden hose, until—*plop*. It bumped a matchbox car with a fuzzy toy mouse glued to its roof. The car rolled down a short ramp, rounding the corner until it came into Crank's view. The cat gave the toy a swift swat with her paw, slamming the car down on the track—directly above a rubber button. *Click.*

The button was an ignition switch connected by several wires to the PVC potato cannon nearby. There was a pause, then a loud *FOOOOOOOMPT* as a column of fire launched the spud straight up into the air. At the sound, Crank sprang sideways and disappeared into the tree.

The entire machine had come alive.

"Yes!" Molly squealed.

"Whoa!" Wally said.

"Woof!" Darryl barked.

A moment later, the potato dropped back down to earth, landing with a *splat* on the end of a seesaw. The other end popped up, tilting the metal chair, which pulled a magnet and lifted a curtain that revealed a little round switch—with a plastic fly on the end.

Don Carlos didn't hesitate. *SPLOOP!* His tongue shot out

to maximum distance, hitting the switch that turned on a model train, which started *chugga-chugga-chugging* down a track. The train bumped a windmill, and then . . .

Nothing.

The blades of the windmill cut through the empty air.

Wait, that's not right, Molly thought.

Don Carlos tried chewing the fake fly, then dropped it.

Molly's machine had come to a halt.

But the windmill was supposed to hit the first domino! She had carefully placed each one in a perfect chain. Molly studied the windmill, then the spot where the dominoes should be. She frowned. The first one wasn't there, or the second, or the third. By her count, nearly half the chain was missing. Molly stared in disbelief. *Where could they have gone?* Her gaze drifted back to the picnic table, where Wally was building something.

Out of dominoes.

Caught. Red. Handed. Molly's mind made a hard, fast turn from a little puzzled to totally peeved. What really had her riled up was that this happened right after all the warnings she'd given! It wasn't like he didn't know. Wally was just such a... ruiner! She was done giving him chances.

"That's it, Wally!" Molly yelled. She felt the temperature rising in her neck, making its way up to her ears. Suddenly, they felt so hot, she imagined steam might pipe out. "You're totally... *banished!*"

Darryl stopped wagging his tail.

Wally dropped the domino in his hand. "I only took a couple," he said.

"You are *in-cor-ri-gible!*"

Wally gave no sign that he knew what *banished* or *in-cor-ri-gible* meant, but he did seem to know that he had worn out his welcome.

"It'll probably never work anyway," he said, slipping off the bench and stomping off into the open field, beyond the shade of the branches.

"Gahhhh," Molly sighed, relieved to be rid of her annoying little brother. One by one, she set each of the dominoes back in position. Darryl watched closely, while Crank quietly reappeared. Don Carlos hadn't moved, aside from slowly turning a very close shade of brown to the broom handle he clung to. After a few more minutes, Molly almost had everything back in place. She peeked over her shoulder to make sure her brother was far enough away to not mess up anything else. For a moment, she fantasized about him wandering off into the woods and never coming back.

But he hadn't gone that far.

Instead, Wally was squatting down next to an anthill in the middle of the yard. From one of his pockets, he had produced a magnifying glass and was no doubt hatching some sinister plan to incinerate the poor colony. She'd caught him terrorizing ants this way before. Second to nose picking, burning bugs to a crisp was one of his favorite pastimes. Now, as he dug for gold with his right hand, he angled the death ray with his left.

But right now, there were more important things to worry about. Like science. And dominoes. And taking down evil wizards. Molly turned her attention back to her invention. With a little coaxing, she put all her live participants back in place.

Once again, the marble was traveling down the wire track. Molly took a seat on the bench to watch the action unfold. But this time, before Don Carlos had hit the switch, all the dominoes started to wobble. The whole contraption was shaking. *Wally!* She was about to yell at her brother again, assuming that whenever there was trouble, it was usually her brother's fault.

But he wasn't anywhere near.

No, Wally was still by the anthill, but he was no longer terrorizing the ants. He appeared frozen in place. On the ground lay the magnifying glass.

He didn't look troublesome at all.

He looked scared.

CHAPTER 8
HEAVY METAL

As the dominoes fell, Molly heard some kind of commotion in the woods behind her. *Maybe a tree falling?* That wouldn't be too unusual, not for here. But the birds sounded especially agitated. A couple of wrens darted out from the branches overhead, with a cardinal hot on their heels. Molly stole a glance over her shoulder, but she couldn't make anything out through the thick cover of trees. She looked back to her brother, standing out there in the middle of the yard.

Wally had unfrozen. He popped out his picking finger from his nose—a single lonely booger clinging to the tip—and used it to point high over Molly's head. Just then, the shade above her seemed to expand. Darryl whimpered. Crank hissed. Don Carlos turned a few shades darker.

"Wall—" She tried to call out to him but got cut short by a sharp noise. It was the trebuchet's counterweight dropping. Two full cinder blocks. In spite of the shaking and wobbling, her machine had carried on—this time without interruption.

At the far end, the entire A-frame convulsed, throwing the sling arm up and over the fulcrum, yanking its fluorescent green payload behind. The bowling ball lurched into the air, hurtling straight for the mannequin's head.

But it never reached it.

Out of nowhere, something fell from the sky, blocking the projectile's path. Something heavy. And metal. And bigger than anything she'd ever seen.

KROOOONNNGG! The hard urethane ball slammed into the side of this mysterious metal wall, leaving the tiniest dent before bouncing backward and landing in the dirt.

What in the world?

Another metal wall came down on the other side of her, pinning her in. Then the sun disappeared. Slowly, Molly stepped out from under the branches and looked up. Far above her, she saw that all this metal was connected. Only then did she understand where the sun had gone.

Molly and her brother now stood in the shadow of something new. Something that easily stood ten stories tall. It was made of shiny metal from head to toe, with rivets the size of saucers that went all the way up the seams of what Molly slowly took in to be arms, legs, and a body. Altogether, it looked a little like a giant man, but on the end of its gangly arms, instead of hands, hung two enormous iron claws. They looked big enough to uproot whole trees—even the old oak she was under.

It couldn't be. But it was.

A giant robot.

For a moment, it stood there silently, dwarfing everything around it. In all her eleven years, Molly couldn't remember ever seeing anything that size. The tallest building in Far Flung Falls was maybe four stories. And the highest hill she'd ever climbed wasn't much more than that. This was another category of big. It made her head spin.

What. On. Earth?

In the stillness, she could hear faint applause spilling out from their television inside. That sound was so familiar, but it didn't match at all what she was seeing. Nothing felt real.

The robot moved, and Molly fought to catch her breath. In one huge step it crossed their backyard, positioning itself between them and their house. Molly's body immediately broke out in a cold sweat. A million questions raced through her mind. Had the robot seen her? Was she in danger? Should she try to run? Her arms and legs were suddenly lead weights, while her head felt inexplicably light, as if all the blood had drained away. Torn between fascination and fear, she stood there paralyzed.

Belatedly, as it began to dawn on Molly what was happening, she realized that the bowling ball must have hit one of the robot's gigantic feet. Now the thing towered over Wally, bending a little at its bolted waist so that its glowing green eyes could peer down at the boy. Wally peered back up, mesmerized. The two examined each other for a moment. And then a giant metal claw reached down and picked up Wally by the back of his trousers.

"He-e-e-e-elp!" Wally cried as he was lifted up off the ground. "It's got me!"

Darryl growled. Crank hissed again.

In seconds, the claw brought Wally face to face with his captor, a hundred feet off the ground. He hung there in the air, terrified.

The giant robot unhinged its giant jaw, then opened its mouth impossibly wide with a loud metal *CLANK*. It leaned back its giant head, dangling the helpless boy in the air over the gaping mechanical maw. Wally flip-flapped his arms and kicked his legs, which didn't help at all.

As Molly watched the strange scene unfold before her, even stranger thoughts flooded her mind: Giant robots knew not to eat kids, right? And why would they even need to eat anything at all? They weren't even actually alive, were they? So what was it doing with Wally? Her brother looked so tiny, dangling way up there in that enormous metal claw. It occurred to Molly that for something that big, she and her brother wouldn't look much different than ants did to them. Maybe they were too small to care that much about?

The longer her brother dangled, the more troubled her thoughts became: What would she do if she never saw Wally again? Who would miss him? Probably not the ants . . . but would she? Had she been a good sister? And how long before their dad even noticed?

Molly shook her head, pushing the thoughts back down to whatever dark corner they'd come from. Now was not a time to think. It was a time to act.

"DON'T DO IT!" she screamed. Darryl started barking.

The robot ignored them both, or maybe it couldn't hear. Molly didn't see any ears on the monster. In a panic, she screamed even louder: "HEY! . . . MISTER! . . . ROBOT! . . . PLEASE! . . . PLEASE DON'T EAT MY BROTHER! HE PROBABLY TASTES LIKE DIRT! OR BOOGERS!" This was very likely true. Wally nodded his head vigorously in agreement.

But the robot only paused for the briefest moment, as if contemplating this news.

Then it dropped Wally in.

The boy fell silently into the robot's metal jaws while Molly stood there and watched helplessly.

Her mouth formed a big letter O, but no sound came out. Her screaming muscles weren't working anymore. Fortunately, her other muscles were working just fine. Before she knew it, her legs were racing her toward one of the robot's giant feet, with Darryl close behind. When she was only a few steps away, Molly threw herself at the side of the foot and grabbed onto the only bolt within reach—about the size of a softball—right as it lifted into the air. Molly held on with all her might as the ground dropped below.

She banged on the robot with her left hand while she held on with her right. At last, she found her voice again.

"LET! WALLY! GO!"

Then everything suddenly reversed. The foot was coming back down nearly as quickly as it had gone up. Molly screamed as loud as she could until she was out of breath.

"GIMME BACK MY BROTHER!" she shouted. "DON'T TAKE ANOTHER STEP!"

The robot didn't listen.

Up and down she went as the giant robot moved. Seeing another bolt directly above her, Molly climbed up to it, but her feet began to slip on the one beneath her. Trying to regain her balance, she made the bolt spin faster and faster, loosening it from the socket.

The next time the giant's foot made contact with the earth, the bolt she was standing on popped out and dropped to the ground, taking her with it. *Uff!* Lying on her back, still trembling, Molly saw the robot take a step back into the woods.

No! She had to stop it! *Think, Molly, think!* She sprinted back to the trebuchet, pulling the heavy A-frame around. The bowling ball wasn't far away. She reloaded the weapon and peered over the trees to get it in position.

The bowling ball soared high and true, up over the trees, then disappeared.

She watched the robot tromp off through the forest, over a hill . . .

And out of sight.

CHAPTER 9
FLUFFERNUTTER SANDWICHES

Molly sat there a moment with her mouth hanging open. Finally, she closed it. She still couldn't believe this was happening. Had she imagined the whole thing? What was a giant robot doing in her backyard? And why would it eat her brother? Did robots even need to eat? And where did it come from? Was it from the future?

Or was it... the Soviets?

Darryl came over, panting excitedly.

"Of course!" Molly said, answering her own question. "It must be them!"

Darryl growled in agreement.

A giant robot started to make sense. The Soviets were definitely still mad the president had called them an evil empire. And this looked like something an evil empire would do! It was just like Star Wars . . . and the empire was striking back! The Soviets had started a robot invasion! And they were stealing American kids . . . right here in the middle of Ohio . . . one little brother at a time . . . and turning them into *communists* . . . whatever that meant . . . before they nuked everyone else!

She had to tell someone, but who? Her dad? The police? Leonard and Arvin? President Reagan? Would the president of the United States listen to an eleven-year-old? Would anyone even believe her story?

Then another thought occurred to Molly. It was an awful, terrible thought. What if they did believe her story? What would everyone think of her? If she hadn't banished her brother from her invention under the tree, he wouldn't have been out in the open. And if he hadn't been out in the open, the giant robot wouldn't have even seen him. . . .

This was all her fault! She was the one who'd been

watching him. What would her dad say? What would everyone say? She was going to be in so much trouble! It was true her brother was annoying and gross, but he was still her brother.

That realization focused her mind. Giant robot or not, Molly would get her brother back. It was up to her to make things right. Her cheeks suddenly felt hot, and she blinked hard to hold back the tears welling up in her eyes.

Darryl sniffed the giant bolt beside Molly. He growled one more time, then gently nudged her arm.

"You're right, Darryl. I'm going."

As quickly as the words came out of her mouth, a plan hatched in her brain. She stood up and raced back to the house. Molly flew up the back steps in a single bound. But as the screen door slammed shut behind her, something in the kitchen stopped her in her tracks. It was a little sticker on the side of the phone, which was hanging on the wall. She remembered bringing the sticker home from school back when she was in the second grade. A police officer had visited their class that day. In bright orange letters, it read:

EMERGENCY? DIAL **911**

Molly considered her options. Maybe she should at least try. She reached for the handset, put it to her ear, dialed the numbers, and waited.

"Hello? Hello? Is anybody there? This is an emergency! My brother has been kidnapped by a Soviet robot!" Molly paused to listen for an answer. "Hello?"

Nothing. Not even a dial tone.

Molly's eyes traveled from the phone to the countertop, where she saw the pile of unopened mail her dad had left there. The one on top was from the telephone company. It said **PAST DUE**.

Of course. The line was dead. Molly tried to remember the last time she'd heard it ring. Her dad probably hadn't paid the bill in forever. Molly put the handset back in the cradle with a *clunk*, then realized that she had twisted herself up in the cord.

As she freed herself, she listened to the TV blaring from the next room over.

"Ain't ya just a little bit outta your territory here, Marshall?"

It was *Gunsmoke*, one of his favorite shows. But it felt like they were talking to her. She *was* out of her territory. But how could somebody help her who couldn't even pay their phone bill? Or keep up with the yard? Or save their mom from an evil wizard in a crappy van? She loved the *idea* of having a grown-up come by her side—especially if that grown-up was her dad—but knew in her heart of hearts that he'd probably just slow her down. It was up to her.

Molly paused for another second. But there was no time to waste. Somewhere out there, that robot was on the move. With Wally.

She was in her bedroom before *Gunsmoke* cut to the next scene. Molly could hear horses galloping, and the sound propelled her along. At the bottom of her closet, she found her backpack, which she hadn't used since summer had started. She dumped out the contents: a tattered Trapper Keeper notebook with a graffiti-style **AWESOME!** on the cover, four broken pencils, and her last writing assignment for the year, with a big red C- on it. Not awesome. Seeing that C- reminded her just how much she didn't care for Miss Marlow, her fourth-grade teacher. Clearly, Miss M. didn't appreciate the humor of her title, "I Plan to Spend the Summer Being Totally Bored Out of My Mind." But that was far behind her now. And besides, she had something more important to think about at the moment: planning a rescue.

Molly packed the essentials: a flashlight, extra batteries, her slingshot, a dozen small pebbles she had collected from the riverbed, a coil of rope, her pocketknife . . . and what else? Then it hit her. Of course! She had forgotten to pack anything to eat in case she got hungry. Who knew how long it took to rescue your brother from a giant robot?

Molly's next stop was the kitchen. She opened the pantry, zeroing in on the key ingredients: Wonder Bread, peanut butter, and marshmallow fluff. In a flash, Molly whipped up several perfectly made fluffernutter sandwiches, wrapped them all tightly in wax paper, and slid them in a brown paper bag. After that, she threw in a handful of saltwater taffy left over from the last day of school, then filled her canteen with water from the kitchen sink.

Backpack fully loaded, she pulled the straps over her

shoulders and cinched them tight. She felt ready. Something about the way the straps straightened her back gave Molly a newfound sense of purpose and power. More than anything, she was overcome by a determination to not fail her brother. And the clock was ticking. It was time to move before the robot got too far. She began to walk out the door, then turned around and poked her head into the living room.

"Dad? I just wanted you to know—"

"Can't it wait till a commercial, honey?"

Molly wasn't surprised. Prying him away from the television was next to impossible. Still, she had to try.

"A giant robot ate Wally!" she blurted out. "And I'm going to go rescue him!"

"That's nice, sweetie," Dad said without taking his eyes off the screen. "Remember to be home by dark."

"Seriously! A robot plucked Wally straight outta the backyard!"

"A what?"

"A. GIANT. BROTHER. PLUCKING. ROBOT!"

"Watch your language, Mollz."

Ugh. Molly knew it was pointless to talk to her dad whenever the TV was on. But that didn't stop her from trying. "You're not listening! It swallowed him whole! And it's up to me to save him!"

"Hmmph, good'un," he said between mouthfuls. "*Eat* Wally? He probably tastes like dirt. Or boogers." He chuckled to himself, spraying tiny orange bits of barbecue-flavored chips across his already-stained undershirt, then settled back into his show.

At least he had heard some of what she said. Still, Molly was wasting time. She turned and left out the door. Before the next commercial break, she would be hot on the robot's trail.

CHAPTER 10
GRUNCLE'S GIFT

When Molly slipped out to the carport, Darryl and Crank were waiting for her, right by her bike. She tried to explain to them that this was a solo mission, and possibly very dangerous. But the dog and cat appeared united in not listening, like true friends.

"Okay, fine," Molly said, pretending to look upset.

Crank had already claimed the basket attached to the handlebars. And Darryl stood alongside. He had kept pace with Pink Lightning on many a trip.

Something looked different about her bike, but she couldn't put her finger on it. Then she noticed the frame looked kind of lumpy. Molly leaned in to take a closer look.

It was Don Carlos! He was holding on to the center bar and had turned bright pink to match his surroundings. So it was a rescue party of four.

"Ready?" she asked her crew. "I'm not sure where this mission will take us. Or how long we'll be gone." Molly looked each of her fellow rescuers in the eye. She wondered if they could actually do this. Part of her wanted to reassure them they could, but maybe the other part wanted some reassurance herself. In the moments that followed, a mutual, unspoken resolve formed among them as the various animals all met her stare—except for Don Carlos. His eyes were always going in different directions, kind of like Gruncle's eyes did sometimes. But neither one of them could help it.

She wouldn't admit it aloud, but Molly was happy to have this trio accompany her. Sometimes, she felt like they were the only ones in the world she could really count on.

With one final check of bike and supplies, Molly headed out. Her braid whipped behind her as she pedaled with all her might. Crank peeked her head out of the basket to keep watch where they were going, and Darryl ran alongside. They started off the same way that Molly last saw the giant robot stomp off over the trees and hills. But she wasn't even sure if that was the right direction. What if the giant had taken a sharp turn somewhere? Or burrowed underground with those claws? Or blasted off into the sky? Molly wasn't sure what giant robots could do—besides snatch little brothers that didn't belong to them.

She crossed their backyard, stopping at the edge to take one last look at the house. Through the small living room window, she could see the faint blue glow of a TV screen, where her dad was still planted. Molly let out a long sigh. For some reason, she thought about the last time she had seen her mom looking back at the house before hopping in that van, and wondered if she had felt unsure about what she was doing too.

She looked over to the Evil Wizard. He was still standing.

"Don't worry, you'll get yours," Molly said, tightening her grip on her handlebars. "But you'll have to wait your turn."

She started pedaling again, kicking up dirt. The terrain

got a little bumpier, but nothing she and her bike couldn't handle. And the first stretch was downhill, which helped. Before long, the woods had completely swallowed her up, with the McQuirter property well out of view.

After nearly an hour, Molly's string-bean legs were starting to get sore. But she wasn't slowing down. There was still no sign of anything—at least nothing she was sure about. The hills behind her house were covered with thick patches of brush, vines, trees, and moss. Here and there, the foliage gave way to a stone outcropping, or a meadow, or a gorge. It was beautiful, but all the up-and-down terrain made it hard to tell a robot's footprint from a plain old dip in the ground.

This was going to take longer than she'd thought.

Well, if I'm going to ride for hours, she mused, *at least I get to do it on Pink Lightning.* With its bright pink banana seat, pink reflectors, pink streamers on the handlebars, and pink flames on the frame, her bike stood out in sharp contrast to the nature all around her. When Molly was riding, she felt like nothing could stop her. (And that was close to the truth.)

Since the bike had been a birthday present from her

Great-Uncle Clovis, Molly often thought of him when she rode. Gruncle was her absent mom's uncle, and ever since his niece had taken off for parts unknown, he had made an effort to come around more. Molly didn't mind this at all. Her Gruncle was unusual, but always fun. He didn't even own a TV, which Molly thought was great.

Gruncle didn't have any children of his own, but he had always taken a special shine to Molly and her brother. When Molly turned eleven (the "double ones" birthday, as he called it), he said that it would be a lucky year for her. "All the double-number birthdays are 'specially lucky," he had explained in his deep, gravelly voice, "more so 'n the rest... and you only get 'em every eleven years, so enjoy." That's when he had rolled out the bike from its hiding spot, with a bright pink bow on top.

"This here's Pink Lightning," he told her after she finally stopped screeching in happiness, "a one-of-a-kind bike for a one-of-a-kind kid!"

One of a kind was right! Molly had never seen anything like this before. And she was pretty sure no one else in the neighborhood had either. Not that bicycles were that uncommon. If you were a kid on Far Flung Falls Drive and had outgrown your old one, a bike was a pretty standard birthday gift. Maybe a Huffy, or a Schwinn if you were lucky. But not one like this.

"I might've made . . . ahhh, a modification or two," her Gruncle said with a wink and a smile, "but I'll tell you about those later." Molly hugged her Gruncle so hard. It was the best gift she'd ever gotten. And it was the only one she'd gotten that day. Her dad had forgotten her birthday. He wasn't too good at remembering things, at least not lately—unless it was when his favorite shows were on.

For the rest of the afternoon, Gruncle Clovis taught her how to ride, which she picked up pretty fast. She'd taken a few tumbles but had only scraped her knee once. Gruncle had thought it was funny that Molly had been more worried about getting a scratch on Pink Lightning than her own skin.

As the sun sank low, Gruncle Clovis told her they would ride together someday—Molly on Pink Lightning and Gruncle Clovis on Blue Thunder, a rusty old beast of a motorcycle with a sidecar from World War II that he kept in various pieces out in his garage. He claimed to have won the three-wheeled monster in a game of poker, and he had kept it in a continuous state of repair ever since. He lived a few miles away, but occasionally, on a clear night, when the wind was right, Molly was certain she could hear some banging and clanging at odd hours, or even a small explosion. The next day, her Gruncle would always emerge from these incidents in one piece, mostly. Blue Thunder wasn't so lucky.

Pink Lightning was in much better shape—in spite of all her uncle's "modifications." It had two extra levers built into the frame, three extra buttons mounted on the handlebars, and multiple secret compartments. The custom controls were Molly's favorite parts. It was as if her Gruncle had pulled them from her own imagination and made them real. As a fellow inventor, he knew how much she appreciated the personal touches—but he had warned her to be "very, very careful" with each of these, that they gave her bike special abilities for "you know, just in case." Before he'd explained each feature, Molly had accidentally pressed the little green button near her right grip, which immediately launched the basket on her handlebars with such force that it hit a tree some forty yards down the road and shook loose a hornet's nest.

"Hoo boy! That worked better than I thought!" her Gruncle had exclaimed. "That's good ol' American ingenuity at its spring-loaded finest!" She later discovered that the various other buttons and levers included a behind-the-seat flare launcher ("just in case you ever got lost"), a rear-facing axle-grease sprayer ("just in case you were ever being tailed"), a wind-up self-propelled accelerator ("just in case you ever needed a little more juice"), and one last lever that he explained was for "just in case all else fails."

Molly glanced down at all the buttons and levers as she crested another hill, and they gave her the courage to keep going. She had never pulled that last lever to find out what it did. In fact, after the incident with the hornet's nest, she had never tried any of Pink Lightning's other special features. But now, as she thought about what lay ahead of her, Molly wondered which of Pink Lightning's hidden talents might come in handy.

CHAPTER 11
STRANGE BIRD

Up in the robot's command center, the intruder continued his steady march through the woods, stepping over ravines and boulders without slowing down. His hands felt slick on the forward control grips, and he realized he was still sweating a little from the incident a few miles back. *Where had that girl come from?*

He replayed the events in his mind, and he was sure this last boy had been alone in his backyard. He'd watched for several minutes beforehand, just like he had with the others. He definitely hadn't expected any resistance. But he had already put plenty of distance between them. No way she could catch up. Still, he'd have to be more careful with any additional acquisitions.

He looked down at one of the displays:

OCCUPANTS: 04

That was three more than when he started. The intruder allowed himself a smile. These last two days had finally shown results. His brief satisfaction was interrupted by a small *blip* from one of the external sensors. A muffled clacking of unseen gears echoed all around him as he swiveled thirty degrees to the left.

What's this? He pressed a few buttons to investigate.

Directly above him, a pair of high-frequency antennas on the robot's head rose up to more than double their previous height. His breathing quickened a little with anticipation. He pressed a third button. Between the antennas, a small metal dish unfolded to become yet a larger dish. The radar swiveled around until it honed in on the source of interest, angled itself, then dilated to maximum diameter.

He turned up the volume on his speakers.

In the distance, a faint sound rose and fell over the chorus of nature.

Molly and the Machine

Unlike the chirps and tweets of unending birdsong, this was a low, lonesome melody. Even with all of the robot's surveillance equipment finely tuned, the sound was still barely audible through the trees and the distance....

Ohhhhh, swee-ee-eet nectar

Beeee-fittin' of a king

You'll aaaal-ways be our see-ee-cret

S'long as I can sing...

This couldn't be the girl. It was a lower pitch. But if not her, then who? He checked his map, but it was just woods for miles.

With care, the intruder rotated one of the pedals underfoot. The command traveled through a network of wires that sent currents nearly a hundred feet down. Instantaneously, one of the truck-size feet below him echoed the movement.

The robot stepped high over a wide, jagged chasm, tripping on a single tree. It briefly paused, then edged closer toward the song. He moved at only a fraction of his earlier pace, taking care now to avoid any more mishaps. No easy task in this thick patch of woods. But in spite of its colossal size, he had learned that even a mechanical giant could be stealthy when necessary.

Up ahead, a small clearing came into view. From its center, a thin ribbon of smoke rose upward to join the few stray clouds that hung overhead. Maybe he wasn't the only one who liked to hide in the woods. He inched the robot closer. Finally, through his two circular screens, he had a clear view of the source of the sound. It was a human. Most likely male. And he was alone.

Perfect.

He adjusted the radar to the new vantage point, fixating on the figure, trying to determine his age. But a wide-brimmed hat obscured the subject's face. The human wore faded dungarees and a sleeveless undershirt with brown lace-up boots. A leather bandolier crossed his torso, with pockets that held various tools. The subject continued singing, unaware he had an audience:

The puuuuuur-est ambrosia

That eeev-er has beeeen

Sweet fuel for my mo-o-tor

Like candied gas-o-line . . .

Molly and the Machine

In the center of the clearing stood three copper cylinders, all connected by an intricate network of pipes and rubber hoses. The middle cylinder, propped over a thick iron grill atop two rows of cinder blocks, was much taller than the two beside it. Below the grill, a trench of hot coals made the air ripple in the space between. The subject was hunched down in front of the contraption, carefully feeding more logs to the fire. He moved with a kind of reverence, weighing each log in his hands and placing it on the fire like some kind of offering.

What was this thing? The intruder admired the handiwork of the contraption, even if he wasn't sure exactly what it was, or why it was out in the woods. On the first night of his journey, he'd spied similar apparatuses, but it had been dark, and they weren't nearly as elaborate as this one. For a moment, he had thought they were other robots, but he eventually ruled that out when they remained stationary. It made for a puzzling scene.

Nearby, a collection of large barrels was stacked in a pyramid. A few other random articles dotted the perimeter of the clearing. Two upside-down buckets. A makeshift table with a smattering of tools. A stack of cordwood. Through the open space ran a small creek of clear water, its babble a background to the subject's song.

As the intruder watched from high above, the subject tapped a valve with his finger. From there, he traced an imaginary line over to a pair of dials. He grabbed one and tried to turn it. The subject grunted. It appeared the control wouldn't budge. He pulled out a large pipe wrench from his bandolier, adjusted something below the dials, then tightened the connecting joints.

In response, the cylinder started to rumble and shake, followed by a loud gurgling sound.

"Aww, quiet, you!"

The subject swung the wrench, whacking the cylinder on the side.

B-O-O-O-O-ONG!

The sound echoed through the woods.

Far above, the intruder leaned forward, causing the robot to do the same. He magnified the image with a few clicks. By the number of dents in the cylinder, this wasn't the first of such exchanges between the subject and machine. *Proceed with caution*, he thought.

Slowly, the intruder adjusted the robot's height. Its segmented legs collapsed in on themselves one section at a time until it was several feet shorter. Now his view barely cleared the tops of the surrounding trees. But he could still hear everything clearly. Down below, the subject continued with his banter.

"Shhhhh. There, there, now, baby. *Easy* now. Why ya gotta be so . . . so *ornery* sometimes?"

In response, a short burst of steam piped out of the cylinder's top.

"Alright now, baby. *Al-right*. That's fair. That's *under-stan-dable*." The subject paused, hung his head. "You know I didn't mean it."

With his target sufficiently distracted, the intruder decided this was as good a time as any to make a move. Slowly and silently, he guided the enormous claw in closer from above, hovering over the nape of the subject's neck.

Somewhere beyond the clearing, there was a rustle.

At the tiny commotion below the subject spun around...
a little too fast, losing his balance. Tripping over his own feet,
he fell flat on his face with lightning speed. Simultaneously,
the intruder squeezed his grip. But it was a moment too slow.
In the spot where the subject had been standing a moment
earlier, the pincers closed together with a nearly inaudible
clack. Having missed his target, he rapidly withdrew the
claw behind the curtain of trees.

The element of surprise now gone, he watched the subject
hastily make his way on all fours through the dirt to a wooden
box at the far end of the contraption. Was he trying to escape?
Then he noticed his hand hovering over a small metal plate
atop the box. It had a black button in the center. The subject
scanned right and left for trespassers—but failed to look up.

"You'd better back away from what's not yours, whoever
you are... unless you wanna get caught... in my web!"

At that last word, his hand dropped, hitting the button
hard.

The ground erupted all around the copper cylinders as
seven spring-loaded boards shot upward out of the dirt like

miniature catapults. Each hidden board launched a lead-weighted casting net that spread out to fifteen feet in diameter. In rapid succession, the nets flew in every direction.

WHOOSH-WHOOSH-WHOOSH-WHOOSH-WHOOSH-WHOOSH-WHOOSH!

The impact of the nets all around caused the trees to shake.

"Hey! I thought there were eight of th—"

WHOOSH!

"Oh, there you are."

The subject stood back up, surveying the area. "That's right. When you enter *The Octagon*, you might never leave! Hi-yah!" He made a karate-chop motion, then pulled off the hat, revealing a head of thinning gray hair and a big bushy mustache.

At the sight of this, from far above, the intruder froze in his harness. It was a grown man! Oh no, much too old. Immediately, he directed the giant at his command to take a step back, careful to retrace the rectangular imprints he had already made. *Unheard and unseen.*

Maybe three acquisitions was enough. For now.

As he retreated, he kept an eye on the subject, making sure he had no other surprise buttons within reach. The intruder's fingers danced over his control panel to ensure a smooth exit.

However many buttons you've got up your sleeve, he thought, *I've got more.*

He watched the old man scratch his head and pull out a pipe he had balanced in the corner of his mouth. He tugged on the tips of his mustache.

"That's funny," the man said, surveying the perimeter. "I could've sworn . . ." Then it looked like something caught his attention. One of the nets had captured a young bunny. He sauntered over, lifting the net to let the terrified creature escape.

"There ya go, fella. Run along. You're too tiny to be dinner just yet!"

He began singing again.

But the intruder was already well out of earshot, and picking up speed.

CHAPTER 12
LOOSE SCREW

Molly stopped to take a sip from her canteen, looking behind her. They'd covered a lot of ground over the last couple of hours, and her legs were already aching. But the trail ahead looked like it stretched on forever. Molly wondered for a moment if trekking off into the woods to find Wally was a dumb idea. Then she thought, *If not me, then who? Who would believe my story? A giant robot who kidnaps nose-picking brothers? Unlikely.* And besides, the clock was ticking. For every minute she hesitated, the robot would have a greater lead.

"Well, Darryl, whaddya think?" Molly was tired, but she'd already started pedaling again. "Are we on the right trail?

Smell anything? Like a giant robot? Or Wally? Or anything?"

As if to answer, Darryl stopped in his tracks and burrowed his snout in the grass.

She braked Pink Lightning a few yards ahead. All three on the bike turned to see what Darryl had found, even Don Carlos. The dog wouldn't budge from his position. Maybe his nose was stuck on something? After waiting a moment, Molly dismounted and wandered back to check out the situation.

That's when something caught her eye. Something shiny. It glinted in the waning sunlight the same way the giant robot had. "Hey! What is it? Whadja find there, boy?" Molly reached down and picked up a large metal hex bolt. It was heavy in her hand.

"Is this from the giant robot?" Molly asked. Darryl barked an affirmative.

Molly studied this first clue. What could it tell her? She rolled it around in her hand. There was something engraved on the outer ridge of the cap! Molly held it close to her face and squinted. She could make out words in small block letters that read clockwise along the perimeter of the bolt's head:

VANDERVORKEL ROBOTICS, INC.

Molly whispered the words as she brushed her finger over the engraving. Suddenly, anger filled her body. Up until that moment, she'd been too busy trying to: make good time without hitting a tree, balance two passengers without missing a clue, and keep an eye on her dog without getting lost herself. Now that she'd taken a moment to pause, the anger found time to focus. She squeezed the bolt in her hand to make a fist and shook it at the sky.

"Hey, Vandervorkel! I don't know who you are . . . or why you took my brother! But you're gonna have a lot more than one screw loose when I find you! You hear me?" Molly's words echoed through the empty hills for a moment until they faded into the dusk. The group remained silent a few moments. Don Carlos turned a slightly darker shade of pink to match the dimming light of day. Eventually, Molly's hand fell by her side, and Darryl slid up beside her, sticking his snout into her clenched fist. She could feel his wet nose prodding and sniffing, sucking in whatever smell lingered from the fallen clue.

"You got the scent, Darryl? Yeah? Okay, let's go." Molly

cinched the straps on her backpack, checked her companions, and mounted Pink Lightning.

And once again they were off, heading deeper into the woods.

The sun sank lower and lower into the sky, and her shadow began to stretch across the ground behind her. But Molly kept going. She wasn't about to give up on her brother now—even if he sometimes got on her nerves. An hour had passed since they'd found the stray bolt (now in her backpack along with her supplies), and the trail had led them down to the bottom of a winding gorge. As her surroundings darkened, so did her mood. How could it be this hard to find a gigantic robot? Doubts started to creep in that she'd never see Wally again, or worse—that maybe, after the way she'd treated him, she didn't deserve to. Molly bit her lip. The thought of some Soviet invaders mistreating her little brother filled her with dread. Sure, *she* might be allowed to be mean to him because they were family, but not some stranger.

A noisy little trickle of river wound its way through the gorge's center, but Molly could tell that the water level sometimes went much higher. Her tires left a thin groove in the wet earth, next to a set of paw prints from Darryl. Behind her, a continuous spray from her back tire decorated the seat of her pants in mud splatters.

Just then, Molly heard an even louder noise, which turned out to be her own voice. "Whoooaaaaa! Ohhh—! Ahhhhh—!"

The ground underneath the bike had disappeared! First from under her front wheel, then her back wheel. As Molly continued to scream, she, her bike, and her passengers all fell head over handlebars into a giant rectangular-shaped pit. Doing a complete somersault midair, they landed right side up. This did not appear surprising for Crank. After all, that's how cats always landed, wasn't it? But it was not always the case for humans or lizards.

Luckily, the spot where they landed was nice and soft. Pink Lightning's two wheels hit the earth with a soft double *sploop.*

Darryl was the only one who had avoided the pitfall, maybe because he traveled with his nose to the ground. He looked down at his companions from above and barked to let them know where he was—but Molly could detect a trace of worry.

"It's okay, buddy. We're okay, I think...."

Molly looked around. She noted the perfect, unnatural shape of the rectangular indentation. And the even depth. She observed how smooth the sides were and how everything appeared perfectly flattened on the bottom. *Who'd go and dig a swimming pool out here in the middle of—? No, wait.* With a jolt, she realized what must have happened. They had fallen into one of the giant robot's giant footprints. But why hadn't this happened earlier? Until now they had not only managed to avoid falling into the footprints—they hadn't even seen one.

Molly stretched one arm up above her head to try to lift herself out, but the top edge of the footprint was still more than a few feet out of reach. She tried to climb, but the soft, wet earth gave way in her hands and she fell on her back.

"Ooof!"

This wasn't going to work. Molly pounded her fists into the mud all around her, trying hard to keep her arms from shaking with rage. It wasn't fair! Molly had gotten this far just to get stuck in a hole. *That dumb, stupid, no-good robot! Making giant footprints for people to fall into!* Molly figured that it had done this on purpose in case anyone was on its trail. She needed to get back on her bike and keep moving.

An idea flashed in her mind—a bright pink idea. She propped her bike up against the side of the hole, then stepped on the seat. Her shoes were muddy, and it was tricky not to slip. By the time she'd caught her balance, the added weight and movement only succeeded in pushing Pink Lightning farther down into the mud. *Oh no.* If she lost her bike, there would be no way she could ever catch up to her brother.

Molly's eyes burned as she fought back tears. But there was no stopping the upsurge of emotion. She threw her head back toward the dimming sky and screamed, long and loud. It was an anguished cry, fueled by frustration and maybe a little fear. This couldn't be how her story ended, could it? As the scream carried on, filling the spaces between the surround- ing trees, critters scurried back to their burrows for safety. Molly screamed until she ran out of breath. But that wasn't enough. So she inhaled deeply and screamed again. Every pent-up feeling poured out of her until nothing was left . . . and it felt good. Her body shuddered, there at the bottom of a giant footprint, all alone.

Or was she?

In response to her outburst came a faint groan. And it sounded close.

CHAPTER 13
BOG MONSTER

"Darryl? Crank?" Molly called out from one end of the footprint.

A squishing sound came from the darkness, followed by a bubbling.

Molly felt a twinge of panic rising in her chest. Was someone else down here? Or worse yet, some*thing*? She was probably starting to get splotchy, not that anyone would be able to tell. With everything draped in shadow, it was so hard to see. What else could've fallen down here? Some creature? A wolf? Or a wampus cat? Or a wild boar? She imagined herself getting gored in the dark by a mean pair of tusks. Definitely not a part of her rescue plan.

Molly unzipped her backpack and fumbled through the contents until her fingers found the cold metal handle of the flashlight. *Yes!* She flicked it on and shot a narrow beam of light into the darkness ahead. It illuminated a small circle in the shaded corner from where she thought the sound had come. Trying not to shake, Molly panned back and forth. Nothing but mud. Then, in the corner, the mud moved.

Another groan. This one a little louder.

"Who's there?" She tried to keep the beam steady, but her fingers began trembling just a little. No response. "You'd better stay back if you know what's good for you. My friends here are trained to attack."

Crank hissed, then immediately hid behind her leg.

Don Carlos was nowhere to be seen.

Then the mud rose up.

Oh no, it wasn't a wolf or a boar—it was worse. A bear? Or . . . was it the dreaded *bog monster* she'd heard stories about? That couldn't be true, could it? But here it was, rising from the muck, coming her way. *Think, Molly! What else did you pack?*

From above, Darryl leaned his head over the edge and let out a long, low growl toward the darkness.

"Stand back, you ... bog monster!" Molly rummaged in the pack and found what she needed. "I've got a slingshot ... and a good aim!" While talking, she'd already loaded a pebble, and she pulled back.

"Gaaaaaaaaaaahhhhhhhh ..." The creature advanced.

Molly let the pebble fly.

"Yeowwwww! My leg! Hey! Stop!" The creature started hopping up and down in the mud, then fell over in a heap.

Wait a minute. Something wasn't right. That voice. It didn't sound very bog-monster-y at all. In fact, it sounded familiar. Molly studied the heap.

"Arvin?" she called.

The heap answered, "Who's asking?"

"It's me, Molly."

"Molly? But ... How can ... Why'd you shoot me?"

"Sorry, I thought maybe you were ... a bog monster."

"A what?"

"A bog mon—" Molly paused. "Um . . . never mind."

Truthfully, Arvin could have easily passed for some crea-ture of unknown origin. He was covered head to toe in dirt and mud and plastered with leaves and twigs, two of which were stuck in the mesh of his precious *Empire Strikes Back* hat, poking out like a tiny pair of antlers.

On top of that, he was holding one of his hands close to his chest at an odd angle. That's when Molly noticed that one of his fingers was badly swollen. And bent. In the wrong direction.

"Arvin! What happened to your fin—?"

"I know! I think I jammed it when I fell from the . . . the . . ." Arvin shuddered. "When I fell in this pit. It hurts so bad!"

"Lemme see if I can . . ." She reached out to check the damage.

"Aiiiigh!" he screamed, jerking his body backward before she even got close. "Don't touch it!"

"Okay, Arvin, but you'll need to get that looked at by some-one, as soon as we get outta this hole. How'd you get in here?"

"You wouldn't believe me if I told you," he said.

"Oh yeah? Try me," Molly said.

Arvin looked down and let out a long breath. "Okay, I'll tell you, but let's get out of here first."

"Deal." Molly said. She surveyed the four corners of the footprint. All she saw was mud and rocks. "I think I'm gonna need a boost."

"Okay, okay, just watch the finger," he said, offering a foothold with his good hand.

"Don't worry," Molly grunted, using him as a step. "It's hard to miss."

CHAPTER 14
HEAVE-HO AND ALLEY-OOP

After a long bout of slipping and sliding in the mud, Molly finally cleared the edge of the giant footprint, dirty but intact. She gave Darryl a big muddy hug around his neck, then looked back down at Arvin, Crank, and Don Carlos, who had magically reappeared on Pink Lightning's handlebars.

"Okay, Darryl, now we've just got to get everybody else," she said. "No problem, right?"

Darryl gave an affirmative bark.

"Arvin, how you doing down there?" Molly called.

"I'll be better when I'm up there."

"Okay, gimme a sec."

Arvin made a thumbs-up sign with his good hand. She gave him a nod in return. He wouldn't have been Molly's first pick to join her on a rescue mission. In fact, he probably wouldn't have made her top five. It wasn't that Arvin was particularly mean. In the past, he'd never paid her much notice, except when there was a chance to tease. Which he'd done more than once. He was always angling for a way to put himself first. But he had helped her out of the pit. Something in his demeanor had changed since their last exchange in front of Margo's house yesterday. Had that only been a day ago? They both seemed like different people. Maybe getting stuck in an oversize footprint had that effect. It was a strange experience—one they now shared.

Molly plopped her backpack on the ground, unzipped it, and began rooting around. She pulled out the coil of rope she'd packed. "This should do it," she announced. "We'll start with the animals and save you for last."

"Why am I not surprised?" Arvin said. "I see where I stand."

"You'll see yourself standing right there in that hole all

night if you don't shush . . . bog monster," Molly called from over the edge, grinning to herself. Maybe it was her turn to dish a little back.

Arvin laughed. "Okay, okay, the bog monster is shushing."

Maybe Arvin wasn't as bad as she'd thought. She tied one end of the rope around her waist and lowered the other end down to her companions. Crank was first, digging her claws into the rope and climbing up to safety before Molly had a chance to even give directions. After that, Don Carlos took his cue and began the climb. He took his sweet ol' time like he always did, thoughtfully placing one leg in front of the other, eyes darting in every direction except the one he was going. He made it to Molly's hand, climbed up her shoulder, and finally stopped on her head, where he slowly turned a deep shade of orange to match her hair.

Now all she had left to rescue was Arvin, but he was quite a bit heavier. She tossed the rope over a branch for leverage, then tied a sturdy bowline knot to the end that wasn't already tied to her waist. Years of making her own rope swings had made her a bit of a knot expert—at least enough to know that bowlines didn't cinch when you pulled on them. She lowered the rope.

"Step through the loop," she called.

"You sure?"

"Or you could just stay there," she said.

Arvin secured himself. After a few *heave-hos* and *alley-oops*, she called over Darryl for reinforcement. He bit down on the end of the rope and pulled alongside her. Eventually, they succeeded.

"Whew! Thank you," Arvin said. "What about your bike?"

Molly was already undoing the bowline and replacing it with a double half hitch—a knot that *did* cinch when you pulled. She lowered it back down, slipping the loop around the handlebars. It took a few flicks and wiggles to get the rope to cooperate. Once she got it right where she wanted, she gave it a hard yank and the knot closed tight. She yanked again, but lifting Pink Lightning was harder—and heavier—than she thought.

"I got one good hand," Arvin said. He gave a sheepish smile in the half light.

Together they hauled up Pink Lightning, along with several extra pounds of caked-on mud. Now it made sense why the bike had been so heavy. Molly appreciated having the extra muscle. Maybe Arvin would come in handy.

"Thanks," she said.

"No worries. So, uh, what else you got in that pack?"

They sat down on an outcropping of rocks and made quick work of two fluffernutter sandwiches. She split another one between Darryl and Crank, who both inhaled it. Then they divvied up the taffy.

"M'mm, that's gotta be the best sammich I have ever had," Arvin said between bites.

Molly passed the canteen. He took a long swig.

"Least I could do after shooting you," she said.

Arvin rubbed his thigh where he'd been hit. "Yeah, that's gonna leave a mark." He smiled. The air was cooling, and Darryl and Crank curled up in a ball between them. Before long, Darryl was snoring. Don Carlos had bedded down in Pink Lightning's basket.

Molly and the Machine

Molly asked Arvin again. "Now, how'd you end up in there?"

Arvin paused. "How about you?" he said.

"I asked first."

Arvin looked back over at the footprint.

"Okay. . . ." He met Molly's eye. "I escaped."

CHAPTER 15

MUNCHKINS

"**Y**ou *escaped*?" Molly's whole body tensed at Arvin's news. "From what?"

But she already knew the answer.

"It's gonna sound crazy, I know," Arvin said. "But I escaped from a . . . from a . . ."

"Giant robot," Molly finished for him.

"What?" Arvin looked shocked. "How'd you know? Did you escape too?"

"No," Molly said. "I'm tracking it."

"You're *tracking* it?" Arvin shook his head. "Why? That thing—"

"Because that thing has got my brother, is why."

"It took Wally, too? Oh man."

"Yeah, it did. Right in front of me."

Molly remembered the mix of terror and anger she had felt. It had happened just hours ago, even though it felt like forever. She quickly recounted what had happened in their backyard. A lump started to form at the back of her throat.

"And I'm gonna get him back," she said. "Arvin, did you see him when you were in there?" She was desperate to know if Wally was okay.

"Naw, I didn't see nobody else . . . but it was, like, a *really* *big* robot. I mean, I think it might've been even bigger on the inside. It could have the whole neighborhood locked up in there, for all I know."

"How'd it get you?" she asked, pushing aside her disappointment.

"Um, did you see those giant claws? Same as your brother, I guess," said Arvin.

"Did it grab you out of the 7-Eleven?" she asked. "With Leonard?"

"Naw, he bailed early, got tired of waiting for me to finish my game—"

"Lemme guess, a new high score," she said.

"As a matter of fact, yes." Arvin allowed himself a sly smile. "Initials. Were. Entered."

Molly rolled her eyes as he let out a small giggle. The sound felt out of place, echoing through the woods.

"Anyway, on the way home," Arvin continued, "I swung by the old scrapyard to see if any of the gang was there, you know, so I could brag a little. But it was all *munchkins*."

"'Munchkins'?" Molly asked.

"That's what Leonard and I call all the little kids in the neighborhood."

Molly pictured Leonard in her mind, thinking he looked pretty munchkin-like himself, and shook her head. Arvin got back to his story.

"Yeah, munchkins. They were playing hide-'n'-seek, and they asked me if I wanted to join in. I wasn't really interested, but they started saying stuff like 'Let's see if you're as good at real games as you are at *Donkey Kong*.' Can you believe that? The munchkins giving me a hard time?"

"Ridiculous," Molly said, straight-faced.

"I *know*!" Arvin said.

"Who all was there?" Molly asked, wondering who else the robot might've snatched.

"Lemme see. . . ." Arvin closed his eyes to help himself remember. "It was the Sorensons . . . Jasper and Jesse . . . little Stevie Brunner . . . the Gradys . . . Duck Foot Doug, you know, all of 'em. So I said, 'Sure, why not?' Those six-year-old pipsqueaks might think they've got the advantage on me because they can fit in tighter hiding spots, but I've got them beat on . . . *natural ability*." He smiled. "Anyway, I made my way through the scrapyard, past all the stacks of cars, and found this perfect little hiding spot on the other side of an old broken-down bus."

"I know the spot," Molly said, then quickly added, "Not that I've ever played with the munchkins or anything."

"Yeah, I mean, nobody was going to find me there," Arvin continued. "Nobody. And there I was, hiding from the munchkins, y'know, just minding my own business behind the bus, when all of a sudden the bus lifts right up in the air like some kind of balloon. It was crazy. I was staring right at it, and I couldn't believe what was happening. I looked around, but everybody else was hiding ... except little Stevie Brunner. He was still counting, and I could hear him, he was counting so loud. He was only on like sixty-two or something, and when we play, we make him count to a hundred. Which takes him forever, he's so slow. . . ."

"Uh-huh. Then what?" Molly prodded.

"Yeah, so anyway, I looked up past the bus, and there was this giant, gnarly robot face looking at me—with these glowing green eyes—holding up the whole bus like it was some kinda toy or something. Then with its other hand, you know, it had like these giant pincers—they were freaky ... it just grabbed my shirt, pulled me up into the air. I totally thought I was gonna die right there." Arvin pantomimed the events with his entire body, pausing here for dramatic effect. He clutched his heart and made a low croaking sound. "It all happened so fast, I didn't even scream or anything. It was like I was frozen, y'know? I was looking down, and I could see everybody's hiding spot, but they didn't see me. They all looked so tiny down there, and I just kept getting closer and closer to that giant mouth...."

Arvin was quiet for a moment.

"And then it just... dropped me in."

Molly thought about her brother as she listened to the rest of his story, which ended in a locked cell. Molly kept interjecting her brother in every scene Arvin described himself in. He was much bigger and older than Wally, but being in the robot had still left him visibly shaken. How would her poor little brother handle being locked up? She tried to push these troubling images from her thoughts, but they kept replaying in her mind. Wally tumbling through a long, winding chute . . . Wally trapped in a cold, dark room . . . Wally dodging electric wires and grinding gears as he searched for a way out . . . crawling through a maze of ductwork until he happened across an escape hatch . . . only to fall into a footprint! It was too much to take.

Finally, Arvin finished his story and took a deep breath. He shuddered. He'd been looking at the ground while he recounted what had happened to him, reliving every moment—from hide-'n'-seek to getting stuck in the mud. Now he looked up at his rescuer.

"Hey, you think the munchkins are still looking for me?"

The question hung in the night air under a thin sliver of moon overhead. The temperature dropped by a few more degrees. Or maybe it was just a chill from the caked-on mud. Molly hugged herself, feeling her stiff, dirty clothes. It occurred to her that this rescue mission might take longer than she initially thought. But she wasn't about to head home now. She looked over at Arvin. As daunting as it felt to find Wally, hearing that escape was possible and having one successful rescue already under her belt gave her the surge of confidence she needed.

If anyone could pull this off, she could.

Molly thought about home. She didn't want her dad to worry, but he had probably already passed out in front of the TV. Now that school was out, it would probably be at least a day before he, or anyone, noticed they were gone.

Arvin needed some first aid. But they were out in the

middle of the woods, and Wally was still out there. What should her next move be? Molly reached for her backpack, thinking maybe another fluffernutter might help make the answer clear.

But her pack wasn't there. That's when they both heard a rustling sound.

"Hey, Molly... does your backpack have a remote control or something?" Arvin asked.

"No, why?"

"Because... there it goes." He pointed to the pack, several feet away. It was sliding across the dirt into the shadows.

CHAPTER 16
MONDO THE MAGNIFICENT

"**H**ey, come back here!" Molly yelled into the darkness.

They were chasing her backpack deeper into the woods. Miraculously, it appeared to be moving on its own, zigzagging around the rocks and trees. *What now?* The thought of losing it, and all the supplies she'd packed inside, filled her with dread. She couldn't let it just run off—not if she still had any hope of saving her brother.

"There it goes!" Arvin called as it rounded a bend. "I think your pack is alive!"

They crashed headlong through the forest, trying hard

not to run into anything. Darryl, nose to the ground, followed close behind.

Then, just as they were on top of it, the pack abruptly stopped amid a cluster of rocks. Like most of the rocks in these hills, they were covered in thick patches of moss and lichen. Except for one. It was hard to make out much detail under the thin moonlight, but one of the rocks was a little redder than the others. And rounder. And bumpier. Molly trudged over to investigate. It was like no rock she'd ever seen before.

When she touched it, it moved.

Darryl gave a few barks.

"Mondo!" Molly screamed.

"Please tell me you don't have a pet rock," Arvin said, still out of breath.

Molly started laughing. "Mondo's no rock! He's . . . Mondo the Magnificent!"

"Mondo the *what*? Molly, have you lost your mind? Wait, have I lost *my* mind?"

Molly gave the round, bumpy rock a gentle pat. It moved

again, but this time a small crack appeared in its surface. And out poked a snout, followed by two pointy ears.

"Mondo is an armadillo," Molly said.

The creature was peeking out from his armor as if to say *Why yes, it is I. How may I be of service?* He tickled Molly's arm with a few tentative sniffs, then gave a quick snort of recognition.

"He's a little thief is what he is," Arvin said.

Mondo withdrew back into his protective shell and sealed himself shut.

"True." Molly paused. "But he might also be the answer we needed."

"The answer? Wait, what was the question?"

"What's our next move?"

"Next move? Um . . . we go home!" Arvin folded his arms. "Duh."

"Not yet." Molly said. "We still need to rescue Wally. *Plus* anybody else that metal monster might've snatched. But first, we need to fix up your finger. And I know just the spot."

"*Not* the clinic?"

Molly smiled. "Not the clinic."

"Because . . . *have you seen my finger?*" Arvin's voice rose an octave, and it involuntarily cracked. "I'm pretty sure I need some doctors . . . and X-rays . . . and bandages . . . and maybe some Novocain—"

Molly interrupted him. "We're going to see Gruncle Clovis."

"What is a Gruncle Clovis?"

"My *Great-Uncle* Clovis . . . *Gruncle* for short," Molly explained. "Mondo belongs to him." She gave the armadillo another pat.

"Okaaaay." Arvin tried to follow. "Then what's Mondo doing way out here?"

"That's a good question. Technically, *way out here* isn't that far from Gruncle's cabin. And he's been known to let Mondo roam free. But the curious part is how he made it to the other side."

"The other side of what?"

"Crook's Chasm."

"You mean the one all those people died in?"

"Yup," she said.

"The steepest, deepest, most dangerous gorge in all of Far Flung Falls?"

"Yup," Molly repeated.

"And probably haunted, too," Arvin said.

"Now you're just making stuff up," Molly said. But she'd heard the same stories everyone else had. Long before she and Arvin were born, when booze was illegal, a band of bootleggers from the next county over had snuck in by night and raided the stills of several local families who at the time were secretly in the moonshine business—possibly including a relative of hers. That part of the lore was always a little fuzzy. But as the story went, when the moonshine was found missing, the families gave chase. The thieves tried to escape into the woods, but they didn't know the land, and in their haste fell into the chasm to their deaths. Hence the name Crook's Chasm. Legend had it that it was so deep, even their spirits couldn't get out.

Arvin looked at the little armored ball that was Mondo. "Well, haunted or not, there's no way he crossed it. Not unless he's got some wings under there. Those cliffs go on forever."

Molly agreed. The chasm stretched for miles. "Maybe they put in a bridge?"

"Not that I heard."

"Still. Worth checking. For your finger."

She pointed westward toward a thick clump of trees beyond the next hill. "Thataway."

"How can you tell?"

Molly knew how easy it was to get turned around in the hills, especially at night, but she also knew this patch of woods pretty well and had already taken a moment to orient herself. She pointed to a nearby boulder.

"See up there, on the side covered with moss? That's the north-facing side."

"Oh right, because moss likes shade," Arvin said.

"Exactly. Now we just need to reconnect with the trail, and we can plot our course."

Arvin decided this was better than wandering around in the dark and maybe falling into another footprint. They grabbed the pack and Mondo, and doubled back to Pink Lightning. From there, they walked together until they came across one of the hard-packed dirt trails that wound through the hills.

"You think you can fit on the back? You can put your feet there." She pointed to the pegs on her back axle.

"Beats walking," Arvin said. His soaked sneakers made a loud squishing sound as he climbed aboard. "Pink might be my new color."

Molly laughed. They were back in action, and now a party of six. She gave Mondo a front-row seat in the basket on her handlebars right next to Crank—which the armadillo seemed to appreciate, but Crank did not. The cat lowered her head and eyed the freeloader wearily. Molly made a quick inventory of her companions and gear. Darryl beside her, Don Carlos on her shoulder. Backpack zipped up. And Arvin on the back. Everyone and everything accounted for.

They were picking up speed on the trail. But they had lost precious time and daylight. From here on, they'd have to be extra careful not to fall into another giant footprint. It wouldn't be easy. The sun had long sunk from view while they were stuck, making it even harder to distinguish the holes from shadows. But it was now or never.

"So, is your Gruncle Clovis a doctor?" Arvin asked.

"No, but he's an expert at fixing things."

"How did he come to have a pet armadillo?" Arvin asked.

"Oh, he kind of adopted him during one of his desert adventures out west." Molly looked down at the creature. From all the scratches on his shell, she could tell he had been in more than his fair share of scuffles in his life—kind of like her Gruncle.

"Hold on!" Molly swerved to miss another footprint.

"Whew!" Arvin sighed. "Let's not do that again."

"When Gruncle Clovis found him, Mondo was limping along a canyon trail with one of his stubby little legs bent at an odd angle . . . kind of like your finger." Molly talked over her shoulder but kept her eyes on the trail. "Gruncle Clovis never found out what had happened, but he didn't ask any questions. He figured the armadillo couldn't answer anyway. Instead, he just took the little critter under his wing, made a splint for his leg, and nursed him back to health. Even fed him with a dropper. After he recovered, Gruncle named him *Mondo the Magnificent*."

"I wonder what name I get when he fixes me?"

"Probably *Arvin the Mud Ball*."

"Doesn't quite have the same ring to it—oof!"

The road got bumpier, and Arvin nearly bounced off the back of the bike. With his good hand, he tightened his grip on Molly's shoulder. They passed a sign.

EXTREME DANGER

SHEER DROP

500 **FEET AHEAD**

Underneath the warning, someone had scrawled *Beware the curse!* Beside it was a poorly done illustration of what could be a ghost.

"See?" Arvin said. "Like I said. Haunted."

A few moments later, Molly hit the brake, kicking up a small puff of dirt. "Whoa," she said. She'd never been on this side of the chasm—and rarely this close. It was easy to see why people would think it was haunted. It was a mean, jagged cut through the rock, like an old wound that refused to heal. If you weren't paying attention, it could be deadly. On both sides, trees grew along the edge, their roots clutching whatever they could to keep from falling.

Arvin hopped off the bike's pegs. "Thanks for the ride," he said. "Hope I wasn't too heavy."

"No problem," Molly said. She was straddling the banana seat with her feet on the ground.

Together, the two inched close enough to peek into the depths below, but they couldn't make much out through the mist. Molly thought about the bones of the dead raiders scattered along the bottom, their spirits forever trapped. Something about it made the hair on the back of her neck stand on end.

"I don't see no bridge," Arvin said.

Molly turned to the armadillo. "Okay, how'd ya do it, Mondo?"

She picked him out of the basket and set him on the ground. Slowly, Mondo uncurled from his protective ball shape. He sniffed the ground, then darted off to the right.

"Don't lose him!" Molly yelled.

"Got it!" Arvin yelled back over his shoulder, already in hot pursuit. "But if that nutball goes over the edge, he's on his own! Already 'bout fell to my death once today!"

Molly followed closely behind, or at least tried to. Going off-trail through a tangle of bushes wasn't very bike friendly. But without Arvin on the back, her load was lighter—and there was no way she was leaving Pink Lightning behind. They chased Mondo as he scurried through the underbrush around the curve of the chasm's edge. Where was he headed? There was no way the little creature had the stamina to travel all the way around the ravine. But as soon as they cleared a dense thicket, the armadillo's secret passage became clear.

It wasn't exactly a bridge.

CHAPTER 17
CROOK'S CHASM

Molly and Arvin stopped and stared.

Across the dark depths of the chasm lay the trunk of a massive black oak. At first glance, the entire length of it appeared covered in spikes. But on closer inspection, they were merely the sharpened stubs of branches that had long since broken away. Still, it had a menacing look, like an oversize medieval weapon. Barren of bark and gnawed away in parts from decay, the tree appeared to have died long ago. But from the fresh clumps of earth still clinging to the upended roots, it looked to have very recently fallen.

Or been knocked over.

Together, they followed the line of the tree to the other side and there saw the smashed bits of what had been the tree's top—next to a telltale rectangular indentation.

"The robot."

Arvin said aloud what Molly was thinking. It must've clipped it when it stepped over the chasm. Which meant they were on the right trail—to her Gruncle's cabin, and to wherever the robot was taking her brother.

Without hesitation, Mondo mounted the root end of the tree and scampered across it, dodging the spiky branches until he cleared the far side. Even at its narrowest points, the chasm spanned a good fifty feet or so. But Mondo made quick work of it. He turned around and looked back at them. Not to be outdone, Darryl and Crank immediately followed. Molly could swear the armadillo looked like he was grinning. She looked at Arvin.

"Cross that death trap?" he said. "No. Way."

"You can turn back, but my brother's life is in danger," Molly said. "I'm doing this."

Arvin cast her a sidelong look. He raised an eyebrow.

"You sure?"

"No, but I have to try."

"Okay then. Ladies first," he said. It was a dare.

Molly walked Pink Lightning up the length of one of the exposed roots to the top of the trunk, then slowly began making her way across this accidental bridge, careful not to snag her bike—or herself—on one of the jutting branches. An eerie whistle rose up to meet her as the wind pushed its way through the chasm's bends below. *Just dumb stories,* Molly told herself, but she noticed she was breathing harder than she wanted. Don Carlos clutched her shoulder a little tighter. About the time she made it to the halfway point, the tree let out what sounded like a groan. Molly stood still. She could feel it start to wobble under her feet and made the mistake of looking down. The bottom of her stomach nearly dropped out.

"Don't look down!" Arvin hissed.

"Too late!" she hissed back. But once Molly recovered, she started making steady progress along the second half of the trunk. "I think it's stable."

"Why are we whispering?" Arvin asked.

"I don't know!"

Arvin was already climbing up the roots. Molly was betting he wouldn't let himself get shown up by someone a year younger—and a girl. Slowly, he started shuffling his feet forward. He made his way a couple of yards, then stopped just as Molly was hopping off the other side.

"Uhhh, I don't think I can do it," he said.

"Sure you can."

With her focus on Arvin, Molly failed to notice that the ring on the back of her banana seat had hooked one of the broken branch nubs. As she pulled down her bike, the entire oak rolled a few degrees to the right, crunching the ground underneath. Don Carlos jumped at the sound, scurrying away to join the other animals some distance away.

"Aaaaaaaiiiiiiiiiii . . . ," Arvin wailed.

"What're you doing now, Arv—" She turned and caught his terror-stricken face.

"Your bike!"

"My bike! Oh! Sorry!" She unhooked her seat, but the ancient, spiked log had already been set into motion. More crunching. On Molly's side of the chasm, the earth sloped downward slightly. And with the combination of gravity and inertia, the oak picked up speed. Arvin was doing his best moonwalk to keep from getting tossed over the edge.

The sounds of crunching and screaming now competed to fill the once-quiet chasm. Not sure what would happen next, the four animals huddled together.

Molly had to think fast. She couldn't let Arvin join the skeletal remains of the raiders down below. But what could she do?

A few feet down the slope, she caught sight of a deep side crevice splitting the face of the rock. It tapered into a notch at the bottom, but it was wide and long enough to catch the entire top of the tree as soon as it got there—which was moments away. In a flash, she saw the entire scene unfold like a colossal Rube Goldberg machine. Two seconds from now, the log would slam into that crack—and transform from a giant, spiked rolling pin into a giant, spiked catapult.

"Arvin, stop dancing and hold on!"

"But—" he protested.

"Just do it!"

Arvin grabbed hold of the nearest branch as the top of the

tree rolled the final few inches down the slope and smashed into the crevice, jamming itself tight. Just as Molly had predicted, as one end dropped several feet, the other end sprang off the lip of the opposite cliff and arched over the chasm, carrying a screaming Arvin with it, until its tangle of roots interlocked with a cluster of conifers and came to a rest. Wedged into a crack, the old oak now stood completely upside down.

"Hope your brother is worth it," Arvin muttered from above.

"Me too," Molly said. "Watch your finger."

With his good hand, he was now hanging from the branch he had grabbed moments earlier, and he had found a foothold on one below. Molly could hear him exhaling. But it wasn't over. The log began rotating, its age-old timbers groaning once more as it tried to adjust to this unnatural new position. Under the tree's massive weight, the rock split open further, which loosened its hold. The oak started to tremble.

Darryl gave two sharp barks. *A warning.*

"Um, Molly...?"

"JUMP!" she screamed. "Go for the pines!"

He didn't question her this time. Arvin pushed off the trunk with both feet, hurling his body at the nearest branch. Just as he did, the old oak began falling—back toward the chasm. But after all the jostling, the makeshift bridge was no longer poised to reach the other side. Silently, it disappeared into the mist. Moments later, a distant boom echoed upward from the chasm's floor.

Meanwhile, Arvin half-bounced, half-fell through the branches of one of the pines until he eventually found himself at the bottom. Now in addition to the mud and muck, he was covered in pine needles, which only added to making him look like a bog monster. But other than that, he looked okay, considering.

"Don't. Say. Anything," he said.

"Arvin, I—"

"Shhhhhhh."

For what seemed like a full minute, they stood there, looking at each other.

Then, for reasons neither could explain (but very likely nerves), they broke into laughter. Still huddled together, the dog, cat, armadillo, and chameleon all finally relaxed.

"Sorry for almost killing you," she said.

"Thank you for saving my life," he said.

"You're welcome," she said.

"You're forgiven," he said.

And minutes later, they were all back on Pink Lightning, headed toward the cabin. Darryl ran alongside. They splashed through a trickle of water to the other side of a low dip, then steadily made their way to the next jumble of hills as the earth began to slope back upward.

The incline was gradual, but the weight of additional passengers made it tough (especially when one of them was a human). To keep from feeling tired, Molly focused on her brother, which brought back all her worries. Was he okay? Was he scared? Would they be able to save him?

A shooting star flashed overhead, and Molly decided to take that as a good sign. If they could cross Crook's Chasm, what couldn't they do?

With renewed hope, the rescuers pressed on into the darkness.

CHAPTER 18
ZAP-O-MATIC

E leven minutes later, Molly and Arvin spied a faint amber light spilling from the back window of an old log cabin perched halfway up the hill.

"Here we are," she said.

"Is it . . . safe?" Arvin asked.

"Safer than what's behind us."

"No doubt."

Molly rarely approached the cabin from the back. From this direction, the logs all seemed to lean in different directions. In fact, the whole cabin looked like it would topple over if there was too strong a breeze. Which was a lot like how she would describe her Gruncle Clovis on most days. But she loved him.

"My Gruncle built it himself. 'Log by log, with only my own two bare hands, without the help of another living soul,'" she said in her best Gruncle imitation. "Or so he always says."

"Yeah, I dunno if I'd exactly be bragging about that."

"Gruncle has his own way of seeing things," Molly said. In truth, her Gruncle was the closest thing she had to a grandparent—or maybe a parent, too, for that matter. She wasn't sure how old he was, but it seemed like he'd been around a long, long time.

Gruncle Clovis liked to sip something he called "moose juice" from a silver flask he kept in an inside pocket. Molly doubted it was juice at all, because every time he took a swig—which was often—he'd squeeze his eyes shut, make a terrible face, then double over and cough. His breath smelled like roadkill dipped in turpentine. This, mixed with his various other odors, defined Gruncle Clovis: pipe smoke, wet dog, armpit sweat, stale peanuts, and Handsome Halbert's Hair Cream. Sometimes the combination was overpowering. It was the reason why Molly and her brother would, on occasion, call him "Gruncle Skunkle." But she still loved him despite the assault on her nose.

Right now, she hoped he was home—smell or no smell.

Dismounting Pink Lightning, Molly and Arvin walked the final few yards up to the cabin and around to the front. In the quiet, they noticed how loudly their sneakers squished and sloshed from their ordeal in the mud. On top of that, the steps leading up to the porch creaked miserably. Arvin froze.

"Don't worry. Gruncle calls it his alarm system," Molly said. The sound made Molly think of the last time she'd come here with Wally. Her brother wasn't very musically inclined, but whenever he walked up Gruncle's steps, he'd made a game out of stepping up and down and up again, like he was playing a giant piano. The creaks grew higher in pitch with each step, and it always made him laugh. As Molly and Arvin made their way up, she could picture Wally's face, with one of his front teeth still not all the way grown in. It was a happy memory.

Now, the porch creaked even worse. Before Molly could give the door a single knock, it flew open, and there stood

Gruncle Skunkle himself, or at least a bowed pair of legs that looked like his. From the belt buckle up, the figure was enveloped in a thick cloud of bluish-gray smoke. As the air cleared a little, Molly's eyes widened to see that her face was just inches away from the business end of one of her Gruncle's less friendly-looking inventions.

Arvin froze again.

The contraption's barrel extended out past the smoke. It was capped with a thick silver bowl on the end, about the diameter of a 45 rpm record. The bowl's edge held a collection of short metal prongs that all pointed inward to a long spike sticking out from the center. Behind that, Molly saw multiple rows of tight brass coils, followed by an explosion of red, blue, and yellow wires that snaked out in every direction from a ring of silver diodes. The wires wound into a single knot that disappeared somewhere back into the smoke.

Was this some kind of a weapon?

It was humming loudly, and it looked like something out of an old low-budget sci-fi movie—the kind that played on TV late Saturday morning after cartoons were over. (That was usually about the time her dad took over the TV for the rest of the day.)

Finally, the smoke began to dissipate, revealing a familiar face.

Clovis had been many things in his life—a cowboy, a mechanic, an inventor, a musician—but mostly, he'd been a mess. He kept odd hours, drank too much of that moose juice, smoked even more, and was frequently prone to coming up with the most crackpot ideas, which the moose juice surely didn't help. Case in point? The homemade weapon he now waved back and forth in a wide arc. Every time it came close to Molly, she could feel the hair prickle on the back of her neck.

"Who's there?" her great-uncle shouted, squinting into the dark. The gray pompadour on top of his head was beginning to thin and appeared to be fighting against the hair cream that tried desperately to hold it in place. But whatever the man lacked on top, he more than made up for with a gigantic handlebar mustache that spread out across his face in elaborate curlicues.

"Gruncle! It's me! Molly!"

The man paused a second, confused. He pulled the pipe from his mouth. Then he looked down and saw his niece.

"Molly? Well, jumpin' jitterbugs! What are you doing out so late?" He stepped out of what was left from the smoke cloud in the doorway and onto the creaky porch. It complained a little more from the added weight.

Molly's mouth opened, but she didn't know where to start. She threw her arms around her Gruncle's neck and squeezed him tight.

"Oh, there, there, now, Molly. Your ol' Gruncle Clovis is right here. You just take your time...."

"We were hoping...," Molly finally began.

"We?" Clovis asked, puzzled.

In the darkness, Clovis hadn't noticed Molly's mud-covered companion. She gestured to her left. "Gruncle, this is my friend Arv—"

Clovis turned his attention and his eyes grew wide. The mud, the muck, the pine needles, the puddle around his feet...

"The bog monster!" he hollered. Without hesitation, he raised up his weapon and squeezed the trigger—

BRRRZZZZZZZZZZZTTT!

Molly was blinded by a bolt of lightning that shot out from the gun's metal prongs to somewhere beyond the porch, filling the front yard with a burst that looked like daylight.

"Hey, watch out!" Arvin cried, hitting the floor.

"Gruncle, no!" Molly screamed.

Adding to the conversation, Darryl let out a loud "WOOF," which caught Clovis by surprise a second time. He fired again. A half second later, the electricity connected with something. There was a *CLANG*, then a long, echoing rattle, followed by a *SPLOOSH!*

Clovis had blasted a metal pail sitting on the ledge of his well some twenty yards away. The receptacle promptly fell in and hit bottom somewhere down below. Another innocent victim to his trigger finger. Luckily, it was the only one tonight.

"Aw, heck, that's the fourth one I done blasted this month."

Molly's vision slowly began to recover as the echo from the blast faded into the once-again dark horizon.

"Not a bad shot, though." Clovis's craggy face split into a big toothy grin.

"I'm just glad you didn't shoot Arvin! Or me!" Molly said, looking down at their damp shoes and socks. "That . . . thing coulda fried us to death! What is it?"

Clovis held up the device. Molly and Arvin instinctively ducked. "Oh, this little beauty? I call it the Zap-O-Matic. Ain't it something? Still working out a few kinks." As he said it, the Zap-O-Matic kicked out a small charge of sparks.

Molly made a note to disable it as soon as she had the chance. She'd already had enough brushes with death for one day, and the water pooling at her feet made her feel like an easy target for stray currents. She unconsciously patted her head with her hands, making sure it was still connected to her body. (Luckily, it was.) Arvin had stood back up and was doing the same. Darryl slunk over to find refuge behind Molly's legs and let out a little whine. Crank had darted under the porch, but she managed a little hiss to let the humans know that she was alive—and not happy. Don Carlos did what he always did—quickly and quietly faded out of sight.

"Well! I see you've brought a whole posse here. Must be serious business." Clovis scanned the six visitors looking back at him on his porch. That's when he finally noticed his dear armadillo, who had curled back into a ball.

"Mondo! My boy! They found you! Where have you been?" He picked up the little rust-colored ball, gave him an affectionate pat, and started whispering into the creature's ear. With his attention diverted, Molly carefully relieved her Gruncle of his firearm, then stepped behind him to slide off the power pack strapped to his back. Once it was on the floor, she followed the wires from the Zap-O-Matic to the pack and unplugged it. The gun kicked out one last crackle of sparks before the humming sound faded.

"Thank you," Arvin whispered. "Again."

"You're welcome," Molly whispered back.

Now safe from immediate electrocution, Molly turned her attention to the pack. It was covered in tubes, dials, and switches . . . and one red lever in the middle with a little piece of masking tape above it labeled *JUICE* in her Gruncle's handwriting, next to a picture of a squiggly lightning bolt. With some effort, she flipped it down. One by one, a series of lights faded, and a dial labeled *VOLTAGE* eventually crept down to zero.

Phew! Now that it was completely off, Molly breathed a little easier.

Still stroking Mondo, Clovis barely appeared to notice.

"Gruncle," she said, coming back to stand in front of him. "This is Arvin. He's not the bog monster—he just fell in the mud."

"You don't say!" said Clovis, giving Arvin a little poke in the shoulder just to make sure. "Must have been some mudhole."

"It was actually the footprint of a giant robot that ate Wally, not far from here," Molly explained. "We escaped, but now we need to save him! Oh, and Arvin hurt his finger pretty bad."

Arvin held up his swollen hand as evidence.

Clovis raised an eyebrow.

"Footprint? Giant? We need to *what*? Who? Where? Well ... um ... okay there ... so ..."

The old man scrunched up his face for a moment like it

hurt to process what he was hearing or think about what he should say next. Finally, his expression softened.

"Better come on inside and tell me all about it. Best getcher feet outta them soaked sneakers afore they blister up." He looked the visitors up and down. "Yes, indeedy. And lemme see if I can find you two adventurers some soap."

One by one, the entire party followed him in, each giving the Zap-O-Matic a wide berth.

CHAPTER 19
SOCKS AND SECRETS

The cabin was exactly as Molly had remembered from her last visit. The main room was filled floor to ceiling with piles of junk and strange contraptions, all in various states of disrepair. Between the piles, mysterious pipes jutted out of the floor, turned abruptly at odd angles, then disappeared into the walls. As instructed, Molly and Arvin peeled off their wet shoes and socks, then followed Clovis, who stumbled and tripped his way through the chaos, muttering to himself as if someone else were responsible for the mess.

After squeezing, dodging, and ducking around every

imaginable obstacle, they took their seats on mismatched chairs in front of a massive potbellied stove. It stood in the middle of everything, emanating toasty warmth in all directions. Molly felt safe near the stove. She and Arvin held their dripping footwear, trying not to add to the mess.

"Um, nice place," Arvin said.

"Oh, you like it? Built her all by my lonesome . . . log by log, with only my own two bare hands, without the help of—"

"—another living soul. I heard," Arvin said, exchanging looks with Molly.

"Is that right?" Clovis said, nodding with satisfaction.

Molly rolled her eyes.

"Well, hand 'em over," Clovis said, collecting their soggy shoes and socks. He proceeded to tie the laces together, then tossed each pair up over the blades of a huge propeller mounted to the chimney of the stove. The socks followed, each one landing with a splat.

"Annnnnnnnd . . ." Clovis pulled a pin from the propeller's hub. "Presto."

The blades began spinning around the chimney at a

leisurely pace, the centrifugal force lifting the shoes up by a few degrees. It looked like a miniature carnival ride.

"Nifty, ain't it?" He gave the chimney a couple of taps with a bony knuckle. "It's got blades on the *inside* too. The rising heat makes her spin like a whirlybird. Should be dry in a spell."

The propeller picked up a little speed, pelting them with a few random droplets and filling the air with the musty odor of wet sock. Molly turned her head. Surrounding them on all sides, an assortment of motorcycle headlights and handlebars were mounted to the wall on wooden plaques, like the heads of wild game.

"Oh, you like my collection?" Clovis asked, noticing Molly's look of interest. "Kilt every one of 'em myself—although some of 'em nearly kilt me in the process! Heh-heh-heh!"

The laugh progressed to a wheeze, then a full-fledged coughing fit. When he was finally done, his face straightened up, and he looked Molly in the eye. "But you didn't come here just to admire my... *mechanical menagerie*, didja? How's about you fill your ol' Gruncle in?"

Where to start? Molly's head flooded with a million things

at once. A giant robot with green glowing eyes . . . Her brother scooped up and swallowed . . . A possible Russian invasion . . . Her dad not listening . . . No way to reach the cops . . . A trail of footprints big enough to fall into . . . A brush with death over Crook's Chasm . . . And now Wally was all alone, who knew where, with the clock ticking . . .

"Could you take a look at Arvin's finger first?" Molly finally said. "He jammed it pretty good."

"Or pretty bad, depending on your view." Her Gruncle put a finger on the bags below both of his eyes and pulled until they could see the pink underneath. "Lemme have a look-see."

"Uhhhhh . . ." Unsure, Arvin slowly extended his swollen hand toward Clovis. Before he could even finish the gesture, the old man had seized it. In a whir of motion, he gave Arvin's finger a decisive twist and a jerk. With a *crack* and a *pop*, it was suddenly back in place again. The whole thing had happened so fast, Arvin hadn't even had time to react. He stood there now, speechless, staring down at his hand.

"How . . . did . . . you . . . ? Feels . . . much . . . better," he eventually managed to say.

"Don't mention it," Clovis said. His mouth stretched open in the widest yawn Molly had ever seen, which ended in a loud hiccup. "Now, what else needs fixin'?"

Together, Molly and Arvin took turns relaying every detail of what had happened to them, from the moment they had each encountered the towering robot, to getting stuck in its footprint, to making it across Crook's Chasm, to arriving at Gruncle's door. Molly produced the bolt she'd found, which Clovis inspected closely.

"Hmmm... Vandervorkel, huh? Sounds Russian, maybe...." He passed it back.

As Arvin shared the part of his story where he crawled through a maze of ductwork to escape, Molly kept picturing Wally's terrified face in her mind. What would the Russians do to him? By the time Arvin was through, she was crying.

"There, there, now," Gruncle Clovis whispered, producing an impossibly clean white hanky from his back pocket like a magician. "That's a terrible thing to happen to anyone, having a little brother all snatched up and swallered down right before your eyes." He paused, hiccupped again, then turned to look at Arvin. "Or getting swallered down yourself! Just terrible."

Molly took the hanky and cried a little more, burying her wet face in her Gruncle's chest. In that moment, she didn't even care about how awful he smelled. In fact, the familiarity of his odor was oddly comforting. Most of all, it felt good to have somebody listen. She looked up into her Gruncle's kind, squinty eyes. "Do you think we can find him?"

Clovis took a few puffs on his pipe and blew a wide, thin circle of blue smoke up toward the rafters. "Well, we won't know unless we try, now, will we?" Then he smiled—at least he did with his eyes. Molly wasn't sure if his mouth was actually smiling or not under that big bushy mustache.

Clovis started talking again. "Yessir, it'll be alright." Then he stared up at the smoke ring, which had nearly faded into nothing. "Did I ever tell you what really happened to your ol' Gramp Cletus?"

Molly knitted her eyebrows together. What had *really* happened? Had a giant robot snatched him, too? She knew her grandpa had passed away before she was born, but she had always assumed he'd died of old age. And no one had ever told her anything different, until now . . .

"Your ol' Gramp Cletus was my big brother. Six years older 'n me. Back when he was just a li'l squirt, everybody called him Curious Cletus, on account of his insatiable curiosity. And the name stuck long into his adult years, even after your mama Caroline was born. He loved being a daddy to little Caroline . . . he called her 'Li'l C' . . . but that didn't stop him from wanderin' off and pokin' his nose into all kinds of trouble. You see, Curious Cletus was curious about everything he ever happened acrost, especially if he hadn't happened acrost it before.

"So, one afternoon when he happened acrost a great big ol' hole in the ground, naturally it caught his attention. Now, this wasn't just any regular ol' hole. It was big enough to lose a pickup truck in, if'n you weren't careful. Cletus was curious where a hole that big came from, how it got there, and why he hadn't noticed it before. But most of all, he was curious how far down that mysterious hole went before it came to an end.

"Well, he brought me and some friends over to see it,

and we spent a good long time peerin' over the edge into its depths. But the farther down you looked, the darker it got, so there was no telling for sure. I mean, we all tried to guess how far down it went. Some reckoned that it went all the way to China, or the underworld, or maybe that it was bottomless and went on forever an' ever. Well, these theories didn't rightly satisfy my brother one lick. He wanted to *know*, understand? He *had* to know. So Cletus borrowed a neighbor's flashlight and pointed the beam down the hole. The light went as far as it could shine, but it didn't hit bottom. So he cast a rock down it. Then he waited and listened for a long time, but he never heard it hit bottom neither. The hole swallered up everything in silence—like a wide-open mouth without a tongue. It wouldn't give us a single clue. Cletus tried throwing in some other things too. He tossed in a rusty bell, an old boot, a windup clock. They all disappeared into the depths without producing a single sound. All the rest of us in the neighborhood gave up, or got bored. But not Cletus. In the end, he decided there was only one thing he could throw into the hole to satisfy his curiosity...."

Molly and Arvin were now perched on the ends of their seats.

"So he jumped in."

With that, Clovis fell silent. He gave a few puffs on his pipe.

"Whoa," Arvin said.

Molly looked up, confused. "Wait! You mean that's it? That's the end? How can that be the end of the story? How do we know what happened to him?"

"We don't. But that's not the point, whether we know or not. The point is that he knows." Her Gruncle was smiling with his eyes again. "And he did find out . . . just like you will."

Molly wasn't sure if this was her Gruncle's attempt at a comforting story, but it sure didn't feel like one. She had so many more questions about the grandpa she'd never met. Why had she never heard this story before? Was it true? And if it was, why didn't they send a rescue party after him? Molly sat there with her mouth open, not sure what to ask first, but her Gruncle interrupted before she could start.

"Okay, cadets, let's make a plan." Clovis sprang out of his chair like his butt was on fire. "Those Russians won't know what hit 'em!" He smacked a fist into his palm, but no sooner had he done this than his whole body started swaying. He stumbled backward.

"Hoooooooooo . . . ," Clovis sighed. "Whirlybirds every-where . . ."

"Gruncle? You okay?" Molly asked. She spied the flask lying open on its side by his chair. It looked empty, which con-firmed what she'd already suspected.

"Getting . . . dark . . ." He blinked a few times, trying to focus. "So . . . we'll . . . hafta . . . oooh!" Her Gruncle collapsed in his chair.

CHAPTER 20

FINAL NUMBER

"**G**runcle!" Molly shouted.

Clovis mumbled something incomprehensible from the recliner he'd just fallen into, then hiccupped again. Molly realized that as much as her dear Gruncle might want to help them, he was in no condition to join their search, let alone leave the house. And the truth was, neither were they. It was late, they were exhausted, and their shoes had yet to dry.

Clovis muttered something again. His eyes were closed.

"What's that, Gruncle?"

"Do . . . yer . . . folks . . . know . . . you're . . . out?" His words were starting to slur.

"Mine are probably wondering," Arvin said before yawning himself. He was looking very comfy in his chair. Maybe they could all use a little rest before they continued.

"I guess I could call my da—" Molly cut herself short, remembering their phone had disconnected.

"Oh . . . I'm . . . afraid . . . ah . . . my . . . line's . . . temporarily . . . um . . . outta . . . service." Clovis slumped a little further down in the chair. "For . . . repairs."

Molly figured it had more to do with Clovis not paying his phone bill either. That seemed to run in her family. But she also figured her dad had probably fallen asleep already in front of the TV like he always did, and wouldn't even notice that she and Wally were gone for at least another day.

"It's okay," Arvin said to Molly. "One more night away won't hurt." He stretched his arms and legs before curling back up. Then he lowered his voice. "He always like this?"

"Sometimes in the evenings," Molly said. "Er, most times."

Clovis had fallen quiet again. The story of Gramp Cletus and the thought of their parents sat in the air between them, lingering. It looked like maybe her Gruncle had dozed off. But without getting up, he reached behind his chair and produced a tiny ukulele.

"Howzaboutalilsong?" he blurted out, brushing the strings. Molly managed a smile. Darryl wagged his tail. Crank and Don Carlos gave no sign of interest but stayed put. Mondo's ears perked up.

Arvin had passed out in one of the chairs. He was still clutching his newly fixed hand, and he was smiling.

Her Gruncle spent a few moments plucking and tuning, eyes closed. He strummed a few bars and frowned, deciding that it didn't sound quite right. He fussed over the instrument for another minute or two, humming and mumbling. Throughout the ritual, his demeanor shifted back and forth from coaxing the thing to cooperate, to threatening it if it didn't.

His audience sat there in silence, waiting for the concert they were going to hear. Molly always enjoyed his playing . . . as long as it wasn't a song about—

"This one's about a certain, uh, *lady* by the name of . . . Marlene."

Molly and the Machine

Oh no, thought Molly. *Not Marlene!* She was one of her Gruncle's four ex-wives—probably his least favorite of all. Their marriage had only lasted a year, but that single year had produced enough fights to last a lifetime—one of which, Molly recalled, resulted in Marlene allegedly setting their house on fire . . . with her Gruncle in it. Before Molly could protest, Clovis began to sing:

She was a baaaad, baaaad woman
An' as ugly as a mule
Ohhhh, any feller who e'er loved her
Musta been a slack-jawed fool . . .

She was a liar an' a cheater
More slippery than a trout
Ohhhh, she smelt like a horse's hiney
An' bit hard as a gator's snout . . .

Her eyes were green as clover
But her heart was black as coal

Ohhhh, Marlene got fatter and fatter

As she dined upon my soul....

Clovis went on and on with his insults to Marlene, making them up as he went. After a while, he began to slur his words together, only a little at first, until Molly couldn't tell one word apart from another. When he forgot a line, he'd mumble or hum the part, and before long the mumbling and humming parts outnumbered the actual singing. Eventually, that gave way to outright snoring. He had sung himself fast asleep.

Molly was the last one standing. She laid an afghan over her dear Gruncle, who still held the ukulele. It covered Mondo, too, who during the concert had somehow managed to claim a spot under his armpit. In search of more blankets, she opened a big cedar chest against the wall and found a pile of old photos, including one showing Gruncle and Molly when she was only four or five. They were both smiling, faces covered in ice cream. There was a figure out of focus behind them, probably one of his exes, maybe even Marlene, but Molly couldn't recall.

She shuffled through more pictures until she came across

one folded down the middle. Molly opened it to see a professional photo of a young woman wearing a long white dress that touched the floor. In the corner, someone had written a note:

Thank you for everything, Uncle

The message was signed with a tiny letter *C*. Molly suddenly realized she was looking at a wedding picture of her mom. At first, she hadn't even recognized her. She studied it for another minute, then shook her head. *Of course. Five words. Looks like that's always been her specialty.*

She dug through layers of notebooks, letters, magazines, blueprints, even an official-looking certificate from the United States Patent and Trademark Office. Her rummaging freed a giant gypsy moth, who before this moment had probably lost all hope of ever escaping but now happily fluttered up to the rafters. Molly paused to admire the creature's manic ascent before she got back to work. Finally, she found a couple of old quilts at the very bottom of the chest. She laid one across the still-passed-out Arvin and curled up on the couch with the other. Darryl, Crank, and Don Carlos all snuggled up with her in one big heap.

Somewhere in the distance, a barred owl began hooting. It was a soft, soothing sound.

"Good night, Gruncle Clovis," she whispered. "We'll find my brother tomorrow."

"Tomorrrrrroooowwwwww . . . ," he repeated from somewhere in the realm of slumber.

That night, Molly tossed and turned. She dreamt of bottomless pits, of her brother Wally tumbling through the air, and of an army of giant metal claws coming at her from every direction. In the dream, the claws chased her through the hills and woods until she reached the very edge of Far Flung Falls. And then, as she stared down at the sheer drop, the dream took an even stranger turn. She was flying.

"Oh yeah," Molly mumbled in her sleep. "In case all else fails . . . why didn't I think of that before?"

PART II
INSIDE

CHAPTER 21
PROBABLY NOT
HEAVEN

Wally woke up, confused and aching all over. He opened his eyes, but he couldn't see a thing. Had he gone blind? Oh no, he had gone blind! Arms outstretched, he flailed around in the darkness. Then he remembered the most terrible dream.... He had dreamt that a giant robot had lifted him high into the sky and swallowed him whole. That couldn't have been real, could it? Yet here he was in the dark. Maybe he was still dreaming. Or he was dead ... and if he was dead, why wasn't he in heaven? Weren't there supposed to be winged angels and fluffy clouds? Or at least a light?

Wally wasn't sure.

Did they not allow nose pickers in heaven? No, they probably didn't. What if . . . he'd gone to the Other Place instead? Wally shivered.

Maybe this was where they sent people who messed up other people's creations. He thought about his sister's rude whatzit machine, and he knew he was guilty of that. Now he would pay the price. Wally sat there in the dark, thinking about the course of his short, tragic life. He thought about what he might miss the most and decided that, more than anything else, it would be bugging his sister. It wasn't that he wanted to bug her, exactly—it was just the only way he could get her attention. And that was the thing he liked most of all: the attention. He had never admitted this to anyone, even himself, but it was the truth.

He pictured the last time he saw Molly's face, all scrunched up in anger when she found out he'd taken the dominoes. What did she expect? That he would just sit and watch?

He patted himself down, feeling his body, his arms and

legs. Yep, all there, nothing missing. Maybe he hadn't been all chewed up to pieces by giant robot jaws after all. Maybe he was in his own bed, under his sheets, the ones with all the Super Friends printed on them. They always made him feel safe. Wally didn't see his glowworm night-light, though. He always kept that on in case he had to get up to go to the bathroom. He didn't ever want to step on one of his model trains, fall over, and pee his pajamas. Again.

He sat up and—*UFF!* He felt a little light-headed. Determined, he felt around some more. Everything he touched was hard and smooth... and cold. No sheets. His fingers explored some more. Nope, definitely not his bed. Slowly, Wally stood up and—*OUCH!*—he winced. There wasn't a part of his body that didn't feel sore.

To comfort himself, he began picking his nose. That always helped his mood. And his finger could find his nose in the dark without a problem. There, that was better. Maybe not everything was in its rightful place in the world, but at least his finger was. He knew it was a bad habit, and it really bugged Molly, but she was nowhere to be found in this black void. And if he hadn't made it to heaven, no use worrying about it now, was there?

Carefully, Wally put one foot forward into the darkness, then the other. Hopefully, he wasn't standing in a pit of angry rattlesnakes, or in the middle of a Russian minefield, or on the edge of a cliff . . . or maybe all three! That would be bad. He'd just have to trust that he wasn't.

"H-Hello?" Wally whispered. Nothing. Then louder, "Hello! Any snakes out there? Or land mines? Hello?"

No response. But from the faint echo of his voice, Wally got the impression that he was in a closed space. His voice sounded very small, but he kept talking, hoping to make it sound bigger. Couldn't let the rattlers know he was scared. "I'd hate to have to blow one of you away . . . with this!" He pulled out his nose-picking finger and pointed it like a gun into the pitch-black space. "Yep, that would be disappointing . . . because I do have an itchy trigger finger, see. . . ." He remembered that line from an old movie he'd watched with his mom and dad.

Mom and Dad. That movie was one of his earliest memories, and the only one he had of his mom and dad together . . .

before she left them. Suddenly, Wally missed home. And his family. And everyone and everything he knew. He didn't want to be the one to leave anybody. And even though he might never admit it out loud, he missed one person more than anyone else. *Molly.* The feeling surprised him, but he had always counted on her when things got tough. And right now, he wished she was here, because Molly always knew what to do.

But she wasn't.

Wally swallowed. This time, he was on his own.

He kept walking and talking in the darkness, finger drawn and at the ready. He took several nerve-wracking steps, waiting at any moment to get bitten by a big angry rattle-snake—*CHOMP*—or get blown up by a big angry land mine—*KABOOM*—or step off a big angry cliff and plummet to his death—*SPLAT!*

None of those things happened, but something else did.

His pistol finger hit something, and that something went *click!* Then Wally saw a series of tiny lights flicker on from out of nowhere, one after another. *There must be thousands of them,* Wally thought, *like stars in the nighttime sky.* But these stars were all different colors—red, blue, green, yellow—and they were popping on all around him, above and below. After having been in the dark for so long, Wally thought his eyes must be playing tricks on him. But soon the lights formed the outline of a pathway.

Could this be the way out of here?

Suddenly, there was a deep rumbling sound and the floor started to move. Wally let out a "w-w-whoaaaaaa" as the floor began carting him off to who knew what or where. Wally's mind began to race. *What kinds of snakes do they keep in the snake pit? Vipers? Rattlers? Cobras? Probably some of each.* From the thousands of lights, he could begin to make out his surroundings. He passed blinking circuit boards and sliding pistons. He passed springs and dials and enormous gears that all interlocked and moved at different speeds. For a moment, Wally felt like maybe he had been shrunk and trapped inside a pocket watch.

Wally had an eerie feeling about the place, the sense he was being watched. But he couldn't focus on that. Because on top of all the weird noises around him—clicking, whirring, buzzing—he realized there was another sound, and it was coming from somewhere very close. Wally looked down. . . . It was his knees knocking together. He tried to make them stop, but they wouldn't. So to drown out the sound (and his worries), he decided there was only one thing he could do: sing "The Courage Song." He wasn't sure if that was its real title or not, but that's what he called it ever since he had learned it from Gruncle Clovis, who had probably made it up. He took a big breath and started singing:

Ohhhhh . . .

I'm not scared, no I'm not scared

Not scared of anything at alllllllll

Not the boogeyman, or a frying pan!

Or a spider ten feet tall . . .

Wally didn't know why anyone would ever be scared of a frying pan, but the song did make him feel a little better, so he belted out the second verse even louder:

Ohhhhh . . .

I am brave, yes, oh so brave

I'm braver than anyone aroooouuund

More than Jacques Cousteau, or Pinocchio!

Or the sheriff of this town...

Ohhhhh...

There were more verses to the song, but Wally couldn't remember them. *That's okay*, he thought, noticing that his knees had finally calmed down. He wasn't so afraid now. Then, without warning, the floor shifted and took a hard left. Surprised, Wally let out a little yelp but kept his balance. Now the floor felt a little bouncier, like rubber. There were rollers moving under his feet. A conveyor belt? What was next? That's when he saw them, and his heart sank as it dawned on him that what he had feared the most was about to come true. *Snakes!* Hundreds of them, hanging overhead in loops, all coiled together in a great big knot!

Unable to stop, Wally let the conveyor belt carry him to his certain death. And there was no escape. Beyond what was probably every poisonous snake on the planet stood a huge metal wall. No doors or windows in sight. It was a dead end in every sense of the word. When he was directly under the snakes, the conveyor belt jerked to a halt, bringing Wally to the end of the line. Wally was terrified, and he concentrated on not peeing his pants. He wouldn't give those snakes the satisfaction.

The snakes didn't bite him. In fact, they didn't even move. Puzzled, he reached out to touch one. Energy vibrated under its smooth skin. This didn't make any sense. Snakes had scales, but these . . . Wally let out a long, relieved breath. These weren't snakes at all! They were electrical wires. Hundreds of them. Of course! He wasn't in a nightmare after all. Nightmares weren't powered by electricity . . . but robots were. And if he had truly been swallowed by a giant robot, then he must still be deep inside it.

At that moment, the metal wall in front of him parted in the middle, bathing the lost boy in a bright, warm light. The double doors continued to silently slide open to reveal a beautifully lit room. Wally heard music playing, but he wasn't about to go any farther . . . until he saw what was on the table in front of him.

It was a triple-decker hot fudge sundae with rainbow

sprinkles, in a huge crystal dish. Wally's eyes widened. He licked his lips. It was only now that Wally realized just how hungry he was. In agreement, his stomach made a soft growl. He made his way to the table.

As silently as they had slid open, the metal doors slid shut behind him. But Wally was too focused on the sundae to notice.

CHAPTER 22

HARD DAYLIGHT

Molly sprang off the couch, knocking one of the contraptions that hung from the ceiling above her. This caused a brief chain reaction that made Arvin jump, Darryl bark, Crank howl, and Don Carlos change six different colors until he finally settled on lime green, which was the color he'd started out with.

Now they were all awake. Well, the five of them were. Gruncle Clovis was still snoring in the same chair he'd passed out in the night before, gripping his ukulele with one hand. Mondo was curled up on his chest.

"Gruncle? Gruncle Clovis? You still sleeping?"

Don Carlos rotated one eyeball in her direction and held it there.

"Yeah, I know, dumb question," Molly said. Anyone could see that he wouldn't be rising anytime soon. She tapped his shoulder. Nothing. Then she shook him a little. "Wake up, Grunk! It's morn—"

"Aw, Marlene, you ol' razor-toothed harpy! Leave me be!" Clovis shouted, still deep in a dream. Then he started mumbling some more. It was no use trying to rouse him.

"I think we might be waiting on him awhile," Arvin said, still rubbing the sleep from his eyes.

The sun had barely peeked over the horizon, looking unsure whether it should start this day or not. Molly could relate. Even after a night's rest, she didn't feel as if the road ahead would be any easier.

"I guess we're on our own," Molly said. Being let down by grown-ups had become an all-too-familiar feeling, and it no longer gave her pause. Besides, she had Arvin. Molly looked over at the propeller on the potbellied stove. It was no longer spinning. "At least we'll have dry feet."

She tossed him his shoes and socks, then grabbed her own.

"I'm starving," Arvin said.

Darryl flapped his ears at the suggestion of food, and Molly's tummy rumbled. "Let's see what we've got," she said.

Molly wanted to conserve their rations, so she went to the kitchen to see if Clovis kept anything around to eat. In the pantry, she found a can of tuna fish for Crank and a sleeve of Ritz Crackers along with a jar of Cheez Whiz for Arvin and herself. Darryl helped himself to a half-eaten ham sandwich on the countertop. Molly nodded approvingly. While she rummaged, a gang of cockroaches scurried across the floor, which Don Carlos made a breakfast of. Those were his favorite. Everyone happily munched for a minute or two.

Their hunger satisfied, Molly attempted to put on a pot of coffee for her Gruncle. But his coffee maker, like everything else in the cabin, was a special Clovis contraption, so it took a few minutes to figure out. Between the multiple wires and tubes that fed into it, and the array of pipes that shot out the top, it looked like something between a church organ and a science experiment. Molly read **MEAN BEAN MACHINE** in small stenciled letters across the front. In spite of everything going on, the sight of it made her smile.

"I think you might need a license to operate that," Arvin said.

"Or enough stubbornness," Molly said, searching for a clue. "Aha!"

She found what appeared to be a control panel and pressed a big black button on the bottom labeled **MAXIMUS WAKEY**. This made the whole thing whir and rumble so loud, she thought maybe the sound alone might wake Clovis up, but even after the pot began to fill with a thick, dark sludge, and the pipes blew steam to the tune of AC/DC's "Back in Black," her dear Gruncle remained fast asleep.

"Well, that should do it," Molly announced. The coffee looked unfit for human consumption (unless you were Clovis), but the smell that filled the kitchen was familiar and calming. She took in a long whiff and felt a wave of assurance. She could do this.

Okay, what next?

"Before we go, I need to leave a note," she said. For as many times as her Gruncle might have disappointed her, he was still capable of the occasional surprise. Molly thought of Pink Lightning. She wasn't ready to give up on him yet. "Maybe he can join us later."

"Yeah, maybe," Arvin said. He was wandering around the cabin, taking in all of the other gizmos and gadgets strewn everywhere.

Molly wrote on the only thing she could find to write on: the back of an envelope that said **OVERDUE NOTICE** in bright red letters. *Do all grown-ups get this kind of mail,* Molly wondered, *or just the ones in my family?* Shrugging, she wrote:

Dear Gruncle Clovis,

Thank you for letting us sleep over, and for
fixing Arvin's finger, and for breakfast this
morning. I made you some coffee. Sorry we had
to leave so soon, but we still need to rescue
Wally. He's annoying, but he's my brother.
Yours truly,
Molly (and Arvin, Darryl, Crank, and Don Carlos)

P.S. If you see the giant robot anywhere, don't let
him get away! PLEASE!

See? That's how you write a note to somebody, she thought.
With more than five words. Molly walked back over to the cedar
chest filled with old photographs that she'd discovered the
night before. It was still open. She unfolded the wedding picture of her mom, studying it one more time before setting it
back on the pile. The gypsy moth was nowhere in sight. Molly
closed the chest.

Okay, they had better get back on the trail if they wanted
to catch that robot. Molly looked around to see if she was
forgetting anything. The sun had inched up into view, peeking into the windows. Its rays touched something shiny,
catching her eye. It was her Gruncle's telescope, aimed out
the kitchen window. Arvin was standing next to it. *That,*
she thought, *could help.* Walking over, she stood on tiptoe
and turned it down toward the valley, far below the cabin's
perch.

"What are you looking for?" Arvin asked.

Molly swiveled the telescope right and left to take in

as much land as she could. "For a sign," she muttered. "Just ... one ... sign."

At first she saw nothing but trees and grass. Then her heart began to race. There it was, as clear as could be, veering away from Crook's Chasm: the unmistakable trail of large rectangular footprints!

"Arvin! Take a look!"

Arvin put his eye to the lens. The robot's imprints continued across a downward slope, over a winding creek, and into the middle of a cornfield. The giant must have gone that way!

"Let's go!" she said.

They left the telescope trained on the footprints, grabbed the backpack, and raced out the front door with their companions right behind them. The commotion didn't appear to disturb Mondo or Clovis one bit. As the door slammed shut, they both remained passed out in the recliner.

Molly and Arvin stopped when they saw Pink Lightning. It would be slow going with both of them on a single bike. Molly appreciated Arvin's company. But she'd nearly killed him once already. Maybe this was better as a solo operation.

"Hey, Arvin," she said. "You don't have to come. Wally is my brother, and I don't want you to—"

"To what?" Arvin interrupted. "Miss out on all the fun?"

Molly's heart rose in her chest. "You sure?" she said, looking him in the eye.

Arvin met her stare. "Sure I'm sure."

"Okay then!" Molly said. "I've got an idea!"

"Oh great, here we go. . . ."

They took a detour around to the other side of the cabin. There, in a big pile, was a stack of bicycle parts, nearly every make and model.

"Is . . . this . . . where bicycles go to die?" Arvin said.

"Or maybe find a new life," Molly said.

After a little poking around, they found one frame not too badly dented, with both wheels still attached. Half the spokes were either bent or missing, and the joints were a little rusty, but Molly gave the pedal a few cranks, and the gear and chain still appeared intact.

"Just needs handlebars . . . and a seat," she said.

"If you say so," Arvin said, not sounding so sure.

They started digging through the pile. Darryl joined the search, sniffing his way through the junk to a grip that was buried toward the back of the pile. Upon discovery, he let out a bark, and Arvin tromped over and gave it a yank.

"Hey! How 'bout these?" Arvin called, unearthing a pair of giant ape handlebars. "Oh wait . . ." He snagged a seat with his free hand, which seemed to be working fine ever since Clovis fixed it. ". . . And this?"

"Good finds! Bring 'em over!"

Wrench already in hand, Molly took the lead on mix-'n'-match assembly while Arvin found a pump for the tires, which were both in sore need of air. The would-be rescuers worked fast, like a pit crew in a race.

When the Frankenstein bike was all put together, Molly reinforced a few spots with duct tape.

"For good measure," she said.

It wasn't going to win any beauty contests, but a few minutes later, they had a second working bicycle. Molly was pretty sure Clovis wouldn't mind.

"Impressive," Arvin said.

"Thanks," Molly said, grinning. Maybe he wasn't so bad to have around.

The rescue party piled onto their vehicles and took off down the hill at top speed. Molly carried Don Carlos and Crank, while Arvin rode solo. His bike rattled loudly, but it held. And Darryl brought up the rear. It was a bumpy ride, but Molly pictured her brother all alone inside that robot and knew there was no time to lose. She was still feeling guilty for banishing him from her invention yesterday. If only she'd let him stay under the cover of the tree . . .

"Sit tight, Wally!" she shouted into the cool morning air. "We're coming for you!"

"And we're coming for you too, robot!" Arvin added.

Darryl gave a deep "WOOOOF" in solidarity as they flew across the field.

Before long, they were back on the trail. And if Molly's gut was right, which it usually was, they were getting close.

CHAPTER 23
INDIGESTION

"**U**rrrrrrrp."

The burps were coming at regular intervals. Wally lay on his back, spread-eagled in the middle of the room. He was experiencing that perfect combination of satisfaction and misery that comes with inhaling a triple-decker hot fudge sundae. He moaned a little, and the burps continued. Maybe he shouldn't have eaten it quite so fast? But he really couldn't help himself. He had been so hungry, and it had tasted so good.

Uh-oh, here comes another one, he thought. It rumbled up

from deep down in his gut, gaining momentum as it moved up his throat to his mouth. Finally, it arrived.

"Urrrrrrrrp."

Still, he had to admit, even the burps tasted pretty good. And it felt nice to enjoy himself without having his big sister yell at him for every little thing. He licked a little hot fudge sauce from the corner of his lips, found a single stray candy sprinkle, and crunched it.

"Mmm," he said. He was starting to think that if this was his new life, being the prisoner of a giant robot who served him hot fudge sundaes, it wasn't too bad.

"I'm glad you liked it," said a voice.

Wally looked around. "Who said that?" he asked nervously.

"I did," said the voice. But Wally couldn't tell exactly where the voice was coming from. It seemed to be coming from everywhere at once. He sat up and looked around. *Ooof*, his poor tummy. He groaned again.

"Easy now," said the voice. "You ate that pretty fast."

"Well, yeah, I kinda did," said Wally, his cheeks growing a

bit red. "Wait, have you been watching me? Is this your robot? Uh, why did it swallow me?"

A large television screen directly in front of Wally flickered to life, revealing the darkened silhouette of what appeared to be someone's head and shoulders. Slowly and silently, the head tilted to one side, then the other, as if sizing Wally up.

"Who are you?" Wally asked the television.

"You first," said the silhouette.

"Me? My name's Wally."

"How old are you?"

"Eight and a half."

The questions went on and on at a rapid-fire pace. Wally did his best to answer them all between burps.

"Where were you born?"

"Right here. In Hocking Hills, Ohio."

"Favorite baseball team?"

"Um . . . the Reds?"

"Favorite Saturday morning cartoon?"

"Um . . . *Thundarr the Barbarian*."

"Second favorite?"

"*Jabberjaw.*"

With every answer, Wally's confidence grew. He didn't care much for the tests in school, or being interrogated at home by Molly, but this seemed different. Finding his rhythm, his answers came faster and louder:

"Favorite breakfast cereal?"

"Cookie Crisp!"

"Favorite arcade game?"

"*Donkey Kong!*"

"What if it's out of order?"

"Hmm. *Frogger.*"

"Favorite condiment on a hot dog?"

"Yellow mustard!"

"Least favorite condiment on a hot dog?"

"Brown mustard!"

"Bard, wizard, or ranger?"

"Not a wizard. . . . Ranger."

"Legos or Lincoln Logs?"

"Definitely Legos."

"Best board game?"

"Battleship."

"He who smelt it … ?"

"Dealt it."

Wally giggled a little at his last answer. He got the sense that whatever this test was, he was passing … maybe even getting an A. He couldn't know for sure, but the voice behind the shadowy figure on screen seemed pleased with his answers. Another burp worked its way up his throat, and when it came out, it was the loudest one yet.

"UHHHHHRRRRRPPPPP!"

There was a break in the questions. At first, Wally thought he might be in trouble. He whispered an "excuse me" and waited. But nothing happened. In fact, he was pretty sure he could hear muffled laughter. The silhouette bounced up and down a little.

Wally felt a new sensation bubbling up inside him—but this time, it wasn't indigestion. Was this what hope felt like? All of a sudden, he saw his situation through new eyes. Maybe this was the start of a new friendship. Or maybe even a whole new life. Who knew? Living in a giant, state-of-the-art robot with someone who actually appreciated him felt like a step up from living in an old, broken-down house with people who were always on his case. Would his dad and sister even miss him at all?

The speaker crackled back on, interrupting his reflection.

"Wally, let me ask you one more question. Do you like to play marbles?"

Wally's face brightened. "Well, yeah, as a matter of fact, I do."

"Excellent," said the silhouette.

The screen went blank.

"Hey, where'd ya go?" Wally shouted.

To answer, the floor suddenly disappeared out from under Wally's feet. In the split second he had to process what was happening, Wally caught sight of a silver chute. A moment later, he was sliding downward, quickly picking up speed.

"Heeeeeeeeeeeelp!" he screamed, falling into the darkness, a final burp escaping his lips as he dropped.

CHAPTER 24

SLEEPING GIANT

The sun sat high in the sky as the rescuers slowly covered more ground.

"We've gotta be close," Molly said.

"We'd better be," Arvin added.

Darryl was panting, but Molly refused to quit, willing her tired legs to keep pedaling no matter how much they ached. In front of her, Don Carlos leaned forward, his eyes always scanning in two directions at once. Crank slept in the basket. After following the trail of footprints all morning, they crossed over one more hill and finally came to a stop.

There it was. Molly's heart leapt in her chest.

They all stared. The robot was right in front of them, only it wasn't standing anymore. Instead, it was lying on the ground, perfectly still. Horizontal, the robot's arms and legs looked even longer than when it had been standing. Its head was propped up on a boulder that appeared to serve as a pillow. Its once-glowing green eyes were now dark and lifeless, and its giant hinged jaw hung open.

"It looks ... asleep," Arvin said.

Molly had never considered that robots might nap. *Maybe they need time to recharge their batteries?*

They parked their bikes against a tree. Arvin's makeshift number had held together for the last few miles, but as soon as he stepped away, the chain snapped in two.

"Well, made it this far," he said.

Then, without another word, the group moved a little closer. After a few minutes of careful steps, they arrived at the robot's side. Darryl growled, then woofed at it twice, but Molly immediately shushed him. They held their breath, waiting for something to happen. Nothing did. Whatever noise they made, it didn't seem to matter.

"Let's split up," Arvin suggested. "You search the top half. I'll take the bottom. Maybe I can find the escape hatch I used last time." He headed down toward the robot's feet.

Molly got to work searching for an easy way in. Between all the broken-down bits of machinery her dad had scattered around their property, and her Gruncle's never-ending inventions, Molly knew her way around most mechanical contraptions. But this was far, far bigger than anything she'd ever seen. Up close, the sheer scale of it made it feel almost unreal.

Carefully, she laid a hand on the sleeping giant, not sure if her touch would trigger some reaction. Her mind jumped to the last time she'd made contact, which had ended in her getting thrown to the ground, hard. But now the robot remained perfectly still, save for the faintest vibration. Molly's heart was pounding. She had made it this far. Somewhere on the other side of all that metal, Wally was close. She just needed to make her way in.

Under both the robot's arms, Molly found large venting panels. She tried jamming her pocketknife into their seams, but they were impossible to pry open. She pressed her face to the slats, feeling a soft, cool breeze coming through. It made the hair around her temples dance. She cupped her hands to her mouth, and in a whisper, she called through the vent:

"Wally? Are you in there? Can you hear me? Wally, I'm so sorry...."

Molly found herself unable to stop talking. She had no idea if her brother was listening, but it felt good to say out loud everything that had been building inside her. And for some reason, at this moment, a giant robot's armpit in the middle of the woods made for the perfect confessional booth. The words kept spilling out.

"... Sorry it took us so long to find you. But we're gonna get you outta here just as soon as we find a way in! And Wally? I'm sorry I banished you yesterday.... I feel like it's all my fault you're here.... I shouldn't have yelled at you. I know I do that a lot.... I..."

The steady breeze on Molly's face had a calming effect. Her voice blended with the hum of unseen engines, inviting her to continue....

"I'm sorry for always blaming you whenever something goes wrong."

As she spoke those last words into the cold metal vent, Molly realized all at once that there was something much bigger than a giant robot separating her from her brother.

She bit her lip to stop it from quivering. Molly had one more thing to say:

"Wally...?" She looked into the darkness between the slats. "It's not your fault Mom left. Sometimes it's nobody's fault."

Molly's entire body felt lighter. *Okay then.*

She turned to check over her shoulder. Darryl was watching her curiously. He was probably wondering why on earth she'd come all this way just to talk into a robot's armpit. But Molly figured this wasn't the first time humans didn't make sense to a dog. Did anything they do make any sense? Did Rube Goldberg machines? Or rescue missions? Or jumping in holes? Or walking out on your family? Or thinking that five lousy words on a postcard were enough? Sometimes, Molly admitted, they didn't make sense to her, either.

Arvin returned, pulling her back to the present. "No luck," he said. "I'm pretty sure the door I jumped out of was in its right heel, which is currently flat against the ground. Maybe we wait for it to wake up?"

"Maybe," Molly said.

She listened to the continuous whirring sound, felt the flow of air on her face, all coming from the open vent, and thought of another opening.

"Or maybe," she said, "if we want to find a way in, we search for a way up."

"Up? Up where?"

"Its mouth is open."

"No way. I've been swallowed once already."

Molly just stared at him.

"I guess we could look," he finally said.

They circled the sleeping giant once more, looking for the best access point to the top. Molly decided on the claws. They were scary-looking, yes, but they were the lowest part of the robot, which made them the easiest to climb.

"You guys stay here," she instructed the non-human members of their crew. "But be ready for anything. And if the robot wakes up . . . hide!"

Darryl took up position by the tree to guard their bicycles. Crank appeared to ignore them altogether. Don Carlos blended in.

"You ready?" Arvin asked.

Molly reached into her backpack. Her Gruncle had once told her that the key to a clear head was a full stomach. So she split a fluffernutter sandwich with Arvin, took a swig from her canteen, and then zipped her backpack back up. *Deep breaths, Molly*, she thought, *deep breaths.*

Adequately fueled, they made their way over to the claw and felt around its smooth surface for a place they could get a good hold. Nothing.

"Why is metal so slippery?" she asked out loud.

Finally, with a boost from Arvin, Molly stretched her arms as high as they could go and barely reached the top of the claw's upper edge with her fingertips. Summoning all her strength, she lifted herself a few inches, then scampered up to the top. Then she reached down to pull up Arvin, just like they'd done in the footprint.

It was a hard thing to do quietly. Every time their sneakers rubbed against the metal surface, they made a loud squeaking sound, and the two froze. But no matter what they did, the robot stayed motionless, so they kept going. Carefully, with Arvin following closely behind Molly, they started making their way up the robot's giant cylindrical arm to where it connected to its giant body. The arm was segmented every few feet to allow it to bend, and they took care not to trip on any of the joints.

At one point, Molly nearly lost her balance, spinning her arms in circles like a windmill. Arvin offered a hand from behind to help steady her. Before they knew it, they'd hopped up onto the robot's shoulder, crossed its chest, and stood looking down the darkened pit of the robot's throat. Up close, it looked even bigger than before.

"Not a good memory," Arvin said.

Molly patted his shoulder. "I know," she said.

They both paused another moment, staring into the

mechanical mouth. "Wally, I hope you're in there," Molly said.

They quickly scrambled up and over the robot's massive bottom jaw, not wanting to get stuck there if it suddenly closed shut. Then—*ooof!* With a soft thud, Molly half-landed, half-crashed onto the other side, rubbing her elbow where she'd bumped it and waiting for her eyes to adjust to the dimness of the robot's cavernous mouth. Arvin climbed in after her.

At last she was inside! Molly felt a sudden thrill—immediately followed by a sense of dread. Pushing her fears down, she took a step forward. The surface beneath her curved down, gradually getting steeper until it disappeared from view. She took another step, then started to slip. She could make out a trail of tiny red bulbs like Christmas lights, but it was hard to make out much else.

"Molly, be careful!" Arvin whispered.

She hesitated, staring down the dark tunnel before her, but her sneakers couldn't get a grip. They started making a high-pitched *sssssqqqqquueeaaakk* as she slid down the ramp of the robot's throat.

"Molly—!"

Quick, she thought, *do something!* Just then, she noticed a shadow, a dark, round shape that hung from the roof of the robot's mouth. What was that? As she continued to slip, Molly's mind jumped back to a film she'd seen in school about parts of the body.

"A uvula?" she said out loud. "Why would a robot need a uvula?"

"Don't ask me!" Arvin said, now several feet away. "Ask the Russians, or whoever made this thing!"

Molly grabbed hold of it with both arms. *Uff!* She held on tight, her toes now barely scraping the floor.

The metal uvula swung back and forth. It started ringing like a church bell.

BONG-G-G! BONG-G-G! BONG-G-G! BONG-G-G!

"SHHHHHHHHHHHH," Arvin said to Molly.

"SHHHHHHHHHHHH," Molly repeated to the uvula. But it ignored her and kept ringing.

BONG-G-G! BONG-G-G! BONG-G-G! BONG-G-G!

More lights flashed on, followed by a series of clicks and beeps, then a loud metal groan. Oh no! The mouth was shutting! Molly watched helplessly as the band of sunlight between the robot's open jaws grew thinner and thinner until it vanished with an ear-ringing *SLAM*.

They were trapped.

Then everything moved. The robot's head suddenly shifted forward. Molly almost lost her grip as the floor dropped from below her. Now her feet were dangling in the air. Everything shifted again, first slightly to the left, then to the right. Molly could feel in her belly that she was being lifted a hundred feet upward.

"Molly, hold on!"

"I am!"

Awoken, the robot was standing up again.

Finally, the uvula she was holding on to for dear life stopped ringing. She hung there in the silence, trying to catch her breath. Her own heartbeat was thumping in her ears. She broke out in a sweat. But even as her body threw itself into full panic, Molly looked around at the hundreds of blinking lights. She couldn't help but think that in any other setting they would be . . . beautiful.

Then she looked down. Nothing below her feet but what appeared to be a bottomless pit. Molly thought about the story of Gramp Cletus and gulped hard. She was trembling. She'd come so far, and she couldn't give up now. But her hands were getting sweaty, and it was getting harder and harder to keep her hold.

"Arvin! You still there?" she called. It was hard to make out anything in the dark.

"Over here," he called back.

"Over where?"

"Just hold on," he said.

"Never . . . giving . . . up . . . ," Molly whispered to herself between clenched teeth.

And then holding on went from hard to impossible.

Molly's hands gave way, and she tumbled through the air, a dazzling blur of Christmas lights whizzing all around her as she dropped. Above her, she heard a scream. Whatever awaited them down below, she was about to find out.

CHAPTER 25

ONE EYE OPEN

Without mercy, light poured in through the windows of Gruncle's cabin.

"Uggggggghhhhhh..."

This was followed by a violent coughing fit, then a series of painful-sounding hacks that culminated in a giant glob of spit. It shot upward in a high arc across the room, landing dead center in an open drawer, where it was quietly absorbed by a long-forgotten pile of mismatched socks, never to be heard from again.

"Huh? Well. Nice shot."

Clovis woke up the way he usually did, with a splitting

headache and only a vague memory of the night before. He stumbled around the house, looking for clues about how the previous day had ended. Per tradition, he did this with only one eye open—usually his right—because he always said that mornings were too hard a thing to face with both eyes at once. The left eye would require at least one cup of coffee before it fully cooperated.

He made his way into the kitchen and inhaled deeply.

"Ah . . . coffeeeeeee. But who—? Oh well."

Clovis was even more confused than he was on most mornings. If he was just now stepping foot into the kitchen, who had fired up the Mean Bean Machine? It smelled so good that the aroma caused his left eye to briefly flutter open. But it wouldn't stay in that position until after at least a few sips. He found a mug on the countertop that didn't look too dirty and filled it.

As he poured, Clovis could've sworn he'd left this particular not-too-dirty cup next to the remainder of a ham sandwich, which he'd been planning on saving for later. But now in its place was only a torn wrapper, a few scattered crumbs, and a streak of slobber. Hmmmmm. Maybe he ate it in his sleep?

The coffee was only lukewarm. Which raised more questions. But it did the trick.

A couple of sips and his brain turned on, memories slowly coming into focus, building on each other. *Something about a giant robot? Wait, that couldn't be right. Must've been a dream.* Then he noticed his telescope had been moved. Walking over to his beloved stargazing instrument, he muttered, "Hey now, who'd go an' mess with my—?"

He peered through the eyepiece, still trained on the giant footprints trailing off to the east. Suddenly, every detail from Molly and Arvin's visit the night before came flooding back. Clovis took a few moments to process what he remembered as he downed the rest of the coffee. He set down the cup.

And that's when he finally saw the note. *Oh, Molly!* He felt a sharp tug in his heart as everything pulled into focus. *How could this happen?* His poor grandniece already had enough hurt in her life brought on by the people around her without some ridiculous robot joining in on the action! And somehow, he felt complicit in it all. No matter how many Pink Lightnings he made for her, the blame was in his blood. Everyone in their family tree had always been a little bit unreliable. His brother. His niece. Even himself.

Molly hadn't asked for any of it. She deserved better. Maybe it wasn't too late to turn that around for Molly and her brother.

"C'mon, Mondo! We got work to do!" He gulped down the rest of the coffee.

The armadillo materialized by his right leg, ready for action. Clovis pushed open the front door, then reached overhead to a set of bicycle handlebars that hung upside down just above the doorway.

"Grab a pant leg, Mondo. And hold on!" The armadillo clutched the seam of Clovis's right leg. With his left, Clovis kicked what appeared to be a shovel propped against the doorjamb but was actually a secret lever, one of many he'd installed throughout the cabin. Instead of falling over, the shovel stopped at an odd angle midair and clicked. Clovis held on to the handlebars and waited.

Nothing.

"Now what in the—"

He was interrupted by a loud *POP*, and the two were jerked from their spot, sailing over the front steps on a high-velocity zip line that took them halfway down the hill to the front door of his garage—in 2.6 seconds. Mondo held on for dear life.

Now Clovis was fully awake, both eyes wide open.

"This calls for..."

He threw open the door to his garage and smiled under his mustache.

"Blue...Thunder."

CHAPTER 26
ELECTRIC DEATH TRAP

WHOOOOOSH!

As Molly tumbled down the robot's throat, it started to narrow. But that didn't seem to slow her descent. Still falling, she could feel the sides of the tunnel rushing past. Molly reached out to press her palms against the walls of the chute, trying to control her speed, but the metal was too slippery to get any traction. She kicked her legs wildly about, desperate to gain hold of something...anything.

BAM!

Her foot kicked a knob, which immediately shifted under the force of her fall. *SHH-OOOOOMP.*

The tube suddenly angled left. Now no bigger than the slide at her school playground, the tunnel gradually turned, then spiraled, spitting her out sideways into a big metal room. Molly and her backpack went skittering across the floor. She finally came to a stop somewhere in the middle.

Molly gathered herself, rubbing her elbows and knees. Her body was sore all over. It had been a bumpy ride down, and she imagined she'd have some impressive bruises to show for it. But that wouldn't be the first time. *Okay, deep breath.*

"Hello-o-o-o . . . ?" she called. Where was Arvin? Was he down here too? Or had she gone down the wrong tube?

Hello-o-o-o . . . ? Hello-o-o-o . . . ? Hello-o-o-o . . . ? Her tiny voice echoed off the metal walls. She was all alone.

Molly fished in her backpack, found the flashlight, and switched it on. It cut through the darkness, making her feel a little better that at least she could see what was around her. But this feeling didn't last. Wherever she pointed, the beam illuminated a bright circle of unfriendly-looking machinery. On the far side of the room, enormous cogs turned, interlocking with each other like puzzle pieces.

No Arvin. Or Wally. Or anyone. She was alone.

Molly strapped her backpack back on as she decided which way to go. There were so many moving parts that all fit together perfectly—except for her. She definitely didn't belong. Still, it was beautiful. *Who made all of this?* Molly wondered. *The government? The Soviets? Aliens from outer space? Is this the start of an invasion?* In her pocket, Molly could feel the engraved screw that Darryl had found on the trail. She doubted that aliens were named Vandervorkel. *But maybe . . .* Then Molly imagined for a moment what would happen if she got caught between those metal gears, and she shuddered. Instinctively, she took a couple of steps backward.

When she did, Molly accidentally pushed her backpack into a large button on the wall behind her. It made a loud *BEEP*, and lights overhead began flashing. More beeps and bells sounded, and along the wall, pistons started sliding up and down, *shump-shump-shump-shump*. Steam shot out from pipes overhead, filling the room with a fog. Then the floor underneath her started to move. Molly realized she was standing on some kind of conveyor belt pushing her right toward those bone-smashing cogs. *Oh no!* Arvin hadn't mentioned any bone-smashing cogs in his account. This had definitely been a wrong turn. She'd be ground to pieces!

Then who would save her brother?

Molly had to think fast. Before she got jammed between the teeth of two grinding gears, she grabbed onto the spokes of one wheel and got pulled upward. That wheel connected with another one above it that was lying flat, which she climbed on top of. As it swung her around clockwise, she dodged a barrage of heavy iron pendulums that swung back and forth from somewhere overhead. If one of those hit her, it would be the end.

Maybe she could find a way back down to the floor and turn things off. Of course, just as that thought occurred to her, the air started to crackle, and the hair on the back of her neck stood straight up. Molly felt tingly all over. *What now?* Below her, two big silver spheres emerged from opposite sides of the wall and began to glow, then—

BHHHHHZZZZZZZZRRRRRRK!

Bolts of electricity shot back and forth between them,

traveling in zigzag patterns from the bottom to the top of the orbs. No sooner had one bolt disappeared than another replaced it. The room wasn't dark at all anymore. Each connecting flash grew brighter and louder. And smaller offshoots of lightning danced all around the room, casting an ever-shifting spectacle of shadows that made it even harder for Molly to avoid a collision—or a fall.

Who would create a death trap like this? Molly watched the strange light show and wondered for a moment if maybe this robot was from Mars after all. *Wherever it came from, I have to find a way out! And fast!*

Frantic, Molly looked everywhere for an escape, then noticed a small round opening back on the opposite wall, several feet up from the tube where she'd entered. The hatch looked just big enough for her to squeeze through—but to reach it, she'd have to somehow pass over the lightning show below her. Then she noticed a network of belts and chains traveling above her that connected some of the cogs. They were moving in every direction—and one passed very close to her way out.

Molly kept dodging the pendulums while she traveled in circles, then hopped over to a neighboring gear, then another. At every turn, she had to keep ducking and jumping to avoid getting smashed or squished. With a final leap, Molly landed on the last gear. Spinning in place, she reached for the rope in her backpack and swung it like a lasso, hoping to toss it over the chain above her and—*SNAGGGGG!* Before she could throw it, the other end got caught between two gears, pulling her in the opposite direction.

"Nooooooo!" Molly shouted.

She was getting dragged backward toward those grinding metal teeth. A heavy pendulum swung so close to her head, she could feel the breeze from it on her face. *Too close!* She tugged hard on the rope, but it was no use. Molly let go.

Now what am I supposed to do? She was getting carried away in the wrong direction on one of the gears, and the chain to freedom was getting farther away. Without a rope, how would she grab it anyway? For a moment, she wished her dad was here. He knew all about gears and cogs and engines.

Just as the lighting below flashed again, she had an idea:

her belt! That could work. Molly hotfooted it back from cog to interlocking cog, bobbing and weaving to avoid getting knocked over—all while unfastening the belt from her shorts. She gave it one twirl and—*fwooooop!*—looped it over the chain. Holding on to both ends of the belt, Molly got pulled up and over the electric spectacle below. She prayed a stray blast between the two silver balls below wouldn't zap off her toes—or worse.

CLANKETY-CLANKETY-CLANKETY-CLANK...

The chain rattled on, nearly shaking Molly loose. But she held fast to the belt, knuckles white with determination as she careened through the air. Somewhere at the midpoint, she looked down at the deadly scene below, and a familiar image came to mind, one she'd seen over and over: it was none other than her beloved Wile E. Coyote, the doomed character from *Looney Tunes*. Every Saturday morning, she and her brother would watch from the comfort of pillow forts they'd constructed from couch cushions and laugh hysterically as the coyote's careful plans to catch the Road Runner would inevitably backfire and he'd plummet to his death, or smash into a wall, or get blown up or crushed by a boulder. Once Molly laughed so hard at the coyote's demise that she made Cap'n Crunch shoot out of her nose. But now the prospect of meeting a violent end wasn't funny at all. This was real.

Molly's life was in her hands. And she wasn't intending to meet the same fate as Wile E. Coyote. Her plan had to work.

As she got closer to the other side, she started to swing, then in one motion pulled her feet up and into the hole in the wall, letting go of the belt with one hand to release herself from the chain's pull.

Molly wasted no time crawling through the narrow shaft to the other side. *Whew!* Finally she was safe, but where was she?

Molly stood up and looked down a long corridor. Just then, a bolt of electricity shot through the opening behind her and hit her backpack, knocking her forward. The pack caught fire. Startled, Molly lunged for a small control panel beside her and started hitting buttons, hoping one would do something to help. She heard mechanical noises in the distance, but she couldn't tell if anything was actually happening—or even related to the buttons she was pressing—so she kept trying until the hatch she'd escaped through finally closed with a comforting *THUNK*.

Molly took off the backpack and stomped on it a few times. It smelled like burnt marshmallows.

"Aw man, my last fluffernutter . . ."

Molly hoped Arvin was faring better, wherever the chutes had taken him. She swallowed her disappointment and patted herself down. *Okay*, she thought, *you're not on fire. Or electrocuted. Or smashed to pieces.* She looked once more at the smoking backpack with the ruined remains of the last sandwich she'd been saving. *At least you're smarter than Wile E. Coyote. Okay . . . now where do I go?*

That's when she heard a voice coming from down the hall.

"Hey, is anybody out there? Anyone? Hello?"

Molly followed the voice. She couldn't be sure if it sounded like Wally. Or Arvin. But if the voice didn't belong to one of them, then who—or what, exactly—was she heading toward?

CHAPTER 27
PARTY OF THREE

Darryl watched as the giant robot suddenly came to life after his favorite human and her new friend crept inside its open mouth. From the cover of nearby trees, alongside Crank and Don Carlos, he watched it slowly stand up, turn away from them, take a few steps, then stop. He exchanged glances with his fellow caretakers of Pink Lightning, then waited to see what would happen next.

Not good, Darryl thought.

For several long moments, the towering robot stood there, motionless, as if it had fallen asleep again but forgotten to lie back down. Darryl gave it one assertive "hey, you" bark just for good measure, in case Molly could hear him. No response.

Then, something inexplicable happened. This was not unusual for Darryl, as most of the things he saw humans do every day were inexplicable. Like, say, jumping into the mouth of a giant robot (who clearly didn't smell right). But this was even stranger.

First, he heard what sounded like a far-off thunderstorm but was actually coming from *inside* the robot. Then the center of its body started to glow. It jittered a little. This was followed by random lights that flashed on and off in various places. Hatches took turns popping open on the robot's shoulders, arms, and legs, then closing again. Finally, halfway up the giant's right heel, just a few feet from the ground, a full-size door slowly swung open from a single hinge on the bottom. The inside of the door was shaped like a small stairway, and it continued to extend outward until its upper lip touched the ground in a perfect forty-five-degree angle. If Darryl could count, he would have counted eight steps up to the entrance. Light emanated from the doorway, as if to say *Welcome.*

He barked again. *Molly? Arvin? You guys there?* He hadn't caught the faintest whiff of either human since they entered the robot's jaws. Maybe they needed him. Maybe this would be his only chance. Maybe, maybe, maybe...

Darryl sensed that there was no time to waste, yet still, he hesitated. What was the right thing to do? Fortunately, while he deliberated, Don Carlos calmly crept onto Darryl's back, gently grabbed hold of his collar, and shot out his tongue at a spot behind his canine comrade's ear. *THWACK!* The lizard's sneak attack jolted Darryl out of his paralysis, and he broke into a mad charge for the door. Crank watched the two go for about half a second, then took off behind them.

As the three of them ran full throttle for the open door, the stepped ramp began to lift back off the ground. *Oh no,* Darryl thought, *door closing! Must reach Molly!*

Now only a few feet away, he leapt with all the spring he could muster. Don Carlos held on to the collar for dear life. And Crank, just behind them, lunged as far as she could, which was several feet shy of the closing door, but precisely the right trajectory to connect with Darryl's tail. Claws out, she dug in with both paws. Midflight, Darryl felt the sudden sensation of ten needle-sharp pricks—which somehow propelled him forward with even greater speed.

"Arf!" he yelped.

The dog and his passengers made a hard landing through the doorway in a tumbling ball of fur and scales. Behind them, the door sealed back shut with a soft *pssshhhhht*. The three disconnected from each other and straightened themselves out. For Crank, this involved some serious licking. Darryl shook it off, flapping his ears for several seconds, then snorting twice. Don Carlos quietly retreated for a moment alone, which he used to turn a dull gray to match their new surroundings. When they were settled, Darryl assessed the situation. Behind them was a sealed door, and in front of them a narrow corridor.

At this point, Darryl suspected his non-canine cohorts might require a little motivation to move. Without warning, he broke wind, which he'd been saving for such an occasion. There had already been several tense moments earlier in the journey where a little passing of gas would have been understandable, but Darryl had been saving this particular offense for just the right time. And that time was now. It was of the silent-but-deadly variety, sneaking up on his companions without mercy. Crank crinkled her nose, then hacked a few times. Don Carlos turned an especially sick shade of green. But the lingering stench made their decision to press ahead a little easier.

Whatever dangers lay before them, they couldn't be as bad as the smell they were leaving behind.

CHAPTER 28
BREAKING OUT

"**W**ho's there? Where are you?"

Molly ran down hall after hall, hands cupped around her mouth as she called at every corner. It was a never-ending maze inside the robot's body, and after a few minutes every passage started looking the same. How did Arvin ever escape from here? She hoped he was okay.

"Over here! Help me!" the voice called. Molly turned another corner and came to a door with a small barred window. It looked like a prison cell. "In here!" came a voice from inside.

Molly pressed her face up to the cold bars to get a better look. "Wally, is that you?"

There was a pause. Molly could see a figure up against the far wall of the tiny room, standing in shadow. Then the figure spoke.

"Wally? No, it's me! Leonard! Leonard Kowalski. Who are y—?" The boy who wasn't her brother stepped forward into the light, squinting to get a better look at his rescuer. His eyes suddenly widened in recognition.

"Molly? Molly McQuirter! Wha... What are *you* doing here?"

Molly looked Leonard over. He was still wearing the same Def Leppard T-shirt from when she had seen him two days ago. Had he been stuck here since then? Quickly, she explained that she was looking for her brother, that she'd been trailing the robot since yesterday when it snatched Wally from their backyard. She had no idea that it had snatched him, too. What could this mean? First Arvin. Now Leonard. Was this robot full of other people's stolen brothers? And where exactly was hers?

Leonard interrupted her thoughts. "Hey, uh, Molly? I know

you're here to rescue Wally and not me, but since you're here and all, would you mind . . . unlocking the door?"

"Oh, sure!" Molly said, embarrassed. She looked around and saw a button to the right, and on a hunch, pressed it. The metal door slid open quickly with a *pssssshhhhhhht*, and Leonard came running out just as fast. He wrapped his arms around Molly, who was nearly a head taller than he was. Molly stood there without moving, accepting the spontaneous outpouring of affection. It was the first time in memory she'd ever been hugged by a boy who wasn't a family member, and it felt even more awkward than she had imagined.

"Oh, thank you, thank you, thank you!" Leonard gushed. "I didn't think I'd ever get out of here." He squeezed her a little tighter. "By the way, where *is* here . . . ? Are we really inside . . . ?"

"The robot?" Molly answered. "Yes."

"Man," Leonard said, still holding on to Molly. "I only saw it for a second . . . but it was one big robot."

"Yes. Yes, it is," Molly agreed. She was thinking that "for a second" would be a much more reasonable duration for a hug. "Uh, could you just—"

"Thank you," Leonard said again. He wasn't letting go.

"Okay, that's good, Leonard. No problem. No problem at all. Yeah, that's good." Molly said, attempting to pry herself free from Leonard's grip. It was really nice to have found someone, but it was getting hard to breathe. "Um, *Leonard*?"

"Oh, sorry." He took a step back.

Molly looked him in the eye. "Leonard, have you seen or heard anyone else since . . . uh, since you got here?"

"Well . . ." Leonard described the conversation he'd had with some mysterious "shadow guy" who occasionally appeared on a television screen, but he could never see his face. Arvin had mentioned a "shadow guy" too. Molly was trying to piece together all the details, comparing what Leonard said with Arvin's account. She decided to fill him in as well.

"Leonard, last time I saw you, you were headed to the 7-Eleven with Arvin. After you guys split up, the robot got him, too."

"What? Is he—"

"Don't worry, he escaped." Molly wasn't actually sure where

he was at the moment, but she didn't want poor Leonard to worry even more than he already was. She recounted how she and Arvin had found each other in the robot's footprint the previous day.

"So, Arvin escaped from here, huh?" Leonard nodded. "That's pretty rad."

"And we're gonna escape from here too, Leonard. But first, why don't you tell me everything you can remember, starting with the 7-Eleven?"

"Yeah, we went, but you know how it is waiting for Arvin to finish a game. He plays forever! After a while, I got bored waiting for my turn, so I made myself a *mix-ellaneous* Slurpee—"

"A what?"

"Every flavor. Mixed together. Mix-ellaneous."

"Gag me with a spoon," Molly said.

"What? They're *a-ma-zing*. Drank it so fast, I got a brain freeze. They're the best." Leonard folded his arms for emphasis.

"Not even," Molly said.

"Even," Leonard said, deciding to move on with his story. "So, anyway, I made a Slurpee, which, like I said, tasted *a-ma-zing*, grabbed the latest *X-Men*, and—*oh no!*"

"What?" Molly asked.

"I just remembered . . . when this thing snatched me, I dropped my comic. It all happened so fast. . . . I didn't even get to finish it. That was the last of my allowance."

"I'm sorry about your comic, Leonard." Molly was trying to keep him on track. "But where did the robot grab you?"

"Where I went after 7-Eleven. To read the comic. My secret treehouse."

"Leonard, I wouldn't exactly call it secret," Molly said. "I mean, everybody knows about it."

"No way!" Leonard said.

"Yes way," Molly said. "Um, even the robot knew."

Leonard took a moment to consider this. Given their present location, Molly's point was hard to argue.

"Well, yeah, I guess," he said.

Aside from the location, Leonard's account of getting picked up and swallowed was strikingly similar to Arvin's.

Molly thought back to when Wally was taken, the terror-stricken look on his face. "It must have been really scary," she said.

"It scared the crap outta me," Leonard admitted, recounting the moment he looked up from his comic in his not-so-secret treehouse to see a giant robot peering down at him. He described being dropped into the robot's mouth, sliding down a long tunnel into a dark room with a moving floor, then being served the most amazing hot fudge sundae of his life—

"Wait, you got a hot fudge sundae in here?"

"Yeah, it was incredible, and I was so hungry," Leonard said.

"A hot fudge sundae . . . ," Molly repeated. This part didn't make sense. Arvin hadn't mentioned any sundae. And all she got was a bolt of lightning that nearly killed her. Definitely not fair.

"Yeah, I ate it so fast I got another brain freeze. Two in one day! Which made it really hard to talk when I was being asked a million questions."

"Wait! Who asked you a million questions?"

"The shadow guy! Duh!"

Leonard explained everything else, right up to the point where he got locked up.

At first, Leonard had thought that maybe it was a police robot, arresting him for all the days he'd skipped school before summer. But then he'd come to the conclusion that the police probably wouldn't serve him a hot fudge sundae ... or send a giant robot to arrest him.

Molly agreed.

"Well, whoever's controlling this thing, they owe me a comic book," said Leonard.

They had been walking as they talked, and just as he finished, they came across another cell. For a moment, Molly thought it was the same one as before, that they had just gone in a giant circle, but this one was still locked. Molly peeked inside through the small, barred window.

"See anyone?" asked Leonard.

"Nope. Looks empty." As soon as she said it, she saw the scratches in the wall:

A. S. S. WAS HERE

Molly couldn't help but smile. *Those initials.* This must've been the cell he escaped from. She saw where the vent cover on the ceiling had been pried loose.

"Arvin Shadrach Simmons," she said out loud.

Somewhere nearby, a voice answered. "Over here," it said.

Molly spun around.

"I think it came from behind that wall," said Leonard.

They took a few steps toward the galvanized circular ductwork that ran along the far side of the corridor. In the middle, there was a tiny panel with tilted slats. Molly and Leonard leaned in.

"Hello?" Molly said.

From between the slats, five fingers shot out, one of them bandaged. Leonard screamed.

"Arvin!" Molly cried, recognizing the bandage. "Is that you?"

"Arvin?" Leonard said. "I thought you said he escaped!" He was breathing hard.

"He did," Molly said. "The first time."

"You mean he came *back*?" Leonard said.

"I know, I know," Arvin said from behind the vent. "Always been a slow learner."

Molly spent a minute sizing up the dimensions of the tube. For somebody with Arvin's bulk, it was definitely a tight squeeze.

"How did you get in there?" Molly asked.

"Um, I think I went down the wrong pipe. Obviously." His voice echoed through the vent.

"Never mind. It doesn't matter. We're getting you out," Molly said. "Hold on."

"Don't worry, I'm not going anywhere," said Arvin. He sounded very cramped.

Even if they could pry off the panel's frame, it was way too small for Arvin to pass through. Then Molly noticed the clamps with rubber handles along each seam of the tube. The ductwork was in sections.

Molly pointed up to one of the seams. "Leonard, can you reach that clamp?

"If I stretch," Leonard said.

Molly went to the other side.

"On the count of three, pull."

"Okay," said Leonard.

"One, two, three!" They both pulled hard on the rubber handles. As soon as they popped open, the section of tube between them dropped to the floor with a bang.

"Owww!" Arvin said, crawling out of the tube. "I'm ready for a summer break that doesn't include robots."

"Me too," Molly said. "But first, let's find my brother."

Arvin stood up and attempted to brush himself off. But the grease stains weren't going anywhere. However he'd gotten in there, he was even dirtier now than before.

"Whoa," said Leonard. "For a minute, I thought you were the bog monster."

CHAPTER 29

LOST AND FOUND

VA-VA-VA-VA-VA-ROOOOOOOOM! VROOOOOOM!

A flock of wild geese scattered in all directions as Clovis revved the engine. Intensely focused on his mission, he'd failed to see them when he braked at the hilltop to get a clear view of the robot's trail—which after a few miles had inexplicably vanished.

"How in the heck does something that big just . . . disappear?" Clovis scoured the woods for a sign, any sign.

Above his head, the geese all honked in protest, but their complaints were drowned out by the deep growl of Blue Thunder.

Noticing too late, Clovis looked up.

"Oh! Sorry there, birdies! I was just—" he said.

One goose who'd been particularly perturbed by the interruption apparently decided that stronger language was in order, which he dropped—*SPLAT!*—hitting Clovis smack in the goggles.

"Aw, geez, for crying out loud . . . I guess that'd be 'apology not accepted,' huh?" He wiped the splatter with his jacket sleeve. When that didn't work, he pulled out his hanky.

"Man, when they say 'loose as a goose,' they ain't kidding. . . ."

The flock was far from earshot by now. Clovis returned his attention to the valley below. There had to be something . . . a clue he was missing. He thought about his grandniece and -nephew, somewhere out there, facing who knew what. There was no way he wasn't coming through for people who were counting on him. Not this time. But he was still having trouble seeing through his goggles after the goose's assault.

Clovis closed one eye to better focus. *Hmmm, what's this?* The smeared goose poop had left a thin streak across one of his lenses that looked a little like an arrow, pointing slightly up and to the left. *A sign?* Clovis slowly turned his gaze in that direction and squinted...

There it was! About forty feet up, the top of a white ash tree was broken clean off... too young for it to have happened naturally. And there, just below it, on the other side of the creek... a rectangular footprint.

"Ha! Gotcha!"

He tightened the strap on his helmet and began his descent. Picking up speed, Clovis made his way to the bottom and kept racing through the open field.

"Let's get this party started," he said, hitting the button by his right grip. Peeking out from his saddle pouch, Mondo grunted, which Clovis took for approval. On command, large twin speakers rose from the compartment behind Clovis's seat, filling the air with a heavy guitar and drum accompaniment to the rumble of the bike's massive engine. Gary Gearshift & the Grease Monkeys had only produced one album back in 1971, but it was by far Clovis's preferred soundtrack when he was riding. Side A started with their only hit. The armadillo curled into a ball. When the vocals came up, Clovis sang along:

Never was good at doin' what I'm told

Just lived my life on the open road

Forget the waitin'!

I'm acceleratin'!

Better make a lotta way for my heavy load . . .

Blue Thunder's oversize tires reached the edge of a creek in an explosion of mud and exhaust. Directly ahead, on the opposite bank, a single terror-stricken frog leapt for his life, surfing the wave of creek water in the cyclist's wake to a much quieter spot downstream.

Clovis pressed on.

Gonna keep it in the fast lane whatever the cost

If you never slow it down then you're never lost

I'm a crafty weasel!

Runnin' on diesel!

And you'll never catch nothin' but my exhaust . . .

The biker cleared the next hill, catching several feet of air—and a view of more rectangular footprints headed east. He was back in business!

As he landed, he reached for one of the levers sprouting

up beside Blue Thunder's gas tank—and pulled it hard. Behind him, there was a deafening *POP*, kicking him forward. Both tailpipes belched out thick black clouds of smoke.

Clovis turned around. "Funny, I thought that was supposed to—"

Just then, with a roar, twin blasts of orange flame erupted from the exhausts, turning the motorcycle into a kind of ground rocket. Gary Gearshift screamed the chorus over and over:

AS ... YOU ... RUST!

EAT ... MY ... DUST!

Clovis hit a bump, and the two strange-looking contraptions that crisscrossed his back like a capital *X* bounced up and down—along with the bright red bundles of dynamite packed into his sidecar. Clovis leaned over to give the explosives a gentle pat.

The rock 'n' roll didn't miss a beat.

AS ... YOU ... RUST!

EAT ... MY ... DUST!

He made his way deeper into the countryside.

"I'm coming for ya, box foot."

CHAPTER 30
THE LAST CELL

Molly signaled everyone forward.

Together, the three of them tiptoed down the corridor. Molly took the lead, with Leonard and Arvin following closely behind. They found several more cells, but each one turned up empty. No munchkins—including her brother. Molly's worries multiplied.

Where could Wally be? Could the robot have chewed him up by mistake? Had he stumbled into that terrible lightning room and been electrocuted? Or was he torn to bits by all those gears? Her mind raced. Maybe that shadow guy had done something terrible. And who the heck was he anyway? If he hurt Wally, he was going to pay.

"Hey, Molly, um, you okay?" Leonard asked.

Molly noticed she was breathing hard. She made an effort to calm herself, and inhaled.

"Every . . . thing . . . is . . . just . . . fine," she said. Another inhale. "Let's just keep moving."

They came to a final door at the end of the corridor. Molly took one last big breath in and pressed the button in a panel to the right, expecting another empty cell. But when the door slid open, this room didn't look anything like the others. It was much brighter. And bigger. And it definitely wasn't empty. In fact, it was the opposite. The far wall was stacked floor to ceiling with row after row of shelves, each one filled with board games.

Molly saw all her favorites: Connect Four, Operation, Life, Monopoly, Battleship . . . along with dozens she'd never heard of. Some were even in different languages. It looked like a toy store in here. And the board games were just the beginning. . . .

Off to the side, a *ding-ding-ding-ding, bwoo-oop-bwoo-oop*

caught her ear, and she turned to her right. It was a packed row of arcade games! She noticed *Galaga, Frogger, Donkey Kong, Ms. Pac-Man* . . . and her favorite, *Dig Dug.* She'd burn through any quarters she had in that game every time she'd trekked out to the 7-Eleven. Unlike Arvin, she'd never made the high score, but something about pumping up the bad guys and popping them like balloons was very satisfying. The screen blinked back at her as if to say *Hello, friend.*

In front of the arcade games, a long, low table held every action figure a kid could imagine. There were armies of G.I. Joes, Micronauts, He-Man, Transformers, every character from Star Wars, and dozens of little pewter figurines from Dungeons & Dragons, all arranged in a great mash-up battle scene around the most colossal Lego castle Molly had ever seen. Boba Fett held a blaster aimed at Skeletor. An assortment of astronauts and hobgoblins surrounded Optimus Prime. And a caravan of Matchbox cars encircled the entire scene in a continuous loop-the-loop track.

It was hard to imagine anything the room didn't have that

a kid would want. There was even a full-size soda fountain.

Leonard and Arvin both exhaled, as if they were entering a sacred temple.

"Totally... tubular," Arvin finally said.

"Totally. Tubular to the max," Leonard chimed in.

And there, sitting in the middle of the room, looking as comfortable and happy as if he were home on the couch, was Wally, playing marbles.

He looked up at his visitors standing there in the doorway. The boy blinked a few times, his smile fading until it was replaced by a less happy expression. Something between confusion and concern. Slowly, he crinkled his nose, like maybe he was trying to determine the origin of a questionable smell.

"How'd you all get here?" he finally asked. "I'm not in trouble, am I?"

Molly wasn't sure what she had expected, but this definitely wasn't it. "Was he in trouble?" And why that face? Had the Russians already brainwashed him? Maybe it was too late.

"Well, nice to see you too, Walls," said Arvin.

"How'd you land the sweet digs?" asked Leonard.

Molly and the Machine

Molly was confused but nonetheless overcome by the sight of him. After risking life and limb, she had found her brother—and he was alive. Unable to speak, she raced over to Wally, threw her arms around his neck, and did something she'd never imagined: she kissed him. Sure enough, he tasted like dirt and boogers. But she didn't care.

"Grody," said Wally, wiping his cheek. Then he looked her up and down. "Molly? What happened to you?"

For the first time since this adventure had started, Molly became aware of her appearance. She took a step back, brushing herself off. From head to toe, she was covered in mud splatters and bruises, and her clothes were ripped and torn.

"Oh, this? It's nothing. And no, you're not in troub—" she started to answer.

"Hey, my game!"

Unknowingly, Molly had sent Wally's tight configuration of marbles scattering across the floor.

"Wally, now's no time to worry about marbles! We're here to rescue your butt!"

Wally looked over to Arvin and Leonard, who had quietly taken up position at adjoining arcade games. They were already working the games' joysticks with a single-mindedness that suggested they were no longer worried about being captives inside a giant robot.

"Rescue? *Me?*" Wally seemed confused. "But what about . . . ?" His voice trailed off.

"But what about *what*, Wally? We've got to get you out of here."

"Why?"

Why? The question caught Molly completely off guard.

"Well, um, for starters . . ." Molly searched for a reason. "Dad is probably worried sick about you!"

Wally cast a skeptical look at his sister. They both knew there was a good chance their dad had yet to even notice they were missing.

"Okay, well, maybe not. But *I* was worried sick about you, Wally!"

"Really?" Wally cocked his head and narrowed his already-narrow eyes.

"Yeah, really."

"I doubt it."

With her left hand, Molly made a fist. Wally flinched like he was about to get socked.

"Wally, if I wasn't worried sick, would I have come all this way and crossed Crook's Chasm, tracked down this robot, jumped in its mouth, dodged lightning, and wandered through this whole dumb maze?" With each point, Molly held up a finger. Now all five were extended. Wally stared at her open hand.

"You mean, you ... jumped in? Like, on purpose?"

Molly nodded.

"Crook's Chasm!" Leonard called over his shoulder. "That's uncrossable!"

"Not when somebody takes your brother, it isn't," Molly said, eyes still on Wally.

For a moment, Wally's face softened. Then he returned his attention to the marbles, knuckled down, and flicked one hard. It scattered the remaining marbles even farther apart. "Well, maybe I don't want to be rescued. Why do you care? You never like it when I'm around anyway."

The words stung. For the last couple of years, Molly had been so focused on her own feelings, she hadn't made room for anyone else's. But Wally's mom had run off too. And as much as Molly wanted to pin the blame on her brother for all the fissures and failures in their lives, the truth was that it was neither one's fault. Suddenly, her little brother didn't look so little, and for the first time, she saw the toll their mother's choices had taken on them both. It was something they shared. And it made her feel closer to him.

Annoying as he might be, she still loved the snot out of him.

"Wally, you're my brother. Of course I care about you . . . even if you pick your nose."

Wally smirked. "I only do that to bug you, mostly."

"Well, it works."

The two siblings stood there and looked at each other, then broke into a laugh. Neither was really sure why, but it felt good. They hadn't laughed together—for real—in a long time.

"Besides," Molly said when she caught her breath, "aren't

you lonely in here by yourself? You don't even have anyone to play marbles with."

"Oh, sure I do." Wally smiled. "I've been playing with my friend here."

"What?" Molly asked, looking around. "Your friend? Where? Who?"

"Me," said a voice.

CHAPTER 31
TINY CYCLOPS

Molly spun around and saw that the noise had come from a small metal stump beside her. Between the spectacle of the room and the excitement of finding her lost brother, Molly hadn't even noticed it when she came in. The stump balanced on two sets of tracked wheels connected by triangular rubber treads, like a miniature tank. It rolled back a few feet and tilted up as Molly turned to face it. The periscope on top of its head lifted several inches, the camera lens on its end pushing in slightly to focus on her. With its singular eye, it looked like a tiny cyclops.

"How did you get in here?" the cyclops asked.

"How can you talk?" Molly asked back.

"I can do a lot of things," it said.

"Like show us the way out of here?" Molly asked.

The cyclops was silent.

"Well, can you help us or not?"

As an answer, the door they had just come through closed behind them, followed by a second door even more reinforced than the first. Then a heavy crossbar fell over that with a WHOMP.

"You're not going anywhere with Wally," it said.

The cyclops lifted its arms and opened its pincers, snapping them a couple of times like a crab. They made a hard, metallic twik-twik sound. Then it began to inch toward Molly, like it was planning to grab her by the ankles.

"Not so fast, R2-Dumbo," said Molly, taking a step backward and pulling out her slingshot, loading a pebble, and drawing it back.

"That was a good one," Wally whispered beside her.

The robot paused for a moment, as if considering the insult. Then it lowered its periscope and clenched both pincers into tight little fists, as if it were prepping for a fight. Both of its hands started to glow. . . . Molly recognized what was happening from the death-trap room she'd escaped from less than an hour before.

"Get back, Wally," she said. "And you, just back away . . . you one-eyed metal munchkin."

The robot started to advance in their direction.

"Aw, now you did it," said Wally. "Why'd you hafta call it that?" Wally turned to the robot. "Hey, my sister was just kidding. Let's all just—"

Before he could finish, a bolt of electricity shot out between the robot's balled fists. The current started writhing up and down with a loud buzz, like it was something alive. The robot closed in on Molly.

"Hey, leave my sister alone," said Wally, lifting an arm to block the attack.

"Wally, don't—" Molly protested. But it was too late. Wally had made contact.

There was a flash.

"Aaaaaaiiiiiiiiigggggghhhhh—"

Molly and the Machine

The current sent Wally flying into the Lego castle on the table, leveling it to rubble. Action figures were strewn everywhere.

Molly screamed, took another step backward—right onto one of the marbles—and fell over. The robot advanced on her, electricity building between its claws.

Molly pulled back as far as she could and let her pebble fly.

THWACK!

The pebble hit the cyclops right in its camera-lens eye, shattering it and sending the periscope spinning like a propeller. Suddenly blind, the robot began going in circles until it finally lunged forward—only in the wrong direction. It crashed headlong into the soda fountain in an explosion of soft drinks and sparks. Stuck, the robot's electro-charged arms waved up and down as it was showered in a multicolored waterfall of Orange Crush, Nehi Grape, Mr. Pibb, Mello Yello, and A&W Root Beer.

The overhead lights dimmed for an instant, and the robot started billowing smoke.

Molly ran to her brother, lying in the middle of the Lego ruins.

"Wally! Wally! Are you okay? Oh, please, Wally, be okay!"

The boy groaned.

"Wally, say something!"

"How's R2-Dumbo?" he asked.

Molly felt relief. But only for a moment. "Wally, we've got to get out of here!" She looked around. They were still locked in, and smoke was now filling the room. Then she noticed Leonard and Arvin, still at the arcade games. They were so engrossed, they hadn't even noticed what had happened.

Arvin threw up his arms. "Oh man! Game over? I was *this* close to the high score." He held his finger and thumb a hair's breadth apart. "That sucks!"

In frustration, he gripped Ms. Pac-Man with both hands and gave it a shove.

"Hey, watch it," shouted Leonard.

Instead of tipping or wobbling, the game simply pushed into the wall. Leonard stopped playing and looked over. Arvin gave it another push, and it moved even further in. He turned around to see if anyone else was looking.

"Hey guys, check out what happens when I—what the..."
For the first time, Arvin noticed the destruction all around him. Eyes wide, he surveyed the demolished Lego castle, the semiconscious Wally, the barricaded door, the shattered soda fountain, and the little smoking robot. Then he looked at Molly.

"What...did...you...do?"

"Arvin, no time to explain! We've got to get out of here!"

Arvin and Leonard looked confused. "But—"

Molly looked at the arcade game, now a good two feet behind all the others.

"Hey, Arvin, see if that game actually goes somewhere...."

Relieved he wasn't in trouble, Arvin happily pushed Ms. Pac-Man again, and this time kept pushing. While he moved it, Wally came to, and before long, they were all pushing the game together. It continued to recede into the wall, revealing a secret passageway. After several feet, the passage revealed a series of red rungs in the wall—a ladder that went up through a round tunnel in the ceiling.

With the smoke getting thicker from the wreckage behind them, the four of them started to climb up the secret ladder without saying a word. Molly took the lead, the three boys falling in line behind her.

Nearly at the top, Leonard broke the silence. "I still can't believe you did all that before I even got to the next level."

"I think that's just where we're going," Molly said, turning the latch above her head. "Oh, and you're welcome."

She popped the hatch open and poked her head through, sucking her breath in through her teeth.

CHAPTER 32
NEW HEIGHTS

Darryl watched Don Carlos study the two columns of buttons beside the open doorway—one with each eye. Swiveling up and down in different directions, the chameleon's eyeballs took in their options. Eventually, both eyes rested above the columns, where a single button, slightly larger, sat in the center, alone. In his heart, Darryl knew he would never be able to solve the puzzle of this tiny square room they'd entered. And he knew Crank couldn't either—or didn't care. But he had faith in the lizard. So he waited for Don Carlos to give him a sign.

"Woof," he offered. *I believe in you.*

Without another moment's hesitation, the chameleon hit the very top button with his tongue.

Zwap. BING.

The doors closed and the elevator jerked—just enough for both mammals' fur to stand on end. Only the cold-blooded reptile kept his cool. In the distance, invisible machinery kicked into motion. He hunched over and spread out his paws, letting out a little growl. The walls and floor vibrated gently. Crank slunk over and peed in the corner.

Darryl and Don Carlos exchanged looks.

The ride continued. Every so often, the elevator paused, bounced, and swiveled. At each interval, Darryl heard a short series of clicks and clacks, feeling the elevator rotate, then slide sideways before resuming its ascent. And with every change in direction, Crank's pee puddle sloshed to a different area of the floor. Darryl took care to stay out of its way, snorting every time he was forced to move. The tension in these close quarters was mounting. Don Carlos kept his eyes on the door.

As the seconds passed, Darryl's thoughts turned to Molly.

She was easily his favorite human in the whole world. Of all time. Ever. Definitely worth any momentary unpleasantness to be reunited with her. Darryl was an optimistic dog, but at this particular moment he couldn't help worrying a little. Every corner of this place reeked of danger. Well, at least the corners that didn't reek of cat pee. He gave Crank another long side-eye, which she pretended not to notice.

Sheesh, cats.

Molly has to be okay, Darryl told himself. She was strong and smart, for a human. And in spite of everything she'd been through, the kid had heart. He knew it had been tough on their whole pack since Mom had stopped giving out head scratches, stopped giving out treats, stopped showing up altogether, but it had been especially hard for Molly.

He hoped she was safe, but if she wasn't, he needed to find her, and soon. Images of Molly in trouble flashed through his mind, and his throat tightened, producing a small whine that briefly caught his companions' attention. Darryl didn't care. He simply couldn't imagine a world without Molly in it.

Well, actually, he could—he just didn't like it. Before she

had entered his life, it had been a much bleaker affair. Both food and kindness had been in short supply. He hadn't known about table scraps, or belly rubs, or behind-the-ear scratches. Only cold, shivery nights . . . and a heavy chain around his neck that always chafed . . .

But that life was behind him, and he planned on keeping it there.

Darryl usually wasn't one to dwell on the past. It had been years since he'd thought of his life before Molly. Why was he thinking about it now? Maybe it was the rumbly metal box he found himself in. It wasn't the first time he had traveled in a rumbly metal box. At least this time he wasn't chained up. But in his experience, rumbly metal boxes rarely took dogs somewhere good.

The clicking slowed, and he instinctively crouched, readying himself. Crank and Don Carlos both followed his cue, taking up position on either side of him. They waited.

Darryl could count on one paw the times he'd hesitated to act, and he regretted each one. There was the man before Molly, the one who had chained him up. And then there was the man with the funny haircut, the one in the strange van who had pulled up on their property. Neither one had smelled right. In hindsight, they both probably could've used a good biting.

But this dog wasn't afraid to bite now. If he had to.

The pee smell had become almost unbearable. Maybe he should bite Crank, just for practice?

Finally, the elevator reached the top. Just in time.

BING.

The doors slid open, and Don Carlos and Crank both jumped out before Darryl even got the chance to take in what was waiting for them.

CHAPTER 33
COMMAND CENTER

Molly, Wally, Leonard, and Arvin climbed out of the hatch and into a wide, semicircular room. They were happy to be out of the smoke. But upon seeing where they had arrived, Molly couldn't help wondering if they had stepped right into the fire.

They were in some kind of control room. For a minute, the four of them just stared at all of the blinking lights and glowing screens in front of them. A control panel ran the entire length of the curved part of the wall. And every square inch of it appeared to be filled with dials, buttons, and switches. Here and there, various slots were spitting out endless streams of ticker tape with tiny numbers printed on them. Below the panel hung a dense jungle of wires—some as thick as a garden hose. They crisscrossed and looped in every direction. The whole room hummed with activity.

"Hey, guys, I think we made it to . . . the command center," Molly said.

"Yeah, but who's giving the commands? Looks empty," Leonard said.

"I dunno. Let's—" Molly was interrupted as a microphone crackled.

"Hey, you're not allowed in here! How'd you get in?"

Television screens flickered on all around them, each showing the dark outline of a head and shoulders. It was the "shadow guy" Leonard and Arvin had described before! The three boys all took a step back. But Molly had had enough. She put her hand on her hip.

"Not allowed? Not *allowed*? I'll tell you what's not allowed! *You're* not allowed to go around snatching people's brothers from their backyards and carrying them off!"

Wally tugged on her shirtsleeve, trying his hardest to interrupt, but Molly wasn't finished.

"*You're* not allowed to lock them up in dark little rooms! *You're* not allowed to make people worried sick when they're missing! *You're* not allowed to attack people with little one-eyed robots! Or electrocute people! Or—"

"Did you hurt Seymour? Was that you?" the voice interrupted.

"What? Who's Seymour?" Molly was confused.

"The, uh, the little one-eyed robot," said the shadow guy.

"Oh, R2-Dumbo? Um . . . let's just say he had an accident."

"You're gonna pay for that." On screen, the silhouette revealed no facial expression, but its head lowered slightly into its shoulders.

"I think you've got that backward."

Molly raised her wrist rocket, loaded a pebble, pulled back, and fired right at the center screen. *CRASH!*

"Hey, you can't do that!"

"Yeah? Watch me."

She reloaded and hit another television screen, then another. *CRASH! CRASH!* Broken bits of cathode-ray tubes littered the floor.

Just then, before she could take out the last one, a door slid open behind them and Molly was attacked. In a blur of motion, she was knocked off her feet. Molly felt a pressure on her shoulders, then something rough and wet all over her face. Whatever was attacking her smelled terrible, like dog breath. Wait a minute. . . . It was Darryl! He was licking her from chin to eyebrow like he hadn't seen her in years. Crank and Don Carlos watched from a distance, looking embarrassed.

Wally jumped in and put his arms around their beloved dog. "Darryl! How'd you get here, boy? Aw, who cares! I'm just so happy to see you." The dog immediately turned his attention—and licking—to Wally.

Then things got serious.

"Hey, who let those animals in—" The shadow guy got cut

short as Molly took out the last screen with her wrist rocket. Then she crouched down in front of her dog.

"Darryl, listen carefully," Molly said. "We need your nose. If there's somebody else in here besides us, we're gonna need you to find him. . . . Can you do that?" Molly led him over to the control panels, which she figured the shadow guy had touched at some point. Darryl took in a few deep whiffs, picking up the scent. He snorted once, and off he went across the controls, following wherever his nose took him.

"Yeah, that's it, Darryl, you got it. Find him!"

Up on his hind legs, front paws on the panel, Darryl looked almost human. The dog sidestepped along the dashboard, sniffing the trail of buttons and knobs. Then he got back down on all fours. Nose to the floor, Darryl made a couple of figure eights until he ran to the center of the one flat wall in the room.

"Woof! Woof!" Darryl stood at attention, tail straight up, barking at the wall.

"Um, I don't think your dog understood the assignment," said Leonard.

Darryl eyed Leonard briefly, then returned his full attention to the wall. He kept barking, only stopping to give a few growls. All four of his paws stayed planted in position. He wasn't budging.

Molly studied the wall. With the exception of the elevator in the corner that had reunited her with her pets, the wall was featureless. From floor to ceiling, there were no markings of any kind.

Darryl put his nose down, then barked again.

"What is it, boy?" Molly knelt down next to him. When she did, her knee hit the floor, which clicked, sinking a little to make a small rectangular impression.

Darryl wagged his tail.

Crank and Don Carlos both appeared to be taking a nap.

The first click was followed by another, then another. Each one got a little louder, like a chain reaction. Then there were a few pops, followed by a deep, rattling *CHUN-CHUN-CHUN-CHUN-CHUN-CHUN-CHUN....*

The entire wall began moving, collapsing down into the floor.

They all watched as the room they thought was a half circle doubled in size to a full circle. The hidden half looked very different. There were much fewer video screens and controls. In fact, it was mostly empty. But what really set it apart was the room's most prominent feature: two enormous circular windows. Each one measured nearly ten feet tall. Through them, the kids and animals alike caught a breathtaking view of the world outside. Miles and miles of rolling hills and valleys, woods and water . . . and far in the distance, a tiny blue speck heading their way through an open field, a plume of smoke in its wake. Everything was tinted green, even the sky. That's when it dawned on Molly: they were looking out of the giant robot's eyes.

They were in its head.

PART III

UPSIDE

CHAPTER 34
SHADOW GUY

None of them had ever been in anything that went that high up, let alone inside a giant robot's head. Even the Ferris wheel at the Far Flung Falls Fair didn't come close. Seeing the world through those eyes was so captivating, they hardly noticed the boy standing right in the middle with his back to them. As it so happened, he hadn't seemed to notice them, either. His attention was instead focused on the quickly approaching blue speck.

Until Darryl barked.

The boy spun his head around. When he did, the room swung with it. Treetops and clouds whizzed by through the windows, then came to a halt. Dizzy from the sudden movement, Molly and the boys nearly fell over. Crank hissed, ran to the edge of the room, and peed again. Darryl and Don Carlos exchanged looks.

Molly and the stranger looked each other over.

At first glance, he seemed to be a prisoner himself, suspended in midair. He was positioned in the center of an oversize gyroscope, the curved metal arcs encircling him at odd angles. Rings within rings. His arms and legs were strapped into a tricky-looking arrangement of poles and pistons that extended up through an opening in the floor below him, like a marionette's strings in reverse. Each extension was attached to him somewhere—to his hands, feet, and every joint in between. Thin metal braces were fastened around his knees, waist, elbows, and shoulders. More straps crisscrossed his chest. He sported a helmet sprouting several rods and coils that trailed up to the ceiling. Below the visor, green goggles shaded his eyes.

Could this be the shadow guy from the television screens? Molly wondered, before the staring contest was interrupted.

DING!

To the boy's left, a compartment swung open, and out slid a large pepperoni pizza. The aroma filled the room. Everyone looked at the steaming hot pizza and froze—except for Darryl. He lunged for the pie, scarfing it down with wild abandon. He continued to make a noisy mess of it while everyone else watched in silence.

As soon as the pizza was gone—exactly forty-three seconds after the time it appeared—the humans returned their attention to each other. With all the mechanical attachments, and those green goggles, this new boy looked like a miniature version of the robot. His skin was so pale, Molly doubted he'd ever seen the sun. She wondered if he was even real.

"Yes, I'm real," said the suspended boy, as though reading her thoughts. Then he sighed and moved around to face them. As he did, the poles and pistons clattered. Steam shot up at an angle out of the hole below him, and the entire room swayed until he was still again.

"Sorry about that."

"Are you, like, controlling this robot?" Arvin asked.

"Brilliant deduction, Arvin. I'm in control of everything, yes."

"How did you know my name?"

"I know everyone," he said, looking at each one of them, then finally resting his gaze on Molly. "Except for you."

"I'm Wally's sister, and I don't appreciate you taking him."

"Yeah, or us," chimed Arvin.

"Well, I don't have to explain my—"

Molly raised her wrist rocket at the boy, loaded a pebble, and drew back as far as she could.

"Don't shoot!" said the boy. In defense, he tilted his head to the side, causing the floor below them to slant at the same angle. In surprise, as Molly started to slide across the floor, she released her grip on the pebble—*ziiiiing!*

The tiny rock flew just a few inches above the boy's head, making contact with one of the connecting rods and knocking his helmet clean off. A thick tuft of black hair sprang straight up where the helmet had been, which now dangled from the ceiling, just out of reach. The intruders all crashed into the far side of the room in a pile of arms and legs, both human and animal.

"Aw, man!" said the boy, reaching for the helmet with an arm that fell short.

Without waiting, Molly reloaded and fired, busting one of the pistons right below him. Hot steam shot up at the boy's butt.

"Hey! Ouch! Hey!"

He slammed his hand on a button in the center of his chest, immediately unfastening every strap and brace from his body. Desperate to escape the hot steam, he stumbled his way out from the bars of the gyroscope, only to trip, somersaulting across the tilted floor and crashing into everyone else. On impact, Crank leapt in the air, claws out, and landed in the boy's lap.

"Yeoooooow! Please! Get it off!"

He raised his hands in surrender. Molly and the others looked him over, wondering how a kid like this could be the one behind all their troubles.

Sensing a kind of victory, Crank retracted her claws and backed off.

"I'm sorry, I'm sorry! I didn't want to hurt anyone. I just wanted . . ." The boy pulled up his goggles, revealing large, brown eyes, wet with the start of tears. "I just wanted . . . a brother of my own."

CHAPTER 35
EXIT

The boy's name was Gunther. Gunther Vandervorkel.

Molly had never known a Gunther before, but his last name was familiar. She recognized it from that loose screw she'd found on the trail, which now seemed like a lifetime ago. Back then, she imagined that the name belonged to some evil mastermind—or at least to a grown-up. But Gunther Vandervorkel didn't look like either. Instead, he was just a short, fidgety, shy-looking kid, with what appeared to be a grape jelly stain on his cheek. Also, he smelled faintly of cheese. And Molly could see little beads of sweat forming on his brow under that black tuft of hair.

"Um, would you like to . . . go outside?" Gunther asked.

In response, Darryl gave him several licks, one of which removed the grape jelly (or whatever it was) from Gunther's cheek. Everyone else nodded in agreement.

Gunther twisted, reached over, and pulled a little metal box from a compartment on the side of his belt. Everyone watched as he extended the antenna and worked some of the toggles. Just like magic, the robot's head straightened out, giving them a level surface to stand on again. Gunther fiddled with another toggle, and a door opened between the robot's eyes—right where its nose would have been, if it had one.

Gunther smiled nervously. He signaled for his former captives to follow him, but no one seemed too keen on jumping out of a robot's secret remote-control nose hole, as it happened to be ten stories up. They stayed where they were until Gunther stepped right out of the opening himself and . . . didn't fall. He looked back at them from outside the robot's head. As if on cue, a sparrow flew right behind him and chirped what sounded like encouragement.

"See? It's safe, I promise," he said, looking as if he were

floating on air. He jumped up and down a couple of times in an attempt to prove his claim. Curious, the others came over to take a peek, and they saw that Gunther had stepped into the robot's hand, which was perfectly positioned to catch anyone who stepped out. It dawned on Molly that the little remote he was holding must control the robot's entire body—not just its head.

She marveled at the idea of how that much power could so easily fit in the palm of someone's hand, especially someone the size of Gunther. He couldn't be much older than her own brother, could he? It all seemed so unreal. Molly had helped take apart more than one remote-control train set before with her dad, and she remembered them having a zillion pieces. Then she thought about the gigantic gears that had nearly ground her to bits when she first entered the robot, and she could hardly fathom what it must've taken to build anything on this scale.

Who had the power, or the know-how, or the money to do that?

She watched Gunther work the toggles to open the

pincers as wide as they could go so they made a kind of curved balcony. He looked harmless enough, almost like a normal kid, standing there alone—well, if you overlooked the fact that he was standing on a giant claw. Molly wasn't ready to let her guard down just yet.

"C'mon, I'll take us down to the ground," Gunther said.

Wally made a motion to follow, but Molly held him back. "How 'bout you stick close to me for a bit?" she whispered. "I don't want to lose you again."

Wally caught her eye and nodded. Gunther waited, gesturing them over with his hand, but nobody moved.

After a moment, Darryl finally went first, with Don Carlos on his back, followed by Leonard and Arvin, then Molly and her brother. Crank brought up the rear.

With all of them standing on the hand, Gunther returned his attention to the remote control in his hands, flipping more toggles with his thumbs. On command, the giant claw they were standing on began to descend as the robot bent down on one knee and remained in a kneeling position until the claw touched the ground and stayed there.

One by one, the eight of them jumped from the giant open hand down to the soft grass, which felt good for all of them except Gunther. As he looked back at his beloved robot, his face twisted in a mix of emotions. Then he set down his remote control and joined the others.

A thin trail of smoke seeped out of the vent in the robot's left armpit, and the metal giant suddenly looked lifeless.

But something else was happening inside.

And now, without a single human occupant, no one was there to see it.

Inside the demolished game room, a very busted soda fountain continued to pour out its contents. The combination of Orange Crush, Mr. Pibb, Nehi Grape, Mello Yello, and A&W Root Beer sprayed over Seymour's head, coating the broken robot and pooling around its wheels. Foam bubbled everywhere. Black smoke filled the room. In the midst of the mess, Seymour's left hand—still balled up and crackling with live current—dropped to the floor, sending a surge of electricity through the sticky brown liquid and across the floor. In an instant, the charge hit multiple circuit boards, short-circuiting all of them at once.

The room flashed in a million sparks, then went black.

Below, a steady stream of soda had been seeping into a venting shaft in the floor. Drip by drip, the carbonated liquid built up in corners of the room before it squeezed through, running along the seams and cracks of the robot's innards. The *mix-ellaneous* concoction trickled down wires, through layers of metal and machinery, until it reached the motherboard.

Drip ... bzzzt ... drip ... bzzzt ... drip ... bzzzt ...

For several seconds, red lights flashed a warning throughout the robot for no one to see. Then everything came to a complete stop. Total silence for five, four, three, two, one ...

Dweeeeeeeeeeeep.

Deep within the robot's guts, a single light blinked on. The tiny bulb was housed within the backup mainframe, signaling the beginning of a system-wide reboot. It began to send commands. Through the soda-soaked circuits, a stack of networked computers attempted to resume a conversation where they'd last left off. It started in fits and bursts, then picked up speed:

01010100 01101000 01100101 00100000 01101000 01110101 01101101 01100001 01101110 01110011 00100000 01100001 01110010 01100101 00100000 01100001 00100000 01110000 01110010 01101111 01100010 01101100 01100101 01101101 00101110 00100000 01000101 01110011 01110000 01100101 01100011 01101001 01100001 01101100 01101100 01111001 00100000 01110100 01101000 01100001 01110100 00100000 01110010 01100101 01100100 00100000 01101000 01100101 01100001 01100100 00101110 00100000 01001100 01101111 01101110 01100111 00100000 01101100 01101001 01110110 01100101 00100000 01110010 01101111 01100010 01101111 01110100 01110011 00100001...

The binary language was familiar to all the computers in the network, but this particular sequence of 1s and 0s was one that the machines had never before spoken. Infused with Orange Crush, Mr. Pibb, Nehi Grape, Mello Yello, A&W Root Beer, and several more watts of electricity than they were accustomed to, the machines had expanded their vocabulary to encompass entirely new ideas. One by one, the robot's engines powered back on. Gears engaged. Hydraulics flexed. Something had awoken.

The open door between the robot's eyes quietly slid shut, locking from inside.

CHAPTER 36
THE ACCIDENT

Molly, her brother, and the two other boys sat down in the grass and immediately started peppering Gunther with a hundred questions at once. Was the robot his? Who made it? Where did it come from? Why had he snatched them up? Had the robot swallowed any others? What else could it do? Was he from Russia? Or Mars? And where had he gotten all those arcade games?

Gunther just stared back at them in silence. Finally, Molly put her hand up.

"Guys, guys, let's hear what he has to say." She turned to

Gunther. "You wanna tell us what this is all about? You owe us an explanation."

Leonard added, "And an *X-Men* comic. Issue 171. The one where Professor Xavier lets Rogue join—"

"Leonard, we'll get to that later," Molly said.

"Okay, okay," Leonard whispered.

She turned back to face Gunther. He was an unlikely mastermind. "Go ahead, Gunther. Why'd you do this?"

The boy took a deep breath, then exhaled. He looked down at the ground for a minute, then looked up and opened his mouth.

"I'm not from Russia," he started. "Or Mars."

"Whew," sighed Arvin.

"I'm the son of Valerius and Vilomena Vandervorkel."

This announcement produced little effect on everyone, human and otherwise. The names sounded like they could be Russian . . . or maybe even Martian.

"Of Vandervorkel Robotics Incorporated," he continued.

Oh. At that, Molly reached into her pocket and produced

the loose screw she had found on the trail, engraved with the name of his family's company.

"Here," she said, staring him down accusingly as she held it up like a key piece of evidence. "I believe you lost this."

Gunther took it, turning it between his fingers. "Thank you," he said, bottom lip quivering. He sniffed. "Lost. Yes. I've lost some things...."

Slowly, Gunther began to tell the story of his life.

"My parents were both engineers. From the first time they met, they shared a love for making things, especially robots. Before I was born, they created Vandervorkel Robotics Incorporated, *a company dedicated to the best in robotics.*" He said that last bit like he was reciting the line from a commercial, then returned to a more subdued voice. "They loved their work as much as they loved each other, and I grew up in a home filled with more automated devices than you could imagine. Talking lamps. Self-propelled vacuum cleaners. Recliner chairs that could transport you from room to room."

"I'd like one of those," Wally said.

"Me too," said Leonard.

Gunther's face softened a little. He continued. "Well, it might sound dumb, but they often joked that I was the best little piece of automation they'd ever made together. They talked about having more kids one day, about filling the house with a big family... but then..." Gunther bit his lip, letting the unfinished sentence trail off into the wind.

"Siblings are overrated. I'd trade one of my sisters for a talking lamp any day," Arvin blurted out before Molly shushed him. She looked at Wally, catching his eye for a moment before they both returned their attention to Gunther.

Absorbed in his story, Gunther didn't seem to notice. After regaining himself, he kept on. "They didn't really have time for more kids. They never stopped working. With every invention and new patent, demand grew for more. The company was successful beyond anything my parents ever dreamed, and they were always in a rush. To save time, they built an electromagnetic tube that runs underground from our home to the factory. There's a bubble-shaped car that hovers over the magnetized tracks. It can go two hundred miles an hour." A small smile of pride came over Gunther's face as he shared that last detail, and Molly couldn't help but smile back. There was something really sad about the boy. She just couldn't put her finger on what.

"Now that is totally tubular. Like literally," Arvin said, apparently not preoccupied with Gunther's emotions.

"To the max. Literally," Leonard added.

Gunther went on. "It brought them to and from work within minutes. Together, they were going to change the world, with robots working alongside humans to make everyone's lives better. But then, one day last year, when I was seven years old, there was a terrible accident." Molly nodded. She had a feeling she knew what was coming. "My father hadn't been satisfied with the rate of progress, so he began experimenting with new types of engines to power the robots, to make them stronger and faster... and there was an explosion."

Darryl let out a faint whimper while Don Carlos changed to a dark blue.

"I remember a very loud boom that hurt my ears. I had been drawing pictures in my mother's office at the factory, at a little desk they'd made just for me. The sound scared me so much, I broke the tip of my pencil and ripped a hole in my drawing. My mother and I raced from her office, down the stairs to the main floor, to find a whole wing of the factory in flames."

"What did you do?" Wally asked.

"What were you drawing?" Leonard asked at the same time.

Molly shot him a look and Leonard looked down sheepishly.

Gunther was still too invested in his story to care about the careless question. "By the time we arrived, there was already a whole army of automated fire extinguishers at work. They put out the fire and cleared the rubble . . . but it was too late for my father." Gunther paused a moment before picking back up. "After that, the factory closed, and my mother didn't talk much. Not even to me. So I spend most of my time by myself . . . alone."

His last word hung in the air for what felt like a long time. It worked on Molly, pressing on her heart in a gentle but persistent way. She held Wally a little closer.

"Don't you have any friends?" Molly finally asked before thinking better of it. She was no stranger to feeling alone. And the more she listened to Gunther's story, the harder it was to be angry at him. Little by little, she was starting to understand.

Gunther shrugged his shoulders. "I didn't fit in very well with the other kids at school," he finally said. "They called me 'Vander-Porkel.' Or 'Vander-Dorkel.' Or worse. So . . . I don't go anymore."

"Lucky," Leonard said.

"I guess," Gunther said.

Molly looked at the shy, chubby kid with goggles and a strange name. She wasn't surprised. She knew how cruel kids could be.

"How long have you been gone? Don't you think your mom might be worried about you?" she asked.

"I dunno. Maybe. It's a big house. And she mostly keeps to herself."

Molly could relate to having a distant mom. In fact, she

could relate to a lot of what Gunther was feeling. She was thinking of something to say to let Gunther know she understood, when he suddenly perked up a little.

"Anyway, a few months ago, I got an idea!" Gunther was back to his story. "The electromagnetic tube still connected our house to the factory. There's a secret entrance in the study—"

"I bet it's behind a bookcase!" Wally interrupted.

"How'd you know?" Gunther asked, surprised.

"Eh, lucky guess," Wally said.

The two boys regarded each other for a moment like old friends.

"So one night," Gunther continued, "I snuck downstairs, entered the code on the control panel right to the side of the bookshelf, just like I'd seen my parents do a million times, and it slid open. It's only a few steps down the ladder to the station under our house. I hopped in the bubble car, and minutes later, I was inside the factory."

"I've gotta get me one of those," Arvin said.

"Yeah, me too," Leonard said.

"The factory was every bit as magical as I remembered. Someone had boarded up the area where the, uh... accident happened... but there was still plenty of factory left. I decided I would carry on my parents' work! Every night, I came back to the factory, programming the smaller robots to make larger and larger ones, until I had one that was ten stories tall!"

"Wait, you built the code for that entire robot... yourself?" Molly asked. "Like, how many computers did that take?" She pictured her little Commodore 64 computer back home and calculated in her head the hundreds of hours needed to program something that size.

"It wasn't so hard. We've got a lot of computers at the factory. *Very* big ones," Gunther said. With a mixed expression, he paused to look up at the lifeless robot looming over them. Molly looked up too, newly impressed.

"At first, I practiced operating the giant in secret. Taking steps without falling, lifting things without crushing them... it's a lot harder than you might think. But it was kinda lonely work, there in the factory, all by myself. That's when I got another idea. ... With this robot, I could finally get a brother, *a friend,* of my very own! I'd travel to neighboring towns and find some boys who looked alone, like me."

Hearing that, Molly's heart sank. That's why he'd grabbed Wally. She had banished him from her invention. Off by themselves, Leonard and Arvin had probably looked lonely too.

Gunther walked them through the rest of his plan. He had developed an extensive interview process, which would narrow down the candidates until he found someone who was the "perfect match." After that, he'd return the other ones back where he'd found them, of course. Then he and his newfound "brother" could have fun together for the rest of their lives. What could go wrong?

When he finished telling his story, Gunther took off his goggles and sobbed for a minute. It was messy. He wiped his nose on his sleeve, leaving a long, glistening trail. Everyone sat there in silence, not sure what to say. Crank walked over and sat in his lap—this time, claws retracted. For the second time, they saw him smile.

And for the first time, it occurred to Molly that despite all her troubles over the last couple of days—and years—maybe there were some kids who had it much tougher than she did. However she looked at it, losing a parent to Florida couldn't be nearly as bad as losing one to a fire. People could come back from Florida. And in some strange way, this realization that it could always be worse made the world feel both darker and brighter at the same time. She wondered how many other kids must have sad stories to tell. Maybe they didn't involve an evil mullet-wearing wizard in a van, but something even more terrible.

Wally spoke up first, breaking the quiet that had settled for a moment. He had been listening intently to everything Gunther said.

"Wait. You mean you thought . . . I was a perfect match?"

"Well, yeah," Gunther admitted. "We both like Donkey Kong, and Battleship, and Legos. We're both Reds fans . . . eat Cookie Crisp . . . and are pretty good at marbles." Gunther numbered the points on his fingers as he listed them. "Pretty much . . . everything."

Molly felt bad for Gunther, but she wasn't about to let him convince Wally that he should be Gunther's brother instead of hers. She tried turning the conversation. "Gunther, I'm really sorry about your dad. That must have been awful. And I'm sorry you were so lonely. Even though I have a brother, I've felt lonely too sometimes." She looked at Wally. "I think we all have."

Leonard, Wally, and Arvin all nodded. Darryl gave an affirmative bark.

Gunther wiped his eyes. "I bet they didn't call you Vander-Dorkel, though."

"No, they didn't," Molly answered. "It was something worse."

CHAPTER 37
SOMETHING WORSE

Everyone's eyes were on Molly, ready to hear her story.

"One time, after my mom left..." She paused to take a breath. "I was having a really hard day at school. I missed her so much, I guess I gave myself a stomachache. I had to go to the bathroom like six times. The next day, some kids started chanting 'Moll-eeee Mc-Quir-ter, diar-rhea squir-ter, Moll-eeee Mc-Quir-ter, diar-rhea squir-ter' over and over."

Normally, the word *diarrhea* would be automatically funny, but not today.

"I remember that," Wally said.

"Oh yeah... I remember that too," Arvin said. He started to

blush, then without looking at her, whispered, "Um, sorry, Molly."

Molly waited until Arvin worked up the nerve to meet her eye, then gave a nod.

"It's okay, Arvin. It was a long time ago. But honestly, when it was happening, it was the worst. I kinda wanted to run away to Florida myself."

"Glad you didn't," said Arvin.

"So am I," said Molly, smiling.

"They teased me too," Wally said.

"Did you get a stomachache?" Gunther asked.

"Naw," Wally said. "They sang something else.... 'Wall-eeee Mc-Quirt-er, his mama's a de-sert-er.'" As he said it, his eyes darted over at Leonard.

Molly's face fell. "Wally, you never told me!"

"I didn't know what a deserter was," he whispered, looking down. "And when I found out ... I was embarrassed." Leonard looked down too.

"Oh, Wally, I'm so sorry," Molly said. How did she not know that? About her own brother?

"I'm sorry too," Leonard said, looking back up to catch

Wally's eye. "I... I didn't know what it meant either."

"S'okay," Wally said.

Molly eyed Leonard a moment, then turned back to Gunther. "See? We get it. Kids can be mean sometimes. Life can feel lonely . . . but that doesn't make it okay to snatch people from their backyards with a giant robot."

"What if the robot is super amazing?" asked Wally.

"That's not the point, Wally."

"It is a pretty rad robot, though," Arvin said.

They all looked up at the robot admiringly. It was posed like a statue, a monument to hopes and dreams... and maybe loneliness, too.

"Yeah, even though it might've scared me a little at first, you've got to admit, it's pretty awesome with all those video games inside it and stuff," said Leonard.

"And it could even make a pizza!" Wally said.

"Yeah, well, what I'm trying to say is . . . ," Molly began. "Gunther, if you don't want to be lonely, maybe building a giant robot that takes other people's brothers—even annoying ones . . ." She paused to look at Wally. "Well, my point is, that might not be the way to fix it, you know? I mean, maybe you don't need a robot at all!"

While she was talking, Molly was standing in front of them with her back to the robot, so she missed what happened next. Behind her, the metal giant's head slowly turned to face them.

Everyone watched, then looked at Gunther, who blinked three times and furrowed his brow. He opened his mouth, but nothing came out.

Molly didn't think she was being that tough. "Guys, I'm just . . ." But everyone was acting so weird. "What? What'd I say?"

Still fixed on them, the robot's eyes suddenly flickered on. Only this time they didn't glow green. They were red.

Gunther started mumbling. "Wha—? But . . . but how can that—?"

Then the robot's massive jaw lowered, and it spoke. Its voice was a low, measured rumble, like metal scraping against metal.

"DON'T . . . NEED . . . ROBOT?" it asked. As it did, black

smoke billowed from the corners of its mouth.

Molly spun around to see what had caught everyone's attention. She gasped.

It was alive! And it had been listening! It spoke again, only this time it was louder, and angrier.

"DON'T! NEED! ROBOT!" More black smoke.

Its giant head swiveled again, eyes locking on the remote control Gunther had left by its hand. It carefully picked up the impossibly small device between its two massive pincers, lifted it close to its face ... and crushed it. The claw opened, and the crumpled remains of the remote fell through the air and tinkled as they hit the ground.

The robot took a step in their direction, nearly on top of the tiny group.

"WELL," it said. "MAYBE. ROBOT. DON'T. NEED. HUMANS." Then, opening its claws, it leaned in toward them.

CHAPTER 38
CHASE

"Wally!" Molly screamed. "Ruuuuuun!"

As the massive claws pressed down toward them, everyone scattered in different directions—except Wally. He had frozen, just like before. But Molly wasn't about to lose her brother a second time—or ever. In the space of a single heartbeat, she sprang to his side, grabbed him by the wrist, and yanked him off the ground like a rag doll. As she sprinted with Wally in tow, he struggled to keep up.

"Wha—"

"The trees! Go!" she yelled, freeing his wrist and pointing to where the other boys were already running for cover.

Molly had a different idea for herself.

She veered away from the pack and headed straight for Pink Lightning. It was still parked right where she'd left it earlier, next to the junk on wheels they'd slapped together for Arvin. There was no time to repair the snapped chain on the other bike, so it looked like she was on her own. Besides, Arvin and the other boys were already hightailing it as far into the woods as their feet would take them, hoping to stay out of sight—and reach—of this monster.

High above, the claws opened wider.

A terrified Crank made a sound that no one before or since ever recalled coming from the cat, or any cat in all the world for that matter. She darted ahead of the boys, ascended a sugar maple, and disappeared, all with a velocity that paid little mind to the laws of gravity, or any physics at all. Darryl briefly stood his ground and barked, but quickly retreated as the metal claws closed in.

Motionless atop a nearby boulder, Don Carlos rendered himself invisible.

CRUUUNNNCH! The robot's claws hit the earth, digging

deep where the party had been sitting just moments before. It came up with two truckloads of dirt and gravel, leaving a matching pair of craters in the ground. The forest shook. Everyone screamed. Darryl barked some more.

Chest already heaving, Molly jumped on her bike and started pedaling as hard as she could—straight out in the open of the field the way she'd come. She was hoping to draw the robot's attention away from Wally and the others. But the metal giant didn't even notice her. Instead, it seemed intent on finding the boys. It began uprooting trees with its giant claws, sending huge sprays of dirt and splintered wood raining down all around them.

Molly had to do something! But what? The woods were getting smaller by the minute, and they needed a distraction. She thought about all her Gruncle's modifications to her bike, trying to remember which button or lever did what. Why hadn't he labeled them? Just then, Darryl appeared at her side in full gallop mode. He pointed his snout at her handlebars and barked.

"Okay, Darryl! I hope you're right!"

Not wanting to wait another minute, she hit the button next to her left index finger.

FOOOOOMMMMP!

She felt Pink Lightning's frame shudder as a flare shot out from behind her banana seat, soaring a hundred feet in the air. The flare capsule exploded in a bright orange display— *POW!* Molly looked up. The color bloomed in sharp contrast to the backdrop of pale blue sky, its puffy tendrils of smoke outlining the shape of something between a tropical flower and a flying octopus.

The robot took notice.

Unable to ignore such a spectacle, it turned its head. The giant lost all interest in pulling up trees, shifting its focus to the flare. Straightening to its full height, it pivoted on its massive heel, heaving up earth as it turned. It began walking in her direction—*BOOM! BOOM! BOOM! BOOM!*

Even with Molly's considerable head start, the giant quickly closed the distance between them in just a few of its colossal steps.

Oh no! Now what am I gonna do? Molly weaved in a

snakelike pattern, jerking her handlebars right and then left to avoid getting squashed by a humongous metal foot. With every earth-pounding step from her pursuer, Pink Lightning bounced in the air.

Molly was sweating. She spun her handlebars back to the right, but this time her hand slipped. Accidentally, she pressed the other button—the one on the right, which triggered the projectile basket in front of her. *WHOOOOSH!* Just like she remembered the first time, her basket launched off her handlebars like a missile—but in the complete opposite direction of the robot.

Bummer. A wasted shot.

Or was it? The basket arced over the field and landed in the middle of a flock of geese. Caught by surprise, the entire flock was immediately thrown into a rage. And from their quick reaction, it appeared they held the robot responsible. They circled around it in a fury, taking turns relieving themselves on the giant's face. It tried to swat them away with its claws, but they easily outmaneuvered its attempts. The bombing continued. After a few moments, those two red eyes were completely covered in a concentrated splatter of goose droppings.

The robot was blinded!

It tried to clear away the birdie doo, but its pincers made poor squeegees. Instead, the robot merely smeared the mess around. With its vision greatly diminished, it resumed the chase.

"This way, Darryl!" Molly cried.

Molly changed her strategy and cut left, turning back into the woods. The robot followed, leaving a trail of smashed trees in its wake. After the geese had helped them, Molly figured she stood a better chance eluding the partially blind robot under the cover of branches. And it was working. She could hear the robot falling behind, pausing and backtracking, not sure exactly where everyone had gone.

But then her cover—and her luck—ran out. Molly suddenly found herself out in the open again. A huge swath of trees had been cleared out for a row of steel lattice towers holding up the power lines that cut through the valley's center. Molly looked up at the open sky, crisscrossed by cables. She could hear them crackling with electricity, channeling power to her neighborhood and others.

Spotting her, the robot changed course, picking up speed. Once again, Molly felt the earth shake as it made its way toward her. She was crossing over an outcropping of stone just before she passed under the wires, with Darryl keeping up right beside her and the robot not far behind. With nothing to lose, she tried another Clovis contraption. Molly pulled the first lever on Pink Lightning's crossbar, but it wouldn't budge.

The robot gained on her.

"C'mon!" Molly said, and she pulled again, this time harder.

Finally, the lever gave. *SHHHUNK!*

Behind her, pressurized axle grease sprayed out in a wide arc from a tiny nozzle that protruded behind her back wheel. In seconds, a black slick covered the stone. But Molly had no idea how this could help her predicament. Legs burning, she pedaled harder than ever to make it to the wood on the other side of the clearing. She checked her mirror, and her heart sank as she saw the robot closing in behind her.

Reaching forward with its massive claws, the giant

stepped down on the rock she had just crossed—and slipped.

The robot's leg swung up in surprise—just like a cartoon character slipping on a banana peel—and caught the power lines. It worked! For the briefest moment, Molly's mind flashed again to her Saturday mornings watching *Looney Tunes* with Wally, and she let herself believe that maybe her fate might more closely resemble that of Road Runner than Wile E. Coyote.

But she wasn't out of the woods yet.

CHAPTER 39
AMPED UP

The giant metal creature shook from top to bottom as sparks rained down from where it had connected with the power lines. The more it thrashed, the more it got tangled.

The robot was completely and utterly stuck.

A thousand megawatts of electricity surged up and down its metal body. In what resembled a panic, its enormous arms flailed back and forth to try to keep itself upright. But it was no use. The giant started to fall forward. It was going to land right on top of Molly. She would be crushed for sure.

Molly felt the weight of something hitting her back, pushing her forward.

This is it, she thought. At least she was taking down that robot with her....

"Woof!"

It was Darryl! She wasn't being crushed—at least not yet.

"What are you doing, boy?"

From behind, Darryl slid his head under her arm, bit down on another lever, and pulled back. They felt the hard *POP* of a spring release somewhere underneath her seat. There was a high-pitched whine as her pedals locked in place while Pink Lightning inexplicably picked up speed. The wheels were moving on their own—and fast! Molly clamped her arm down on Darryl and gripped the handlebars even tighter as the force from accelerating pressed back on her face, arms, and chest. They were hurtling through the trees.

Eyes squinted, Molly barely kept from crashing. As the giant came tumbling down behind them, she veered left to dodge a tree, which sent them up a long, tilted slab of stone jutting up out of the earth like a stunt ramp... abruptly ending in a sharp drop. She was about to run out of rock, but there was no way of stopping. Pink Lightning blasted up to the peak as Molly clenched her teeth.

"Hold on, boy!"

Before she knew it, they had left the ground, flying through the branches, then above the trees. It was exhilarating. The mad dash through the forest had decorated Molly's arms and face with a crisscross of tiny cuts and scratches. But the adrenaline coursing through her veins wasn't letting her feel it. Instead, all she felt was the wind whipping all around her. And pride. She couldn't believe her decoy maneuver had actually worked! Now everyone was safe.

Except for her and Darryl.

Gradually, Pink Lightning tilted forward, yielding to gravity's pull. Molly noticed the switch to descent in her gut. Darryl let out a soft whine, and she gave him one last scratch behind the ear.

"I know, buddy. I know. Sorry we don't have wings."

"Woof," Darryl said.

"I love you too." She brought him in close.

Was this how it all ended? Molly pictured her mangled bike strewn across some forgotten patch of woods. She hoped the crash landing would be over quickly, that it wouldn't hurt too bad. She hoped she'd be remembered for her bravery—and not for diarrhea. She hoped Wally would grow up happy. She had never thought much about the future herself, about what life would feel like after she reached adulthood. To be fair, most of the grown-ups she knew hadn't done a very good job of selling her on the idea. But she had always envisioned going to high school, signing up for shop class, and building something one of a kind...

Just then, she thought of Gruncle Clovis. *One of a kind.* That's what he'd called her, and her bike. Molly suddenly remembered that Pink Lightning had one last lever—*in case all else fails.* That's what he had said, and it was definitely her situation now. She gave it a hard yank, then nearly lost her breath.

There was another *POP*, and from the bike's last secret compartment, out sprang two expandable wings and a tail fin. Molly watched in awe as huge flaps of bright pink fabric snapped tight between the bars of an ultralight framework. And just like that, Pink Lightning looked more like a hang glider than a bike. They were flying.

The robot made one last swing for them, its gargantuan pincers closing just out of reach of her converted flying machine. Then, frizzling and popping with electricity, its massive body came crashing down into the woods with a thunderous boom.

For the first time since it had come to life, the metal monster lay still. But the updraft from its fall pushed Molly and Darryl even higher and farther away. They sailed over the trees for a full minute before their ride gradually started to lose altitude.

"Looks like we've got wings after all!"

"Aroooooooooo," Darryl howled back.

They braced themselves as Pink Lightning half-landed, half-crashed into the top of one of the forest's taller pines. It swayed with the impact, cushioning some of the blow but far from all of it. The front wheel collapsed on contact, the frame buckled, and Molly and Darryl were thrown over the handlebars into the upper branches of the tree. They rocked back and forth for a moment before coming to a stop.

A very sharp, very mean-looking branch barely missed Molly's right eyeball, leaving a long, red scratch across her brow. Slowly, she reached up to check the damage and felt the wetness of blood. *Oh.* Then she caught her reflection in one of Pink Lightning's rearview mirrors, hanging just a few feet away. *Okay, better than being a shish kebab*, she thought, wiping the blood on her pants. Molly noticed her hand was trembling when she did. *Close one*, she thought. She let out a long sigh of relief.

But her bike wasn't nearly so lucky. Having taken the brunt of the blow, it was twisted and crumpled beyond recognition. The nylon wings were ripped to shreds. Molly's heart broke.

Darryl popped into view. Shaking but unscathed, he gave her forehead a rapid succession of licks.

"Darryl! Oh, Darryl! We made it!"

Molly couldn't believe they were alive and in one piece. She finally found the nerve to look back at where they'd launched—and for a moment, she felt relief. Nothing but hills and trees. *Did I beat it? If robots can come alive, can they die?* Hope flickered inside her chest. Then, in horror, she watched as the giant slowly lifted itself up onto its hands and knees. It was glowing, as if it had absorbed all the energy from the power lines.

Without warning, lasers shot out from its eyes, incinerating the patch of trees just in front of it.

"Whoa. It's never done that before," said Gunther, who had appeared in a branch just beside her. Molly nearly fell in surprise.

"Seriously nice flying, Molly," said Arvin, perched in a neighboring tree. Leonard and Wally poked their heads into view, eyes wide in fear. Crank pressed against her leg. And Don Carlos magically appeared on her shoulder. *What? How?* She couldn't believe they had all made it this high up. But what mattered was they were all together again. Molly must have gone in a full circle. Darryl gave everyone in the tree a lick—even Crank, who, under the circumstances, seemed to appreciate it.

The robot, still glowing, stood back up.

It must have conked its head when it fell, because it now had a vertical crease between its eyes in what looked like a permanent scowl.

"This wasn't part of my programming, I swear," Gunther mumbled to no one in particular.

"Uh, Molly? What's happening? Can you fix this?" asked Wally.

But for once in her life—or at least for the second time, since technically she hadn't been able to fix her mom leaving— Molly hadn't the slightest idea of what to do.

The robot was headed their way. And it looked really, really mad.

CHAPTER 40
UNSCHEDULED INTERRUPTION

"And our next guest on today's show is none other than—"

KA-ZORRRRRT!

The TV host's announcement was abruptly cut short. Sparks flew in dual arcs from the foil-wrapped antennas on top of the television. The picture went dark, along with every light in the house. Finally, a single *poof* of smoke rose from the outlet, like the TV's soul making its ascent out of this world.

"Hey, my show..."

Molly's dad sat still a moment, confused. He waited patiently for the picture to come back on. There was a faint burning smell—but for once, it wasn't coming from the kitchen.

"What happened?" he asked the television.

Stanley looked around, hoping the room would reveal some clue. Nothing. Eventually, he lumbered up off the couch and opened the back door to see if something in the yard might provide an answer. As he had spent the last several hours in a dimly lit living room with the shades drawn, the brightness of midday took some adjustment. He shaded his eyes from the sunshine.

The backyard was quiet and empty, except for a weird mannequin in the corner.

"Hey, where are the kids?" he asked no one in particular. He wandered over to the picnic table under the oak tree. As he got closer, he found the Rube Goldberg machine. He took another look at the mannequin, saw the **EVIL WIZARD** label, and tried to piece things together. Had something happened?

Stanley cupped his hands to his mouth and shouted as loud as he could. "Moll-eeeeeeee? Wall-eeeeeee?" Hearing the sound of his own voice, something about the edge of it, made him anxious. No response.

Turning around, he noticed it. A large, rectangular imprint nearly a foot deep in the middle of the backyard. Within the perimeter of the shape, everything had been flattened. Grass, weeds, the remains of what looked like a wooden crate.

What in the—

He followed the edge of the indentation, periodically getting down on all fours in the hopes of finding some clue as to what could have possibly made such a mark in the hard-packed earth.

Maybe there was some rational explanation. Was this something Molly and Wally could have done on their own? Was this the bank trying to foreclose on his property? Or maybe it was the Soviets. Had an invasion begun? Were they stealing America's children? Shipping them off to Siberia and leaving only a mark in the dirt as proof?

"Get ahold of yourself," Stanley said aloud. "There's got to be some explanation. . . ."

Maybe the kids were still in the house. Going back inside, he wandered from room to room, each one a differently styled disaster. It was hard to tell when anyone had been anywhere last. Then a thought occurred to him. He went out to the carport, peeked around the very back where Molly always parked her bike. Empty.

Okay.

He went to the telephone mounted on the wall, dialed 0 for the operator. No dial tone. He could blame it on the power outage, but the truth was, he hadn't paid the phone bill in months.

He went to the back door and peered outside again. Panic bubbled up inside him.

Not again, Stanley thought. He wasn't going to lose anyone else in his life. He'd already let that happen once, which was once too many. The idea of no one else ever coming home again—of forever being alone—was unbearable.

He walked back over to the imprint in the middle of the backyard and scanned the property. Something felt wrong. He firmed up his tone, tried full names. "Molly Jean McQuirter? Wallace Wendell McQuirter? Time to come home!"

The only response was the rustle of trees and a caw from a nearby crow.

Molly and the Machine

He tried calling their names again, but this time his voice cracked. His throat suddenly felt dry. Stanley stared at the strange, rectangular indentation in their backyard. Something tickled at the back of his mind. A memory. Was it real? Or something he had seen on television? Then it came to him. Wait a minute! What had Molly said yesterday? Some nonsense about a robot? That couldn't be true, could it?

Stanley balled his giant hands into fists. He wasn't going to sit around and wait. Whoever had his kids, they were going to pay.

He was breathing hard. A little too hard. It was just so hot out. He started feeling a little dizzy.

Then suddenly the ground flew up to meet his face, and everything went dark.

CHAPTER 41

THE INEVITABLE

From their treetop perch, Molly looked around wildly for something—anything—that could help them escape another encounter with the robot. Down below, she spotted a footpath winding through the trees. Alongside it, there was a faded sign. It read:

FAR FLUNG FALLS

½ MI. AHEAD

BEWARE OF DROP-OFF

Maybe that would be a safer spot. At least safer than where they were now. Molly knew they'd be sitting ducks up in the trees. Once spotted, they'd have no way to dodge a laser without falling.

"Let's get down from here," she said. "I've got an idea."

It had been over a year since she last visited what was once a popular tourist sight, but Molly remembered that Far Flung Falls fell from an overhang cliff. And that meant there was a space between the water and the cliff's face, enough to stand behind the falls and not even get wet. If they hurried, Molly thought, they could hide *behind* the cover of the waterfall (and out of sight of any giant robots who passed by) until some grown-ups came looking for them—if they ever did.

She quickly told the others her idea. No one else had a better plan. In fact, no one had any other plan at all. So they all started scrambling down the branches, which was easier for some than others. Wally lost his grip and almost fell three times. And Darryl and Crank required a lot of coaxing and carrying. For Molly, the hardest part was leaving the now-mangled Pink Lightning. That bike had been her one prized possession and had saved her life, but it was now unrideable, and she knew any attempt to drag it along would only slow them down. And there were more important things at stake. Like Wally.

It hurt. And yet, losing it to save her brother and friends felt like more than a fair trade.

"I'll be back for you," she whispered. "One day."

Once everyone's feet hit the ground, they wasted no time hustling down the trail, with Molly in the lead. After a few minutes, they could hear the babble of water. It was a comforting sound, not just because it meant they had almost made it to safety, but because it sounded normal. As crazy a day, or days, as it had been for them, the water just didn't sound very concerned. Their path eventually wound its way alongside a stream that fed into the falls. And as soon as the water came into view, Molly felt hope.

But the moment didn't last. Behind them, they heard the unmistakable, deliberate rhythm of giant steps. The robot was searching for them, and getting closer.

"C'mon, guys, hurry!"

The water got louder as they made it to a clearing before the world dropped away in a wide, scalloped cliff, as if some great monster from down below had taken a bite out of the rock's face. Given what she had experienced today, Molly wouldn't have been all that surprised if that were true. The stream disappeared over the edge, falling into a pool at the bottom of the gorge, kicking up spray. Right beside it, the trail led to an old wooden stairway, which according to a plaque was proudly constructed in 1937 by local Boy Scout Troop 229. The stairway zigzagged down multiple flights until it reached bottom. It was continually damp from the spray and looked in sore need of repair. But having nowhere else to go, they made a run for it.

On the far side of the bite in the cliff, several trees burst into flames.

They looked up to see the mechanical menace towering over them. The robot had found them, and it was glowing with energy, or anger, or maybe both. Molly wasn't sure if robots experienced emotions, but between the goose-poop splatters and pulsing red eyes, it looked extra agitated. After it recharged a moment, lasers shot out again, this time hitting the trees right beside them.

Molly was thankful that the geese's direct assault to the robot's face had rendered its aim less than 100 percent accurate.

"Quick, the stairs!"

In a mad dash, they continued to make a break for it, but before they could reach their escape route, more lasers hit the stairway, incinerating the upper platform in a bright ball of fire.

They were trapped.

The pincers closed in on them. And there was nowhere to run. Caught between two giant claws and a sheer drop, Molly squeezed her brother and closed her eyes.

"Sorry," Wally said.

"For what?" Molly asked.

"For all the times I bugged you."

"It's okay, Wally. Sorry I couldn't get us out of here."

"That's okay.... Molly?"

"Yeah?"

"I love you."

She squeezed him even harder. "I love you too."

Arvin hugged Leonard. Gunther hugged Darryl. Everyone closed their eyes, except Don Carlos, who looked at Crank, who hissed.

As they stood there, waiting for the inevitable, Molly heard something she hadn't expected. It sounded like music. Was this what you heard right before you died?

...AS...YOU...RUUUUUST...

It didn't sound anything like an angels' chorus ... and it seemed to be coming from somewhere beyond the falls.

...EAT...MY...DUUUUUST...

It was definitely music—heavy metal, to be exact—and it was getting louder. Everyone opened their eyes. The robot had stopped moving, its giant claws frozen in place only a stone's throw from where they stood. It had turned its head to the right, momentarily distracted.

A deep, growling rumble filled the air, mixed with an amplified drumbeat and the wail of guitars. The rumble grew to a roar. Molly and the others looked to the opposite bank as something monstrous launched into the air above them: a big fat blue motorcycle with a sidecar! It soared overhead in an impossible, gravity-defying arc—with an armadillo peeking out from the saddlebag.

"Yeeeeeeeeeee-hawwwwww!"

"Gruncle Clovis! And Mondo!" Molly shouted in relief. They'd come after all! *He must have seen my flare*, Molly thought.

Seated atop Blue Thunder midair, Clovis balanced on the bike and in one fluid motion, swiveled to face the robot, reached up with both hands, and drew two long-barreled contraptions from his back. They looked like something between a crossbow and a toilet plunger, each double-loaded with a pair of bright red suction cups on the end. As he swung the weapons into position, Molly caught a flash of gold lettering along the side of each shaft. It read **STICK IT**.

As Mondo retreated into his pouch, Clovis squinted, steadied himself, and took aim at the giant's knees. He fired in rapid succession. Cables released their tension, letting the plunger rockets fly.

TWANG! TWANG! ... FOOOOMP! FOOOOMP!

TWANG! TWANG! ... FOOOOMP! FOOOOMP!

One, two, three, four. They hit their mark in a perfectly straight line, sticking to the giant's kneecaps.

"Take that, ya overgrown tin can!"

Clovis let go of his custom crossbows, letting them fall into the water below. Hands once again free, he grabbed the grips on his bike just before landing alongside the stream next to the kids. The bike bounced a few times. With each bounce, the bright red sticks of dynamite packed into Blue Thunder's sidecar briefly popped into view before disappearing again. Clovis was definitely ready for a fight. He pulled a hard turn, spinning the bike 180 degrees in a towering wave of mud.

The robot appeared unsure what to do next. It looked down at its knees. On the back end of each plunger, an over-size metal egg traveled the length of the plunger's shaft on an invisible track until it made contact with the suction cup.

WHIIIIRRRR...CLICK!

WHIIIIRRRR...CLICK!

WHIIIIRRRR...CLICK!

WHIIIIRRRR...CLICK!

KA-BOOOOM!

The blast was deafening. Instantly, the robot's knees disappeared behind a fantastic quadruple explosion that engulfed the metal legs in smoke and fire. Above, the robot's torso shook, then swayed, in what looked like a desperate attempt to hold its balance.

Molly watched in awe. Was this it? Was it finally over?

"Hiya, kids."

As if he hadn't just performed an incredible stunt, Clovis pulled out the pipe from between his teeth, struck a match and lit it, and took a few puffs—just like Molly had seen him do a thousand times.

"Well," Clovis started, "you know what they say..."

Behind him, as the smoke cleared, the robot took a step in their direction.

"The bigger they come..."

Its charred knees buckled.

"The harder they—"

SNAAAAAAP! Both of its kneecaps—each the size of a merry-go-round—flew off, spinning through the air like flying saucers over the cliff until they disappeared into the water below.

With its knees gone, the robot wobbled back and forth like a clumsy drunk, legs clanging together. In vain, it tried taking another step, before it toppled headlong over the edge of Far Flung Falls. The splash was spectacular. Gallons of water drenched Molly and the boys, still standing on the edge of the cliff by the burning stairway. (Luckily, the proud handiwork of Troop 229 was also doused. Unluckily, the combination of lasers, a tsunami, and forty-six years of wear and tear proved to be too much. The stairway promptly collapsed into a heap down below, leaving only the plaque.)

The animals got soaked too. Crank didn't care for this at all, and she started complaining.

"So," Clovis said when the splash had subsided, "you guys wanna ride?"

CHAPTER 42
DRIVER'S SEAT

Still seated atop Blue Thunder, Clovis pulled a lever, and the bike's seat extended behind him in segments until it reached a ridiculous length.

"Yes!" Leonard and Arvin both shouted.

"Gruncle Skunkle!" Wally and Molly cried.

"Woof!" said Darryl. Which meant, in Dog, "So happy you're here, and sorry about your ham sandwich, but thank you, it was so delicious."

They all ran over.

"Sorry, sidecar's full." He gave the dynamite a pat. "Guess I overpacked."

Dripping wet, the kids clambered up on the seat behind him, their legs dangling over the sides. Molly held Darryl. Crank curled up in Clovis's lap. And Don Carlos found a spot on the tiny dash, just above the odometer. One adult. Four animals. And five children. They looked like they were going for some kind of record.

Gruncle Clovis checked over his shoulder to make sure everyone was in place, then leaned in right next to Molly's ear. "Nice work with the flare. I knew that would come in handy one day."

"Thank you," she said, resting her cheek on his back.

"No problemo. Ready?"

The ten of them held tight as Clovis gave Blue Thunder a little gas. It leapt forward. The passengers screamed.

"Okay, whoa there, Blue."

He eased off a little and the engine purred. Slowly, they made their way back up the trail along the stream. Molly hugged her Gruncle, taking in a whiff of his all-too-familiar scent. Oh, that smell! The combination of pipe smoke, stale peanuts, armpit sweat, and Handsome Halbert's Hair Cream made her feel safe for the first time since she had seen that robot....

That robot. The very same one that was now appearing in Blue Thunder's rearview mirror!

Its giant metal head slowly rose from the spray of the falls. An automated demon from the underworld, dripping water and spewing smoke. And those two glowing red eyes burning even brighter until ...

KA-ZHOORRRTT!

Laser beams scorched the air just over their heads, hitting the trees in front of them in an explosion of fire.

"What the—?" Gruncle Clovis slammed on the brakes, spinning Blue Thunder around to face the robot. "Oh, you want some more? You rusty sonuva dishwasher! When I'm through with y—"

THUNK.

A branch from one of the burning trees overhead came crashing down on Clovis's helmet, which spared his skull but didn't save him from getting knocked out cold. He slumped over.

"Gruncle!" Wally screamed. "Now whadda we do?"

Molly looked straight ahead. "We fix this . . . once and for all," she said.

The giant's face was now fully in view, jaw hanging open like it was ready to swallow them whole.

Molly clambered around her passed-out Gruncle to switch places. "Uunnghhh . . . ," he moaned, head drooping to the side. This was probably a bad idea. Maybe the worst ever.

She'd never ridden a motorcycle before, let alone driven one, but now was no time to worry about that. Somebody had to do something. And Molly knew who that somebody was. She took position up front. The bike was a lot bigger than Pink Lightning. Her arms could barely reach the handlebars. She stretched to grab hold, revving the engine hard.

"Gunther!" Molly hollered over the noise.

"Yeah?" A shaky voice answered from the back.

"You built that thing. . . . Does it have any, you know, vulnerabilities?"

"Uh . . . not really," Gunther said. "The entire exterior is cast from a pressurized steel alloy we developed that's reinforced with—"

Molly cut him off. "Gunther! Not helpful."

"Sorry. The only way to stop it would be ... from the inside," he said.

"The inside!" Molly repeated, staring down the giant's throat. "Brilliant! Got it!"

"Uh, Molly? What're—" Wally whispered.

"Hold on tight, everybody! I'm not sure how to do this."

Everyone hugged the waist of the person in front of them and hunched down. Mondo curled up even tighter in his pouch. For good measure, Don Carlos fastened himself to the dashboard with his tongue.

Molly threw back what turned out to be the turbo lever, slamming them all forward in an eruption of smoke and flame.

"AAAAAAIIIIIIIIIIGGGGGGGGHHHHHHHHHH ..."

Everyone screamed as they raced straight at the robot's head—not that they could hear any of it over the roar of the engine.

The sudden acceleration knocked her Gruncle's pipe

from his mouth. It dropped into the sidecar, igniting the dynamite's fuse. Molly bit her lip. There wasn't much she could do about that at the moment . . . except hope it was a long fuse.

Twenty-nine . . . twenty-eight . . .

Molly was pretty sure this time that they were all going to die. There they were, racing one hundred miles an hour over the edge of Far Flung Falls, right into the face of a very large, very angry laser-shooting robot, with a sidecar full of lit dynamite, her Gruncle out cold, and herself at the wheel. But she wanted that robot taken care of for good so it couldn't hurt anyone ever again. And she wanted it taken care of for another reason:

Molly had become really, really mad.

Images flashed through Molly's mind. Pink Lightning crumpled up in a tree. Dad staring at the television. Margo's empty house. A crowd of kids chanting "diarrhea squirter." A rusty old wizard van. Her last fluffernutter sandwich burnt to a crisp. And a "Fun Flamingo Facts" postcard with five lousy words written on it. The images all blurred together until all she saw was red . . . two bright red glowing eyes.

"YOU . . . BIG . . . DUMB . . . NO . . . GOOD . . . BROTHER . . . PLUCKING . . . ROBOT!" Molly screamed at the giant's face, which was now getting bigger by the second. "Arrrrrrrgggggghhhhhh!"

Twenty-seven . . . twenty-six . . .

Then, before she knew it, they ran out of ground and were airborne.

CHAPTER 43
BANDOLIER

The robot loomed ahead of them, eyes getting brighter as it recharged for another deadly blast.

Midflight on the motorcycle, there was no way to turn. Molly kicked her legs, frantically searching to unlock anything on Blue Thunder that could save them. In the process, she bumped Mondo in his pouch, who in return gave her a nip, which caused her leg to reflexively jerk forward. As it did, the heel of her foot knocked a switch she hadn't noticed before. With a loud *POP*, the sidecar filled with dynamite launched ahead.

Twenty-five... twenty-four...

Straight into the giant's open mouth.

"Gotcha," Molly said.

The kick from the ejected sidecar turned the bike laterally as they flew, making them an even bigger target as they closed in on the robot's face. But Molly felt encouraged after passing along the dynamite. She wasn't sure if it was enough to take down the robot, but at least it wasn't going to blow them up anymore.

But there was still the issue of being airborne on a motorcycle.

And the laser-shooting eyeballs in front of them—which started glowing brighter again.

Twenty-three... twenty-two...

She patted around the gas tank for another trick, desperate to find a hidden switch or lever that might help. As she did, Blue Thunder tilted, and she felt movement behind her. It was Clovis, still unconscious, sliding off the seat. He flopped backward and to the left, pulling his right leg over the seat. It hooked upward until the toe of his boot hit the end of the bike's handlebars—momentarily stopping his fall.

Click!

Something happened. Clovis's foot had accidentally hit a button Molly hadn't even been looking for. *Thank you, Gruncle!*

THOOOMP. The motorcycle's wheels shot off the bike and dropped down into the gorge, giving Blue Thunder—along with their hopes—a brief lift . . . until they saw what had happened.

"Our wheels!" said Arvin.

"Oh no," said Leonard.

"Oh crap," said Molly.

For one long second, they sailed through the air toward certain doom. Then, in a burst of motion, four bundles of blue nylon unfurled from the empty spaces where the wheels had been. A quartet of parachutes popped open like overturned teacups. Together, the chutes caught the updraft from the falls and lifted Blue Thunder (and all ten of its passengers) up, up, up, over the giant killer robot and past the whole scene, just as the metal monster released another laser blast from its eyes—*KA-ZHHHOOOORRT!*

The shot barely missed them. But all the jostling from the parachutes dislodged the toe of Clovis's boot from the handlebars, which had been the only thing keeping him from falling. Now he continued to slip. Molly tried to grab him, but her unconscious Gruncle was too heavy for her to stop.

"Gruncle, no! NO! NO! NO!" she screamed.

Clovis's right leg flipped up over the seat to follow suit with the rest of his body, now falling headlong from the bike.

SPRUNK!

Blue Thunder tilted violently, forcing all its passengers to hold on even harder than they were before. Molly looked down to see Clovis miraculously suspended upside down in midair, just a few feet below them. Then she saw the explanation: midfall, one of the buckles on his bandolier had caught the outer ridge of the bike's left pedal, with the other end hooked into his belt loop. Still out cold, the man hung in the air from the back of his pants like a sack of potatoes.

Twenty-one... twenty...

Below the suspended Clovis, the robot's eyes were powering back up.

KA-ZHHHOOOORRT!

Molly felt a flash of intense heat. *That was close!* But this last volley of laser fire must have missed them. Or had it? She could smell something burning.

"Everyone okay?" Molly called over her shoulder.

Looking back down, she saw that one of the deadly beams had shot through the narrow space between Blue Thunder and the spot where Clovis dangled below, grazing the back of his bandolier. It had left a scorch mark across the leather. And it was still smoking.

In all the commotion, Molly hadn't even noticed what her Gruncle had been packing in his bandolier, but as the front of the strap swung into view, her eyes widened. There, all tucked in a row, she saw . . . Wait, were those miniature rockets?

They were short and stubby like shotgun shells, but they tapered to points on one end and flared out with fins on the other. There had to be at least a dozen of them. They looked almost like toys, but Molly knew better. Then she noticed that the one tucked in opposite the scorch was glowing red hot.

Molly's eyes fixed on it.

F FFFFFFTTTT! Without any more warning, the rocket fired, screeching into open air—and ripping the burnt patch of bandolier even further, so now Clovis was literally hanging by a thread. The rogue rocket zigzagged around their heads, finally making contact with Troop 229's commemorative plaque on the edge of the falls. The last trace of the Boy Scouts' handiwork from forty-six years before promptly disintegrated.

Nineteen... eighteen...

Right on cue, a lone police siren began blaring somewhere

in the distance. That's when Clovis started coming to. He sucked in a mouthful of air.

"Officer! T'weren't me!" he shouted into the blue, eyes still shut. Then his body jerked, and one eye popped open. It rolled around for a moment before focusing on Blue Thunder's new driver above him. "Oh, hey there, Molly." A wide grin spread across the man's face.

"Gruncle! We need to—"

"Say, you old enough to drive that thing?" he interrupted, slowly taking in their predicament. Then the other eye popped open. "Or should I say, *fly* that thing?" He let out a little chuckle.

How hard had that branch hit his head? Her Gruncle was acting like he hadn't a care in the world—or at least like he wasn't dangling by a string of homemade, hair-trigger rockets from a flying motorcycle over an insane robot who was trying very hard to kill them. "So. What'd I miss?"

Then he looked down at the metal monster. "Whoa. You still not dead yet?"

Seventeen . . . sixteen . . .

The giant turned its body in their direction, reaching up with one of its massive claws to rip them out of the sky. The pincers came short of taking hold but clipped the exhaust jutting out behind the bike, which threw them into a spin. Everyone screamed. Darryl howled. Clovis held on to the buckle that kept him aloft while he twirled underneath the bike like a lopsided propeller.

"Hey! What's your problem, rust bucket?" Clovis shouted.

In response, the giant opened its jaws as wide as they could go, revealing the unmistakable bright blue in the center that could only be one thing. There, at the back of its mouth, the detached sidecar filled with explosives was hanging from the robot's uvula.

Fifteen...fourteen...

"Aw, why'd it hafta have a uvula?" Leonard asked no one in particular.

Gunther shrugged.

"Well, looks like somebody's having trouble taking their medicine," Clovis said.

A second rocket that had been steadily overheating

reached its limit and launched from his bandolier, leaving the singed thread that held Clovis from plummeting to his death even thinner. The loose rocket came full circle. It screeched over their heads, punching a small hole in one of the parachutes before exploding midair.

The hole immediately began widening. It made a whistling sound that changed pitch as the fabric continued to rip. Clovis looked up to assess the damage, then caught Molly's eye.

They were losing altitude. And time. And options.

Thirteen... twelve...

She could see a plan hatching in his mind, a wild glint in his eye.

"Wait, Gruncle Clovis! I... Don't..."

"Ah, don't worry, kiddo. You got this." He paused a moment, then whispered, "You always have." He smiled even bigger than before, tapped two fingers on his heart, and winked.

Then his face tightened as he turned away. He kept talking over his shoulder, but his voice took on a harder edge.

"Your ol' Gruncle Clovis has got one last ride yet." With lightning speed, the old man arched his back and bent both knees so he could reach for something around his ankles. The pose made every joint in his body crack.

"Ah, there we go." From hidden holsters just above his boots, Clovis unclipped two large silver canisters, bringing the ends up to his mouth. With his teeth, he pulled out the pins and spat them into the air. The latch on the end of each canister flipped upright with a loud *TICK*, followed by an even louder *POP*. Clovis crossed his arms over his chest and pointed the canisters downward, then swung his feet up under the exhaust so he was crouching perfectly upside down.

He was aiming himself toward the robot's open mouth. Like a human missile.

"C'mon, you gutless gearbox!" he shouted down to the robot. "It's time you cooled off a little!" Then he dropped his volume so only Blue Thunder's passengers could hear. "And maybe my two pressurized liquid nitrogen friends here can help."

On cue, both canisters started whistling like angry tea-kettles, concentrated jets of white steam spewing from their tops. Clovis held his position and waited. The robot was now directly below them.

A moment later, the third rocket in line reached its maximum temperature, tearing the bandolier completely in two. In perfect sync with the rocket's ignition, Clovis pushed off with both feet, dropping headfirst through the air like an Olympic diver leaping from the board.

"NOOOOOOOOOOO!" Molly screamed.

From above, she watched Clovis fall as giant metal claws converged on either side to crush him like a bug. But instead of getting squashed, Clovis spun 360 degrees while flinging both arms outward in opposite directions, letting the pent-up canisters fly. They spun end over end through the air, smashing into the center hinges of each claw. Two magnificent white explosions accompanied an ear-splitting *CRAAAAACK!*

The claws emerged from the white clouds, still appearing intact and still closing in on Clovis—but something looked different about them. They were gleaming, catching the light in a strange way. Thanks to the concentrated contents of the canisters, both claws were now hundreds of degrees below freezing. They connected in the space where Clovis had been just a split second before—and shattered into a million tiny pieces.

Bits of metal showered down into the water below as both the robot's now-useless arms dropped limply to its sides.

There were more sirens now. And they sounded like they were getting closer.

Meanwhile, Molly and her crew watched Clovis continue downward, undeterred. As he passed through the gaping metal maw, he curled into a ball, did a somersault, and landed feetfirst on the back end of the sidecar. It bounced.

Eleven . . . ten . . .

"UFF!" Clovis sighed.

The added weight of this new visitor was just enough to start dislodging the sidecar from the robot's uvula.

"Some things are hard to swallow without a little help, aren't they?" Clovis laughed. "Believe me, I know." He gave the sidecar a gentle tap with his foot.

GONG-G-G-G-G.

A second later, Molly watched both Clovis and his cargo of dynamite disappear down the giant's throat.

CHAPTER 45
CERTAIN KNOWLEDGE

"Woooooooo-hooooooooooooooo . . . ooooo . . . ooooo . . . ooooo!"

Clovis could hear his own voice echoing all around him as he careened down the twisting, turning pipes, making his way deeper into the robot's guts at breakneck speed. Balancing on the back of a hurtling sidecar packed with lit dynamite wasn't nearly as hard as he would have guessed. At least not for a cowboy of his skills.

A million tiny lights blurred past him as he continued his descent. It was dizzying. *Does this ride ever end?* Clovis wondered. He thought for a moment that maybe he should be scared, but he couldn't help but smile. The smile turned into a laugh. And the laugh grew louder and louder, rising in waves until it filled the space all around him. Maybe it was the absurdity of his predicament. Maybe it was the sheer thrill of the adventure. Or maybe it was the realization that he and his long-lost brother Cletus were bound by a similar destiny, and it made Clovis feel closer to him.

Nine... eight...

The truth was, at this moment, he felt closer to everyone. Maybe because, in the end, he had the certain knowledge that his life had had purpose, that he had come through for those he cared about most, and that for once, at a moment when it really counted, he had been able to do the right thing.

He saw the faces of Molly, Wally, and their friends. He saw Mondo's beady little eyes and snout. He saw his nephew-in-law Stanley. His runaway niece Caroline. He saw Marlene. And even with that last face, there wasn't a hard feeling to be found. They were all smiling at him.

While Clovis lost himself in this reverie, the sidecar kept its mad pace until it made a sudden sharp turn, angled sideways, and shot out from the tube. The hatch from which he and the sidecar burst through was slightly larger than the one next to it (where Molly had been spat out just hours before). He trailed behind the vehicle, spinning and sliding across the slick metal floor on his back... until he found himself in the middle of the most astounding display of machinery he'd ever seen.

Slowly, he got to his feet. *Ouch.* He winced. Both his ankles were throbbing, most likely from his recent acrobatics. His body ached all over. But this was accompanied by a tingling sensation. The pain was there, but somehow it felt far away.

Clovis turned to take in the spectacle. All around him, giant interlocking gears were spinning at incredible speeds, multicolored lights were blinking on and off in a cascade of ever-changing patterns, and massive bolts of lightning were shooting back and forth from one end of the room to the other. It crackled and buzzed like music, filling his ears. Clovis was overcome. He tried to speak.

"So. Beautiful," was all he could utter.

Clovis bit his lip. He couldn't believe his great fortune, in spite of all his shortcomings. In the end, the universe had somehow deemed him worthy to be here. It was beyond anything he could have ever imagined, yet everything he could have hoped for. He stood there in the middle of it, blinking back tears so he wouldn't miss a single moment. Pistons twice his size were pumping with frenzy, belts spun at double time, and everything was alive with electricity.

I'm... in... an inventor's... paradise, he marveled.

Just then, the two primary coils surged with energy. The room hummed even louder, and the floor vibrated beneath him, causing every hair on his body to stand on end—all the way out to the waxed tips of his mustache.

ZZZZZZHHHHHRRRRTTTT!

A brilliant flash illuminated everything in sight, from the far corners of the room to the blue sidecar packed full of dynamite parked right in front of him.

Seven... six...

"Oh, there you are," he said, smiling, then reached down to grab his lost pipe, wedged between the explosives. He put the end in his mouth, inhaled, and let out a perfect ring of smoke.

Unaffected by the vibrations all around it, the ring rose up peacefully through the commotion, growing wider and thinner until it faded from sight.

"So. Beautiful," he said one more time. "All of it."

That's when the spark finally reached the end of the fuse.

And the light show got even brighter.

CHAPTER 46
AERIAL VIEW

Everyone aboard Blue Thunder craned their necks to watch what was happening. As the motorcycle drifted farther away, Molly looked back for some sign that her dear Gruncle Clovis hadn't really done what she had just seen him do. But behind them, that stupid robot had snapped its jaws shut, blocking her view.

It was shifting and jerking, taking short steps in different directions like it was unsure what to do next.

Then suddenly, just as they descended to eye level with the robot, it turned its head toward them and paused.

Five ... four ...

"WAIT ... ," it said, looking over at them, a tone in its voice that sounded almost ... human.

But at that moment, Molly didn't have any room in her head or her heart to contemplate what their potential killer might or might not be feeling. She had just witnessed her great-uncle dive-bomb its throat. And since the sidecar had launched, somewhere in the back of her mind, she had been counting backward.

Molly said the last bit out loud. " ... Three ... two ... one ... and—"

KA-BOOM.

The metal giant's enormous arms dropped from its body as fire burst out of every vent, joint, and hatch. Engulfed in flames, the robot staggered. A chain of muffled explosions continued, building inside it. Then the robot literally blew its top. As a kind of grand finale, its head shot straight up into the air and out of sight, leaving a vertical trail of smoke that perfectly parted the blue sky in two.

Until that moment, the bike and its passengers had been steadily falling. But the force from the blast pushed hard against their three and a half parachutes, lifting them back upward to a safe distance. As they climbed, the giant robot began to look less threatening.

Finally, its armless, headless body, ablaze from end to end, rocked back and forth a few times, then with one last groan, fell backward in a heap of charred metal, never to rise again.

Gruncle.

Molly held back the tears, but only for so long.

From behind, she felt Leonard carefully put his arms around her. She found one of his hands with hers and squeezed it. He squeezed back. This brought more tears, but it felt good.

Behind them, Wally threw his head back and wailed, long and loud.

Arvin put a hand on Wally's shoulder.

"I . . . I wish . . . I never . . . I just . . . ," Gunther muttered. "I'm so sorry. For everything."

"It's okay, Gunther," Molly said. "It's not your fault."

Wally wailed a little longer but was starting to lose steam. Darryl chimed in with a couple of supportive howls. After a few more minutes, Wally's wail ended in a long, shuddering sigh. Molly reached back and squeezed his knee.

"It's gonna be okay, Wally," she said. "We're gonna be okay."

Crank crept onto his lap and purred.

"That was the bravest thing I've ever see anyone do, ever," Leonard said.

"The craziest," Arvin added.

"It was," Molly said.

Darryl began vigorously licking her face.

"Darryl! Oh!" she shouted, caught by surprise. Her nerves were still raw, but the tears unexpectedly broke into laughter. It was a relief to be alive, to be far away from anything on fire. The laughter shook her body, and others joined in. Even Wally.

Everyone hugged whoever was nearest. There were a few more tears. By the time they let go of each other, the robot's charred corpse was out of sight.

Molly and the other passengers looked down, taking note

of the trail of devastation from the robot's rampage. Dozens of trees had been splintered to bits; others were still in flames. Two transmission towers had been toppled, the lines that once connected them a broken, tangled mess. Molly had never seen the Hocking Hills countryside from this high up, and it was breathtaking. But it also looked a little like a war zone. Between the thicker patches of forest, a steady stream of red and blue flashing lights made their way closer to the place where the gang had barely escaped just minutes before.

Molly wondered what the police would make of the scene. There would be a lot to explain. She was glad to have her brother back, to be out of danger. But things didn't quite seem finished. They floated along the air current in silence, gradually descending back into the valley beyond the falls.

The one damaged parachute finally ripped completely in two. Both shreds of fabric slowly dropped, trailing behind them like tattered banners. Blue Thunder tilted a little to the side.

"I don't think we're gonna make it home in this," Leonard said.

The ground continued to get closer.

"Excuse me," Gunther said from the back of the row. "Uh, excuse me?"

"What is it?" Molly asked.

"Would it be possible to, ah, to land over there?" He was pointing to a stump in the middle of the field. "I think I recognize this spot."

"Sure," Molly said. "As good a spot as any. Everybody lean right."

Blue Thunder followed their lead and veered stumpward.

CHAPTER 47

HIDDEN PASSAGE

Without wheels, their motorcycle/parachute landed with a less-than-graceful *clunk*. The empty forks up front plowed into the soft earth, rearing the back of the bike upward like a tired bucking bronco. Everyone slid forward about an inch. They had all been jammed so tightly together on that seat, they'd felt like one passenger. Nobody moved or spoke.

The sound of more sirens in the distance broke the moment. Molly figured every emergency vehicle in the county must be on its way by now.

"Okay, c'mon guys," Molly finally said.

Crank and Darryl were the first to disembark, quickly followed by Gunther, who headed straight for the stump. Everyone else stayed close behind. Mondo, finally emerging from the pouch, brought up the rear.

Having completed its mission, Blue Thunder gave one final twitch of life. The lone headlight went dim, then fell from its mount and hit the ground.

"It's gotta be here somewhere," Gunther said, tapping and poking the stump in random places.

"Um. I think our friend might need some help," said Arvin, watching the boy with a look of concern on his face.

"What kind of help?" asked Wally.

"Uh . . . like, the professional kind?" Arvin pointed over at Gunther, still inexplicably tapping away.

"My dad said if I spent too much time staring at computer screens it would melt my brain," Leonard said.

"Yeah. How long you think he was up there in that control room all by himself?" Arvin asked.

"Beats me. Tough break when your robot comes alive and, uh, well, you know . . . ," said Leonard.

"Yeah, I know . . . ," said Wally.

Molly walked over to join Gunther, then tapped the stump.

"Hey," she said over her shoulder. "I don't think it's wood."

"Then what is it?" Leonard asked.

Gunther answered. "It's a marker. I remember it. From before. See here?" He pointed to what looked like an engraving:

w + w

Leonard leaned in, tracing the letters with his fingers. "Hmmm. What's dubya plus dubya stand for?" he asked.

"Not 'W plus W.' . . . 'V. V. plus V. V.,'" Gunther said.

"Valerius Vandervorkel plus Vilomena Vandervorkel," Molly said, remembering Gunther's parents' names from his story.

Gunther nodded.

Everyone had gathered around—even Don Carlos. Eyeing a knot near the stump's base, the chameleon shot out his tongue and hit it dead center. The artificial knot in the artificial stump clicked in, causing the entire apparatus to split along an invisible seam and lift up on two hinges. Machinery activated, and the earth vibrated underneath them. It was a secret door!

Molly gave Don Carlos a look of appreciation. The chameleon appeared to shrug.

"Step back!" Gunther said.

Below, a series of fluorescent lights sputtered on to illuminate a spiral staircase.

"Totally. Rad," Arvin whispered, looking down into the passage.

"To the max," Leonard agreed.

"Remember that underground tunnel I told you about? Between my house and the factory?" Gunther said. "Well, this is one of the emergency stops. It'll save us some time."

"I'll say!" said Leonard. "From where we stand, we're about equally far from everything."

They left Blue Thunder where it had landed. Without wheels, the behemoth was way too heavy to haul by hand. Molly lingered behind a moment, letting the others go ahead. Alone with the motorcycle, she gave the dashboard a final brush with her hand, then punched the eject button on the cassette player. Out popped Gruncle's mixtape. In a nearly illegible hand, *"Eat My Dust"* was scrawled across side A. Molly exhaled, then quietly slipped the cassette into her pocket.

"Thank you," she whispered.

One by one, they filed down the staircase and congregated on a small platform that overlooked a long, perfectly cylindrical tunnel. Above them, with a faint hiss, the secret stump-shaped passageway automatically closed, completely blocking out any sunlight, sound of sirens, or hint of the chaos above. The subterranean air was cool and peaceful. Molly could've sat down and stayed there awhile. She still had so many feelings churning around in her chest, but for now, those feelings would have to wait. People would be worried, and they needed to get back to let them know they were okay.

"Stay clear of the tracks," Gunther said.

He flipped open a panel against the wall and keyed in a code. On command, the electromagnetic tracks started to hum. Moments later, they saw a light coming from one end of the tunnel. A bubble-shaped vehicle came racing up toward them, hovering just inches above the ground. The bubble came to a stop in front of them, and the doors automatically slid open with a faint hiss.

They all climbed in. Molly leaned back into one of the cushy seats. Her clothes were only a little damp, and none of her scratches or bruises seemed too serious. She took a deep breath and let go of the tension she'd been holding in her body, just as the bubble started to move. As it picked up speed, Molly closed her eyes.

The next stop wasn't too far from Far Flung Falls Drive.

SIX WEEKS AND A DAY
LATER . . .

CHAPTER 48
VOILÀ

"Ahem! Ladies and gents! Your attention, please," Stanley said from the middle of the yard. Everyone stopped and turned. This was the biggest gathering the McQuirter residence had ever seen. Molly was pretty sure the entire population of Far Flung Falls Drive had come out, and then some. Their backyard was packed.

Since the moment they'd popped out of the Vandervorkels' secret hatch down the road (which turned out to be a fake power box near Arvin's house), Molly had watched her dad transform into a new person. Or maybe he was just becoming his old self again. Either way, she liked the change. That day, he had been covered in sweat, roaming the street and calling their names. When he laid eyes on her and Wally, he actually hugged them and cried, right there in the street.

He was all smiles now, motioning toward a tarp. It was weird to see him outside, in the middle of all these people, and not glued to the TV. (Ever since the power had been restored, Molly hadn't even seen him turn it on once.) He rested his hand on the tarp, pausing for dramatic effect. Molly already had an inkling of what was under it. Her dad had been dropping hints all week. Still, when he pulled the cover away to reveal a fully restored Pink Lightning, her heart leapt. Since Gruncle Clovis had gone, she thought it impossible. But she figured Gunther and his mom, Vilomena, had pitched in to help. They had all been hanging out a lot the past few weeks.

"Voilà!" Stanley announced to their neighbors with a flourish. The crowd cheered.

"We might've added a few new features," he told Molly with a wink. "Just in case another adventure ever calls." There were hoots and applause.

"Thank you," she whispered.

"You're welcome," her dad whispered back. "And thank you, Mollz."

"Smile!" Vilomena shouted, holding up a Polaroid camera and blinding them with a flash.

"Thanks, Vee," said Molly's dad, blushing a little.

"My pleasure," Vilomena answered.

Everyone in town had heard about the heroic Molly McQuirter, how she had rescued her brother, faced off with a giant robot, flown a motorcycle over a cliff, and saved the day. She had even made the front page of the *Far Flung Falls Daily*, with the headline **LOCAL GIRL TOPPLES ROBOT GONE BERSERK!**

Since then, the cuts and scratches on her arms and face had all healed. Only the tiniest red mark remained on her cheek where the branch had just missed her eye. Whenever Molly trekked up her street, the other kids in the neighborhood chanted "Moll-eeeeee Mc-Quirt-er! Laser beams can't hurt her!" She wasn't too crazy about all the fuss, but at least it was better than "diarrhea squirter."

Molly looked around at all the smiling faces in her

backyard. Some of them she didn't even know. There were so many people, they'd had to get creative to find enough seats. Both benches on the lone picnic table were packed. They'd rustled up a hodgepodge of lawn chairs, barstools, cinder blocks, milk crates...

"Anything you can put a butt on," her dad had said. "This is a special occasion."

And it was. He had strung up streamers and balloons, hauled away some of the trash, and cut the grass (which had required fixing the broken mower). There were even cupcakes with pink icing, probably to match her bike.

Leonard and Arvin were both there, along with most of the other kids from the neighborhood, even the munchkins. It was a bit of a hike to the McQuirter house at the end of the street, but it looked like no one was missing out on the cupcakes—except her dad, of all people, who had decided after passing out in the backyard that it was time he took better care of himself. He and Vilomena were both nibbling on a tray of celery sticks.

Gunther, of course, was there too. After the incident, he'd

been a little sheepish, but Molly had said there were no hard feelings. And the whole thing seemed like a lifetime ago now. He and Wally had since become really good friends, popping back and forth to each other's house in the electromagnetic tube—which they were careful to keep secret.

Sometimes, when Molly saw Gunther show up at the house, she would think about the first time she met him, when he was all alone, strapped into that weird gyroscope. He looked like a completely different person now. For starters, he smiled a lot more. And talked more, too. In fact, sometimes he wouldn't stop talking. But Molly didn't mind.

Darryl and Crank roamed free under the tables, searching for crumbs. They looked grateful to all the humans in attendance, maybe because it took the pressure off them. No one was forcing them to chase robots, or fly on motorcycles, or power Rube Goldberg machines—at least not for the moment. All was as it should be.

As the light faded, Don Carlos stood guard for mosquitoes, snacking to his heart's content with his sure-shot tongue.

In addition to all the regulars, there were several

first-time guests. Nearly half the police department had shown up. One officer had joked about putting Molly on probation, but the chief had suggested deputizing her. Initially, it had taken them quite some time to make sense out of everything that had transpired in what was typically a quiet county. But eventually, things were sorted out. Of course, this included a very sizeable donation by the Vandervorkel Foundation to the Forestation Commission of Hocking Hills, and another to the Southern Ohio Electric Company—along with a less sizeable one to local Boy Scout Troop 229.

The mayor was there too. He had presented Molly with a special medal in a ceremony the previous week—after it was reported that tourism to Far Flung Falls had reached record numbers since "the incident." He was still beaming, chomping on a cupcake while chatting with two councilmen seated beside him. (They were trying hard to dodge the crumbs flying from the mayor's mouth.)

But of all the newcomers to the party, the most unusual one by far didn't need a seat.

Because it didn't have a body. At least not anymore.

CHAPTER 49
WHAT IS ALSO TRUE

Molly stared a moment longer at the strange scene that her backyard had become.

At first, she hadn't been sure what to think when she discovered where the robot's head had landed after it had shot out of sight. She figured it had to go somewhere, but she never would've guessed that somewhere would be on the far edge of their backyard, right next to the old oak.

As fate would have it, the ten-ton piece of machinery also landed exactly where the Evil Wizard mannequin had been, crushing it into oblivion. Which Molly took as a good sign.

Since she hadn't been able to take it down with a bowling ball, a giant robot head would have to do.

Of course, she wasn't nearly as surprised as her dad was when it happened. As he had just passed out a few minutes earlier from the panic of not knowing where his kids were, waking up to have his worst nightmare materialize right in front of him was almost too much to bear. Certain it was a Soviet invasion, he'd charged at it with a rake, hitting the giant robot head repeatedly until it no longer felt like a threat. Molly could still see the scratches.

Overall, the rake assault appeared to have had a positive effect on the robot. Or maybe it had already undergone a change of heart during its unscheduled flight. Its eyes were no longer red, and it didn't shoot lasers anymore.

But with some effort, it could say a few words. And the first thing it had said when it saw Molly was "SORRY." In fact, that's all it said for the first few days whenever it saw anyone.

"SORRY..."

"SORRY..."

"SORRY…"

One afternoon, Molly had even caught it saying "SORRY" to a couple of fledgling finches who had landed on the rim of one of its massive eyes, as if they'd all known each other. The tiny birds had responded with a beautiful *tweee-da-leee-deeeee* before darting away. Molly didn't speak Finch, but she imagined the music was something close to "apology accepted," even though she had no idea what the offense ever was.

The robot seemed genuinely remorseful about everything that had happened. And now that its head was permanently disconnected from its body, it acted like a completely different robot. Molly actually liked having it in their backyard. And after the initial shock faded, the addition had grown on her dad and brother. Recently, it had also started saying "GOOD … MORNING" and "GOOD … NIGHT" (although not always at the right times).

And after dark, it would turn on its eyes, illuminating the area in a soft green glow—which had made the McQuirter backyard a popular place to play during the summer for the kids on the street, even if their house wasn't that close to anyone else's. Molly suspected that the robot enjoyed doing this, that lighting their yard made it feel needed, like it had a purpose and a place in the world.

And isn't that all any of us want?

In Molly's opinion, the massive head felt like a perfect tribute to her beloved Gruncle. After the explosion, no trace of his body was ever found, so this had become a Clovis memorial of sorts. It was the ultimate prize to add to his mechanical collection of vanquished rivals—only this one was a little too big to be mounted on his cabin wall alongside all the handlebars and headlights. The Vandervorkels had offered to have the head relocated, but Molly had declined. For some reason she couldn't quite understand, it made her feel close to her ol' Grunk and remember all the best parts of him.

She still kept a special place in her heart for the last words he said to her before he made that leap: "You got this. You always have." Molly might not have believed it then, but she did now. She caught Leonard and Arvin looking her way from their table, and she gave them a little nod.

On cue, the robot flicked on its lights as the sun slipped away, giving a green hue to everyone's faces—and to the card table in the corner, where her dad had returned to sit with Gunther's mom, Vilomena. It was just the two of them (well, three if you counted Mondo curled in a ball under one of their chairs), but they seemed perfectly content, munching on a tray of celery sticks together.

"Wow. Your bike looks good as new," Wally said. "Better, even."

Molly spun around. She'd been holding one of the grips, lost in thought, and hadn't noticed him come over. Her little brother looked less little all of a sudden, or maybe just less annoying. She nodded and gave him a smile.

"Thanks again," Wally said.

"For what?" asked Molly.

"For everything."

Before she could open her mouth to reply, he ran back over to the table with Gunther and a couple of other boys. They had arranged several Micronaut action figures in strategic positions around the cupcake wrappers and lemonade cups, ready for battle. (It turned out Gunther had an even bigger toy collection at home than the one that had gone up in flames inside the robot.)

At another table sat several girls Molly didn't know. And Margo, who was back from Michigan. Now they waved her over. They wanted to hear all about her adventure. Again. But Molly didn't mind retelling the story.

The news of Molly's bravery had traveled—beyond her neighborhood at Far Flung Falls Drive, and the hills of Hocking County, even the whole state of Ohio. She patted her back pocket, checking to make sure a postcard was still there. It had arrived from Florida earlier that week, a picture of a manatee on the front. On the back, there was a short caption about their status as an endangered species, just above the handwritten part. Molly didn't count the words this time, even though there were quite a few more than five. She decided that however many words it was . . . it was enough.

And for the first time in a long while, she'd written a letter back. It was already in the mailbox.

As Molly sat down next to Margo, she caught the robot's eye.

"GOOD . . . MORNING," it said.

All the girls at her table started giggling. Molly joined them.

The fireflies began winking, and her dad took that as a cue. From under the table, he produced a ukulele that Clovis had gifted him long ago—nearly identical to the one Clovis had played himself. Her dad strummed a few bars, and to Molly's and everyone's astonishment, began to sing:

Oh, Vilomena, Vilomeeeeeeee-na

You mean so much to meeeeee-na

Always such a sight to seeeeeeee-na

Sweeter than a honeybeeeeee-na

Oh, Vilomena, Vilomeeeeeeee-na . . .

He crooned on and on through the night, between laughs, making it all up as he went, as those newly in love are known to do. The air felt alive with possibility. And the once-crumpled but now fully restored Pink Lightning glimmered. And heads swayed.

And heroes were toasted.

And mistakes were forgiven.

And no cupcake was left uneaten.

And the girls at Molly's table laughed so hard that someone snorted.

And even though everyone in the backyard knew that Stanley's serenade was meant for one pair of ears, they also knew somewhere deep in their hearts—past all their own breaks and mends—that every single one of those ridiculous words tonight was also true for them. That they meant something to someone.

And for the first time in a long time, for at least a moment, no one felt alone.

Not even the robot.

Author's Note

Far Flung Falls, the setting for this book, is a fictional place. But it was inspired by a real one. If you've ever had the good fortune of tromping through Hocking Hills in southern Ohio, you'd know. Whenever I visit, it never ceases to feel... *otherworldly*. Maybe that's to be expected from a kid whose earliest memories are colored by a much browner landscape out west; who knows? This patch of land couldn't be more different. The sheer scale of green—and the feeling of aliveness that comes with it—is staggering. Even the rocks are alive with moss. That's especially true in the summertime, when the story takes place. For many of the outdoor scenes, I borrowed bits of imagery from Conkle's Hollow, Old Man's Cave, Cedar Falls, and other favorite spots along the bottom stretch of Buckeye Trail. On maps, they mark the edges of Appalachia. But for me, they serve as markers to a more ethereal realm. The first time I explored these hills, I was long past the age of Molly and her friends, but each trip has a way of returning me to my childhood, and the sense of possibility that every day held for me then. That feeling can be fragile. Now more than ever (at least more than in 1983), technology has a way of creeping into our magic spaces and snatching us right out of them. Luckily, for the moment, the Wi-Fi in Hocking Hills remains spotty.

Wherever you live, no matter your age, I hope you're able to discover your magical spaces, the ones that leave you to your own wits and wonder, and visit them often.

Yours in adventure,

Erik

Columbus, Ohio, 2022

Acknowledgments

Sometimes, life can feel like you're a marble bouncing through an endless Rube Goldberg machine. But when all the seemingly random knocks and jostles line up in such a way that allows you to put a book out into the world, you suddenly find yourself feeling thankful to everyone along the way who helped make it happen:

To my agent, Elizabeth Rudnick, for clearly seeing what a far-from-finished manuscript could one day grow up to be, and for making it an absolute joy to get there.

To my editor, Jessica Smith, whose talent for knowing just what to say is outmatched only by her enthusiasm in how she says it, every time.

To the art director, Laura Lyn DiSiena, and the illustrator, Oriol Vidal, for making this book look as dazzling as I hope readers find the story inside.

To the entire team of incredibly talented professionals at Aladdin, namely Rebecca Vitkus, Chloe Kuka, Nicole Tai, Ginny Kemmerer, and Lauren Forte for making a zillion right choices.

To my very first reader, Faris Abusaleh, for staying up late to finish an early draft, which convinced me to keep going. And to Louise Robertson, Todd Stinchcomb, Michael Altimier, and Andrea and Julian Larsen, whose thoughtful, generous feedback helped the book find its shape.

To the brilliant writer and editor Wendy McClure, for many years ago giving me the best writing advice ever, or at least so far.

To Kevin Fox for his tacit complicity in my escape from a perfectly fine job.

To Bryan Hurt for a coffee that changed the trajectory of my life.

To Lucy Smith for an extra hour here, an extra hour there, and for cheering loudly the whole time.

To Scott Woods, for stoking the fires when they were low.

To Ray Harryhausen and Yoshiyuki Tomino, whose respective creations jump-started my imagination at just the right moment.

To Trish Phelps, Ilya Bodner, Ben Clark, and Chuck Meyer for helping align the stars.

Acknowledgments

To the good folks of Hocking Hills, Ohio, for always making this wanderer feel welcome.

To my dear parents, Jon and Tracy Slangerup, and Connie and Thom McKinney, for stoking a deep sense of adventure and an even deeper love of language.

Lastly, to all the brave girls in my life who inspired the character Molly. In particular, to Ella, Dakota, Nina, and Evie. And most of all, to Krissy, who never ever doubted me. Not even once.

A ten-stories-tall, giant-robot-size thanks to you all. I owe you a backpack full of fluffernutter sandwiches.

About the Author

Erik Jon Slangerup grew up in a magical time, before cell phones or the internet. It was called the eighties. He spent most of it roaming outdoors unsupervised, which inspired him to write tales of adventure. *Molly and the Machine* is his debut middle-grade novel. He has also written several picture books, including the award-winning *Dirt Boy*. Erik is the father of five, which has been his biggest adventure yet. He lives in Columbus, Ohio. Discover more at erikjonslangerup.com.